I want to dedicate this book to my children,
Amanda Morgan, Timothy Adger, and Emily Briggs,
who have been unfailingly supportive in my ventures.

In addition, Emily's clever suggestions over the years
have added a great deal to the lives
of the Toad Springs residents.

CONTENTS

Preface

by Ernie Hewitt
Head Deacon at the Church of Everlasting Liability

It was back in 1971, the 100th anniversary of Toad Springs, Florida, when some workmen found a trunk up in the attic of the old house where the Church of Everlasting Liability held their services years and years before. Inside were a bunch of stories written by folks who were livin' in Toad Springs, probably around the 1930s, but they didn't all have dates on 'em.

The workmen took the trunk to the new church building, and one of the deacons found a note inside sayin' the Toad Springs folks had decided to write their own history book about their little town, and everybody who was around and wanted to could put a story in the trunk. Well, after reading some of the stories, the deacons decided to publish some of 'em in a book. It took lots of talking and arguing, but they finally picked some stories and put them in a book called *Seashells, Gator Bones, and the Church of Everlasting Liability* and it helped bring some money into the church. It's a few years later now, and it seems that lots of the people who bought it want to hear more of the stories from the trunk, so here they are.

This book is called *Moonshine, Muffins, and a Boat Named Helen*, and if enough folks like these stories, we could probably print one more.

Feather and Two

by Spurley Narrows

It all started that day when Willeva Pipkin come all the way out here in the woods to see me. I hadn't laid eyes on that woman since she broke my heart all them years ago after she promised to marry me, then changed her mind. Decided I wasn't good enough, I reckon. Anyhow, in all that time I'd managed to stay out of her path. When she turned up here she didn't look much like the cute little redhead with freckles I remembered, but even with her grey hair and extra thirty pounds I could tell it was her.

I was in the garden pickin' them big fat green hornworms off the tomato plants when this old junkheap of a car pulled up out front and the dogs started barkin' their heads off. Willeva got out and started walkin' my way, smilin' and wavin' her hand at me like she's my oldest friend. I holler for her to get the hell off my property, that I don't want nothin' to do with her. She looks surprised, then sad, and her shoulders droop as she turns around and leaves. But then after she's gone I did some thinkin'—recallin' back the way she'd liked me to take her hand when we was walkin' along and how good she smelled and how happy she'd looked when I'd brought her flowers.

A few weeks later she comes back and heads up to where I'm sittin' on the porch. For some reason—I couldn't tell you why—I don't run her off. Maybe it's 'cause she's carryin' somethin' out in front of her. It looks like a dish that's covered up with a piece of cloth. And as she gets close, I can smell it. A rhubarb pie. A hot, sweet rhubarb pie. My mouth starts waterin', and in a split second it takes me back to when she used to make me pies when we was courtin'.

She lifts up the cloth to show me. "Right out of the oven, and I made it just for you. I want to talk to you for a minute, Spurley. Then, if you want me to leave, I will."

I just look at her.

"So," she says, puttin' the pie on a table I had sittin' out there, "nice day, ain't it? It's good to see you after all this time. How you been?"

"I'm fine."

She sits down in the other chair and plops her hands in her lap. "Well, I come to see you today 'cause we got us this real good idea up at the church and we need your help. We're gonna put down the history of Toad Springs, one person tellin' their story at a time. Everybody's gonna write their own account of what it's like to live here, then we'll lock all them papers away for a generation or two. Whoever's around when they take 'em out can read 'em and see what it was like way back when." She cocks her head to one side and smiles. "Now, don't that seem like a good idea?"

"I don't care what you do. Why you tellin' me?"

"We want you to write your story. You got a good one."

"Ain't interested." I look at the dish over on the table and take a deep breath. "You can take your pie and git."

She gives me a sly smile, one that I remember from way back. "Why, Spurley Narrows," she says real nice, uncoverin' the pie. "Pull your horns in and don't be so damned hard headed. Everybody around here's gonna do it. We're makin' our own history book. It'll be interestin'."

"That's a stupid idea. And a waste of time. I ain't never done nothin' worth talkin' about. Ain't nobody gonna want to read nothin' about me."

"Yes sir, they sure will."

I give her a dirty look. "I ain't interestin'."

"Yes, you are. Everybody's interestin'."

"Yeah. Just like you to say that. You still gettin' your nose into everybody's business?"

"Come on now," she says in this wheedlin' voice. "You got to let bygones be bygones. All that weddin' stuff happened a long time ago now. It's water under the bridge."

"Listen, Willeva, I don't even live in Toad Springs."

"But you grew up there. And you're the only fella in the whole town who come home from the Great War with a Purple Heart. Matter of fact, you're the only one who come up with a medal at all, and we want the whole world to know we did our part. We sent our boys over there just like the big cities did. That's why we need you to help us out."

"I ain't talkin' about the war. You can just forget about that. And I don't need nobody to be proud of me. All I want is for everybody to leave me alone."

She leans over and pats my arm. And for some reason, I don't pull away. "And we *do* leave you alone."

"You ain't gonna read my story, 'cause I ain't gonna write it."

"Well then, how about tellin' it to me and I'll set it down for you."

Now I'm gettin' mad. "I don't need nobody to write nothin' for me. I been to school."

"Why, Spurley. I know that. Why, I even recall this one time in the third grade, the teacher'd worked an arithmetic problem wrong. And you showed her how to do it right."

Damn, I think. I'd forgot that. "Oh, yeah. Reckon I did."

"Now, just 'cause we don't see much of you, that don't mean that we ain't thinkin' about you," she says. "I even brought you this rhubarb pie." She glances over at it and smiles. "That shows you we care. So . . . let's have some while it's still warm."

I give her a look out of the corner of my eye, take a deep breath, then go inside. I have to rinse off a couple of dirty plates and forks. Then I grab a knife to cut the pie with and come back out. And after eatin' three pieces, I tell her I'll think about it.

Now, it's true that I was born and raised in Toad Springs, but I didn't have a lot of friends there. When I was comin' up, I never played softball or threw horseshoes with the other young'uns. It ain't that I didn't like 'em, I just liked bein' all by my ownself. Still do. I don't need nobody orderin' me around. I had enough of that in the army. Had enough of fightin' and arguin' too. After I come home from the war, I decided I wanted to live outside of town all by my lonesome and do as I please. I got me this little piece of property out here in the woods by a little lake, and that's where I live to this very day. And I'm just fine with this old shack I got. I grow my own food in the side yard and sell some to the grocery in Turkey Creek for what money I need, shoot me a rabbit or squirrel once in a while, go fishin' in the lake, and I got chickens for eggs and meat. I eat when I'm hungry, sleep when I'm tired, and don't take a bath unless I feel like it.

To this day, I still ain't sure how I got talked into writin' a story for the town's history book, but here it is.

Now, my old dogs, Feather and Two, they was all the company I ever wanted. They didn't ever argue with me, didn't try to order me around, and they left me alone when I didn't want to be messin' with 'em without gettin' their feelins hurt like people do. They kicked up a big fuss when anybody come nosin' around my property and helped me find squirrels and possums and such when I was huntin'. They even went out fishin' in the rowboat with me. They were damn good company, them two.

Now, Feather was black, and he got his name from a white spot on his side that looked just like a feather. And he was Two's daddy. The mama, called Mama Dog, got caught by a panther after she had pups, and Two's the only pup that lived. Two's real name was "Feather Number Two," and even though he was grey instead of black like his daddy, I named him that 'cause he had the same feather mark on his side. I just called him Two for short.

Me and the dogs, we was doin' just fine 'til one day this rag-gedy kid showed up lookin' like death warmed over, nothin' but a bag of bones. It's the only time I ever remember Feather and Two lettin' anybody come up here without barkin' their fool heads off.

I hear the kid callin' from the porch. "Mister?"

I jump, real surprised, 'cause the dogs hadn't made a peep. I walk to the door, and standin' there between Feather and Two is this skinny, dirty kid with long, stringy, brown hair, wearin' torn-up overalls. Looks to be maybe twelve, thirteen years old.

"You got a piece of bread or somethin' I could eat? I ain't had nothin' in a while."

"Sit in one of them chairs out there," I say, pointin' to the porch, thinkin' I'll give him somethin' and then get rid of him. "I'll see what I got."

He sits down, and a few minutes later when I hand him a piece of cornbread, he crams it all in his mouth like he's starvin'. I get him another piece while I'm heatin' up some squirrel and potato stew, and when it's done I hand him a bowlful and say, "What's your name?"

"Sam Smith," he says. His mouth is so full that some corn-bread spews out, but he keeps on eatin'.

I wait 'til he's finished and wipes his mouth on his sleeve, then say, "How old are you?"

"Fifteen."

"Fifteen, eh? You don't look that old."

"I know. But I'm fifteen."

I sit down in the other chair and say, "What you doin' way out here, boy? You lost?"

"No, sir. Just passin' through."

"Where's your folks?"

He shakes his head. "Don't know. I reckon they're still in Georgia."

"They know where you are?"

"No, sir."

"And why's that?"

He don't answer my question, just says, "Thank you for the dinner, sir. That was real good."

I go inside to get a smoke and when I come out he's leanin' back in the chair with his eyes closed, sound asleep. When I get him inside to lie down on the couch, it feels like he don't weigh no more than one of the dogs. He doesn't even wake up, and right off, Feather and Two come over and lie down beside him. Damnedest thing I ever seen, them two dogs.

That kid sleeps right through 'til the next afternoon, and while he's snorin' away, I make some chicken soup and biscuits. When he wakes up, he eats two big bowls full, keeps glancin' at me out of the corner of his eye, then back to the food like I might be gonna snatch it away or hit him. When he's finished, he just sits there, starin' straight ahead.

"Well, Sam," I say, "where you plannin' to go next?"

Two puts his head in the boy's lap, and Sam scratches him behind the ears. "I . . . I don't know, sir. Ain't got no plans."

"How'd you get here all the way from Georgia?"

"Hitched rides. And walked."

"You wasn't headed no place in particular?"

"No, sir. I knew where I didn't want to be, and just figured the good Lord would find me to a better place."

"And in all this way from Georgia, the good Lord didn't find you nothin'?"

"No, sir."

"Well, this ain't gonna be no good place to stay neither. Just so's you know."

He looks down at the floor. "Yes, sir. But thanks for the food. And the rest." He stands up. "I'll be going now, I reckon."

When he starts down the front steps with Feather right beside him, I call out, "Well, you don't have to go right now. I could use a little help around here for a few days. Just a few days, now. If you want to stay on, that is."

He turns around and looks up with a little hope in his eyes. "Yes, sir."

"The back garden needs weedin' real bad. And I let them damned tomatoes get ahead of me. I figure if you work hard on it for a few days, you might could get it done by Saturday."

"Yes, sir. Thank you. I will, sir."

"Long as you see you can't stay here."

"No, sir. I mean yes, sir. I know."

I can tell on the first day that Sam's a hard worker. Knows what's weeds and what ain't, and he pulls 'em out by the roots, don't just break 'em off at the ground. He even knows which tomato suckers to pinch off, and he don't hardly talk at all, which makes me cotton to him right away. Feather and Two are always hangin' out around him, even more than they do me, as a matter of fact.

After supper the next night, I pull out a book I been readin' called *Treasure Island*. When I start tellin' him about findin' buried treasure, his eyes get wide.

"Oh, lands," he says. "I want to know the whole story."

"It's too long to tell," I say. "But you can read it yourself when I'm done."

"But . . . " he says, "it'd be better if you'd just tell it to me. It would take too long to read."

I hold the book out to him. "It's all right. You can have it."

He don't take it. Just looks away.

"What's the matter? Can't you read?"

"Well . . . sir . . . I can write my name. And read a little bit."

"How much?"

He looks at the floor. "Well, not much."

"Maybe that's somethin' I could teach you. I'm pretty good at readin'."

His face lights up, and he gives me the first real smile I've seen out of him. "Oh, yes, sir," he says. "That's real good of you . . . I ain't never got to go to school, you see."

"Never been to school?"

"No, sir. Wasn't none close to where I was livin' . . . up in Georgia, you know."

"Well, I reckon I might could teach you. At least get you started on it, since you won't be stayin' here long. It ain't hard, once you get the hang of it. You're a smart boy. You can do it."

"But . . . how long will it take?"

"I don't know. Depends, I reckon, on how good I am at teachin' and how good you are at learnin'."

We start sittin' on the front porch every day after the chores are done and work on it. He knows how to do some of his letters, but I teach him the rest and how to put 'em together into words. He catches on fast, and before I know it, a few weeks have gone by. By that time, I've got him writin' down somethin' he's done that day, like pullin' weeds or feedin' the dogs or walkin' in the woods.

Time passes right quick, and I have to say that I'm surprised at how much he don't bother me. Sometimes, I even remind myself there's somethin' I want to tell him later on, and I hadn't thought like that in many a year. The only thing that bothers me is that I don't like him knowin' I have bad sweatin' dreams at night. Give me the willies. I know he must have heard me hollerin' when I wake up from one, but he never says nothin'.

One day, maybe a year later while he's off somewhere with the dogs, it crosses my mind that for the first time since I was a kid, I'm livin' with somebody and don't mind too much havin' another person around. Some days, we'd start out fishin' early in the mornin', then come back and fry up our catch for breakfast. He wasn't much for huntin' though, said he wouldn't want nobody huntin' him and didn't like doin' that to other creatures, so he'd work the garden while I went with one of the dogs.

Sometimes, I'd catch him sittin' on the front porch, starin' way off in the distance with a sad look on his face. If I made a noise, he'd jump, then get up and start doin' somethin'. I never said nothin' to him, but it made me wonder what was goin' on in his head. Sounded like he hadn't had no easy life before he got here. 'Course, he never said nothin' about it. Kind of like me and the army, I reckon. He was lookin' better, not so hangdog all the time, and he'd put on a few pounds. He worked hard and kept to himself, and I liked that.

One day we went to the grocery in Turkey Creek to get some flour and coffee and such, and he sat down on a bench out front while I went inside. I look to say a few words to the grocery man—the only person in town I ever bother to talk to—but there's a new guy workin' there so I just go on in. I'm lookin' at a can of baked beans when Sam comes runnin' inside, lookin' scared. "What's the matter?" I ask.

"Nothin'," he says, tryin' to act like he ain't nervous. But he ain't foolin' me. "I just come to see where you was."

Then I notice this great big ole fella in dirty overalls with long stringy black hair who comes strollin' in, frownin'—got a mean look to him. After lookin' around the place, he goes over to the fella at the counter. I'm standin' between Sam and the man so the fella can't see him, and Sam's lookin' pale and scared.

"What's wrong?" I ask in a whisper. "You know that guy?"

He tries to answer, but no words come out.

"That feller after you?"

"I don't know. I hope not."

"That your daddy?"

He shakes his head no.

"You know him?"

"Yes, sir."

"Think he's huntin' you?"

"Could be," he whispers.

"Well, you listen to me now," I say. "You don't want to go with him, I ain't gonna let him take you. Don't you worry about that."

He looks at me and wipes his eyes.

The big man talks to the new fella at the counter for a few minutes, then leaves.

I pay for our stuff and before we walk out Sam looks up and down the road real careful. All the way back to the house he don't say a word, and I don't ask him nothin', 'cause I can see he ain't in no mood to talk. But at supper that night I look over at him and say, "Wonder why that fella would show up here of all places . . . I mean, Turkey Creek ain't exactly a place you'd think to go lookin' for a young'un from Georgia, is it?"

"I don't know," he says.

"Who is that fella, Sam?"

"Just somebody I used to know."

"From up in Georgia?"

"Yes, sir."

"You sure you're from Georgia, Sam?"

"I ain't lyin' that I'm from Georgia. But . . . but my folks moved down here a few years back."

"Down here where?"

"Kissimmee."

"So that fella we just seen, he's from Kissimmee?"

"Yes, sir."

"Well, that's a lot closer than Georgia, now, ain't it?" I take a bite of stew. "And who is he?"

"Stanley. He's married to my mama."

"So, why'd you run off?"

He's quiet for a long minute. "'Cause he said he was gonna kill me."

"Kill you! What you done to deserve that?"

"Nothin'. He just don't like me. I don't know why, for sure. He didn't ever want Mama puttin' her arm around me or fixin' me somethin' special to eat. She says it's 'cause I look like my daddy. Stanley wanted Mama to marry him, but she married Daddy instead, so I guess he was all jealous of Daddy."

"You got any other kin around here?"

"No, sir."

"Tell me, son. Is Sam Smith your real name? It sounds made up to me."

He looks surprised. "Yes, sir! It sure is. Samuel Steven Smith."

"All right," I say. "If you say so." But I ain't sure I believe it. "Don't you think your mama worries about you?"

"Yes, sir . . . she probably does. She'd told him to quit beatin' me and bein' so mean, but he wouldn't stop. He ain't like that with the other kids, maybe 'cause they're all his. And he's only mean to Mama once in a while. But before I left home, I'd told her I was gonna run off. She cried and told me not to, but I told her I was too scared to stay there."

Don't know why, but all that afternoon, the dogs hung around close to Sam, so close they kept trippin' him up when he's walkin' around the place. He'd sit down and pet 'em for a while, and they'd settle in, but when he got up, they went right with him. It was like they was thinkin', same as him, that somebody was after him, but they wasn't gonna let nothin' bad happen to him. And I was thinkin' the same as the dogs.

I'd never said nothin' to him about leavin', and along the way, I started feelin' like he was my own kin. Maybe like a son, and I liked that idea. Every evenin' we'd sit out on the porch after supper and talk about everything that's goin' on in the world.

One night, he says to me, "Mr. Narrows, how come you have them bad dreams all the time? Like somebody's after you?"

Now, like I said, them dreams is somethin' I've always been ashamed of. It's the sign of a coward, it is, gettin' so scared when I'm just sleepin' in my own bed. "You know, boy, that ain't really none of your business."

"Oh, sorry. Didn't mean no harm. I was just askin' 'cause my uncle Pete up in Georgia had them same kinds of dreams. Mama said he never had 'em growin' up, just after he come home from the war. And he's the bravest, best man we ever knew. A real hero. So I was just thinking maybe you'd been in the war too."

I look at him, then out to the woods. "Well, come to mention it, I did go to the war."

"You was in the Great War?"

"That's right."

"You got to go overseas, did you? On a boat?"

I look at him. "On a ship."

"Where? What country?"

"France. We was in France."

"Did you kill anybody?"

I should have figured he'd ask me about that—seemed like everybody did when I first got back—but it caught me off guard. "I don't talk about the fightin'. I ain't never said a word to a soul, and I ain't never gonna, neither. I'll tell you about growin' up in Toad Springs and livin' out here, but I ain't talkin' about the war."

"But why?"

"'Cause there ain't nothin' good to say about it. And don't let nobody tell you different. You don't ever want to go fight if you don't have to."

He sits quiet for a minute. Then I say, "Why don't you tell me what it was like up in Georgia? What town did y'all live in?"

"Brunswick."

"What did your daddy do for a living?"

"He was a fisherman. I don't recall a lot about him, but Mama always told me how kind and gentle he was and that he was real proud of me. He was gonna teach me how to fish when I got big enough. She said we was always safe with him.

"The only thing I remember about him was that when I was maybe three or four years old, he took me ridin' with him on a horse. When we passed this tree I heard baby birds cheepin' and wanted to see 'em, so he stopped. When he held me up to the nest I could see three little babies in there, all with their mouths wide open, and the mama was flyin' around us, tryin' to chase us off. She finally did too."

"He sounds like a good daddy."

"Yep, but it wasn't too long after that he went out fishin' and never come back. Nobody ever found a trace of him. His boat, neither. Figured he must have drowned."

I shake my head. "That's too bad. A real shame."

He looks at the floor and says, "Then Mama married Stanley."

"The fella we seen in the store?"

"Yes, sir."

He looks away to where I can't see his face. I don't say nothin'.

"Stanley ain't nothin' like my daddy." He goes quiet again, but finally, he says, "How come you live way out here all by yourself?"

"I like bein' alone. Ain't got no use for people. Most people, anyways."

"How come is that?"

"Folks are more interested in tellin' lies and stirrin' up sand than gettin' along. That's why. I got no use for troublemakers."

"But don't you get lonesome out here?"

"Nah. I'm used to it."

"But don't you like talkin' to folks?"

"Nope."

"But you talk to me."

"That's different."

"Don't see how . . . "

I had enough of this, so I get up and go inside. My business is my business.

A few years after he come, when Sam turned eighteen, he figured he was old enough to set out on his own, and I have to say, the day he left was a sad one. I'd got right used to havin' him around, liked the company . . . as long as he didn't ask too many questions. He lives over in Tampa now and has a good job with the railroad. Him and his wife and two young'uns come out to see me every month or so. He did finally get ahold of somebody in Kissimmee who told him his mama had died and Stanley took his kids back to Georgia. Sam was real sad about his mama and he prays for her every night. Says it's almost like talkin' to her.

Me, I'm still livin' out here on my own, but I find myself goin' to town more than I used to and even sayin' howdy to folks when I bring vegetables in to sell at the grocery. I miss old Feather and Two, them bein' the best friends I ever had in this world. Feather died when he was sixteen, and Two died at seventeen. Went through some hard times when I lost them fellers. It was like losin' my family. That's just what it was. Losin' my family. I trusted them two and they never let me down. Not once.

Sometimes I think about how different my life would have been if them two had chased Sam away that day he turned up here, like they did every other person who ever came on the property. Instead, they brought him up to the porch.

These days, I have to say that the folks in town are nicer to me than they used to be. Some of the old fellas even asked me to come over to Smitty's Hardware and play checkers with 'em on the porch, and I've gone a few times. I got invited to church and maybe I'll go someday, maybe on Christmas or Easter. That young'un kinda changed the way I see a few things, if you see what I mean. And writin' down my story for the Toad Springs history book made me see things a little different than I did before. Maybe a lot different.

Guess it's turned out to be a good thing I let old Willeva bring me that rhubarb pie when she come over that day. Kind of makes up, just a little bit, for breakin' my heart all them years ago.

Heavenly Days
by Midge Mallet

My husband, Smitty, grew up thinkin' the grass was always greener across the road, or however that sayin' goes. He was always wantin' to do somethin' different from whatever he was doin'. Somethin' more *interestin'*. That was his favorite word, and *that's* how we ended up in Florida in 1920. But it ain't no pretty story.

Smitty's daddy owned the Corner Hardware store on the outskirts of Nashville, Tennessee, and Smitty had to work there when he was a kid. And he sure didn't want to do that for the rest of his life. Right out of high school he went to work at one of them Lion's filling stations, but havin' to smell gas all day made him sick to his stomach. So then he got a job at the Princess Movie Theater, thinkin' he could earn money and get to watch every movie for free, but it didn't pay enough. He was fixin' to try workin' on a cotton farm when his daddy's heart started giving out. Somebody had to take over at the hardware store, and Smitty got the job.

He thought they oughta sell the place, but since his daddy had built it up from nothin', he said it had to stay in the family whether Smitty wanted it or not. We got married while all that hoopla was goin' on, and to tell the truth, I liked the idea of him runnin' the store. I figured then he'd have to settle down.

Every Sunday, when we had dinner at his folks' house, him and his daddy would get in an argument 'cause Smitty was changin' things from the way his daddy did 'em, like buyin' supplies different places and gettin' in new, different lines of stuff. One Sunday, Smitty made the mistake of sayin', "We got to keep up with the times."

"Keep up with the times?" his daddy says, lookin' up with a mouthful of fried chicken, all red in the face. "Keep up with the times?" He slams the drumstick down on his plate, and when he starts yellin', he spits out little bits of chicken all over the table. "What in hell you think I been doin' all this time! I've been runnin' that store just fine for almost thirty years." He wipes his mouth with his hand. "Hrummph. Keepin' up with the times."

"Well, Pop," Smitty says, "I found this new place to get fertilizer for half what we're payin', and besides—"

"Might be cheaper, but it ain't no good. You listen to me, boy. I learned the hard way, and I know what I'm talkin' about."

"All's I'm sayin' is that there's some new suppliers out there."

His daddy slaps his hand on the table. "I don't give a goddamn, Smitty! You got to stick with what you know or in the end you'll be sorry. Just take my word for it."

"You ain't listened to a word I've said!" Smitty hollers back at him.

Then his daddy clutches his heart like he's havin' a heart attack.

"You okay?" Smitty says, reachin' over to touch his arm.

His daddy jerks away. "I'm fine. Just fine. But you're gonna kill me with all this aggravation, Smitty Mallet. You just do what I tell you and I don't want to hear no more about it."

Later I told Smitty not to argue with his daddy. He should just listen to him, then go on and do what he wanted in the first place. But no, he wouldn't do that. So our Sunday dinners always upset my stomach.

After we'd been married about five years and Lillie and Travis had been born, both Smitty's folks died within a month of each other. His mama caught the flu and wouldn't go to the doctor 'til it was too late, and then his daddy had a heart attack in the middle of the night and passed on over to greener pastures. Smitty thought his daddy really died 'cause he couldn't live without his mama.

'Course, Smitty was real sad and all, but before long he starts talkin' about findin' another kind of work. And at the same time, we're havin' money troubles, what with some new fella puttin' in another hardware store just a block away from ours and stealin' all our customers.

Just so happened that DuPont had a great big factory in Nashville and Smitty thought about getting on there. Problem was that his cousin, Ellis, was doin' all the hirin' and him and Smitty hadn't never seen eye-to-eye on nothin', especially after the Thanksgiving just past. Smitty's people all go to his Aunt Katie's for a big fancy dinner, and that year him and Ellis got in a big set-to over a hog Smitty'd sold him just before it died.

Now, Smitty'd taken it in trade for some lumber and he said it was good and healthy last time he saw it, but Ellis said Smitty'd sold him a sick hog on purpose, and things got real ugly. Nasty temper, that Ellis. We had to leave early before we got any of Aunt Katie's blueberry glop dessert she always makes. I sure wasn't happy about that. It was so good that she wouldn't give out the recipe even to her own grandma. Anyway, that's when Smitty started talkin' about leavin' town.

"Midge, honey," he says one night. "Listen to this. They're sellin' property down in Florida real cheap!"

"Florida?" I say.

"This fella called Duke, he told me about this big real estate boom goin' on down there. Says we could be livin' practically on the beach. And for next to nothin'. They need business people like us to move in. It's the chance of a lifetime!"

My heart sinks. "But we ain't got enough money to live on now. We can't—"

"Just listen! We can sell the house and the store here in Nashville. The way things been goin', we're gonna have to sell the store anyway. And we could move to Florida and set up a new business with what we make on the sale and have somethin' other than a hardware store."

"Are you crazy?"

"But Midgie, after we sell everything here, we'll have money to buy down there. And anyways, these folks'll help me get a loan. They got them fellas at the banks eatin' outta their hands, Duke says."

I feel sick to my stomach.

"And he says it looks just like Eden. Like in the Bible. Now, damn if that don't sound like a good deal . . . "

"Smitty, come on. We ain't got—"

"Duke's one of them binder boys I've heard about. That means he can sell Florida property cheap, and we don't even have to go down there to see it. Can just pay for it all here, and they'll have it ready for us whenever we want to move in. And the property's close to Miami, in a little town called Heavenly Days. Don't you like the sound of that?"

I roll my eyes, but he acts like he don't notice.

Duke comes over to the house the next afternoon and when I tell him I can't find Heavenly Days on a road map, he says it's just so new that the map companies hadn't added it yet, but he'd been there himself, in person, and it was the purtiest piece of property he'd ever laid eyes on, just a few blocks off the beach. He even showed us pictures somebody drew of nice two-story houses along a stream, with lots of palm trees and rolling hills, and he said there was freshwater wells already dug on each lot and electric ready to hook up. And the best part's that everything's on sale, but we have to hurry if we want to get one of the best spots. The regular price is five thousand dollars for the lot and three thousand for the house, but just for the next few weeks, the lots and the houses together are sellin' for five thousand.

Soon as I hear that, I smell a rat. "Come on now, Duke," I say. "If it's so beautiful there, why are you folks sellin' so cheap?"

"Well, ma'am," he says, lookin' at me like he thinks I'm some damn fool, "right now, they're goin' like hotcakes. Only a few of the best ones are left, and you'd better hurry if you're gonna get one."

I squint my eyes at him. "Now, that don't answer my question, Duke. That ain't what I asked you. I want to know why they lowered the price so far down. I could see lowerin' it some, but that much? It don't make sense. They'd just be throwin' money away."

Smitty clears his throat. "Come on now, Midge, honey. You don't know nothin' about buyin' property and this young fella knows what he's doin'. He wouldn't lie to us." He looks at Duke. "Would you, son?"

Duke shakes his head and glances from Smitty to me. "Well, just between us, ma'am, now, I don't tell this to everybody, but I'll tell you. They lower the prices on some just to get everybody knowin' about the place. It's a cheap way to spread the word."

I sit back and cross my arms. "Don't sound cheap to me. If it really looked like them drawin's, you'd have a real picture to prove it. And you could get lots more money for 'em. No way they'd lower the price that much."

Duke turns and starts talkin' just to Smitty, and they both act like I'm not even here, so I go in the kitchen and start choppin' carrots for supper.

After he leaves, I say, "Smitty, I don't trust that fella."

Smitty gives me a big smile. "But Midge, honey, Duke can fix it with the bank so we'll have enough for a down payment. Then, with the money from what we sell here, we'll have enough left to open up another business down there, dependin' what we get for this one."

"It just don't sound right to me."

His face turns serious. "We got to do somethin', Midge. We're gonna lose the store for sure."

"And what about the new house? What if it's not built when we get down there?"

"Well, then, I reckon we'd just live in a tent for a while. We'll need one for the trip down anyways. It's way too long a drive to pay for somewhere to sleep every night, so we can be like some of them folks, what do they call 'em . . . oh yeah, tin can tourists.

My stomach's in a knot. "I'm tellin' you, Smitty, this ain't a good idea."

"Oh, hogwash," Smitty says. "I got my mind made up. We couldn't be in worse shape down there than we are here. And we might can do a lot better."

Well, after Smitty and Ellis have one more run-in, this time over who should be elected president, that was it. Three months later, near the end of July, with me draggin' my feet the whole way, we sell our house and the store, pay off the property in Heavenly Days, buy us a tent, pack up the two kids, and head south.

Now, I won't bore you by tellin' you how Lillie, who was six by then, was carsick most of the way and what that did to the back seat, or how Travis, who was four, got an earache and screamed like a banshee day and night, and nothin' I did helped, or that when either one of 'em started to feelin' a little better, it was time for 'em to pick a fight. And I won't tell you how many flat tires we had—well, yes I will. There was four. Or that we had to buy a new radiator, or that part of the Dixie Highway had gotten washed out, or that I found out I hate campin', or that the further south we got, the bigger the skeeters got, and the hotter the weather got 'til by the time we was comin' up on August, I was ready to strangle myself and everybody else in the car. I won't bother you with all that. I'll just say it wasn't the best trip I ever took in my life.

Duke had give us a special map so we could find the place, and I was lookin' for the big sign that said "Welcome to Heavenly Days" like I'd seen in the drawings. Duke said they were all done with the house and we could just move right in. I was sure in my heart it wasn't never gonna happen, but just in case, I let myself daydream that we'd drive right up to our property at 500

Pearly Gates Avenue and the house would be all finished down to the rockin' chairs on the front porch.

Well, come to find out that the Florida map Duke gave us didn't even have the Dixie Highway on it, and that's the main highway in the whole state, so we went to usin' the Texaco map. There was a few hills after we got into Florida, with cattle ranches and orange trees everywhere, but the closer to Heavenly Days we got, the flatter it got. I tried to keep my mouth shut, 'cause by that time, there was no turnin' back—nowhere to go home to. But it was gettin' harder and harder to keep quiet. Finally, I couldn't stand it another minute and said, "Smitty, you notice there ain't no hills around here like was in the pictures?"

"We seen hills, Midge. What you talkin' about?"

"Yeah, we seen hills three hundred miles ago. Ain't been none lately."

"Well, that don't mean there won't be more to come."

"Smitty, I just hope—"

"You look right there," he says, pointin' off at a bunch of scrub land. "There's palm trees right there. And palmettos. They was in the picture too."

The further we drive, the more scared I get. When we do find a road that looks right, we end up on somebody's farm or headed into a swamp—even see three different gators that could have eat us up alive. When Smitty finally gives up and starts askin' folks where Heavenly Days is, they all act like they've never even heard of it, and the longer we look, the madder I get.

Finally, Smitty agrees to go to the police station in Miami to get directions, figured they'd know about every town around. When we go in I'm carryin' Travis on my hip while he cries and holds onto his ear, and his face is all dirty. Smitty's got Lillie's hand and her bottom lip's stuck out in a pout and she's whinin' that she's hungry. But if we give her anything to eat and put her back in the car she'll just throw up. I feel like we're circlin' the drain, but I take a deep breath, and we march inside. When the kids see the great big policeman standin' at the desk, they hush up and watch. I put Travis down, and he sticks his thumb in his mouth while Smitty introduces himself and asks for directions.

The big old policeman says, "Hmmm. I've never heard of that place, let me see. Heavenly Days, huh?" He walks over to a doorway and hollers back into another room, "Anybody in there ever heard of a town called Heavenly Days?"

"Heavenly Days?" a man yells out. "You kiddin' me?" He laughs, then says in a higher pitched voice, "Oh, my heavenly days! Ain't never heard of that." Then some more men laugh, and a couple of 'em peek at us around the edge of the doorway.

The officer comes back with a little smile on his face. "Don't sound like it's in this neck of the woods." He kind of chuckles as he sits down. "Heavenly Days, huh?"

Smitty turns pale and I'm ready to wring his neck.

The policeman puts his elbows on his desk and leans toward us. "You by any chance buy some property there?"

Smitty nods.

"Then I'm real sorry to tell you that you've probably just been cheated outta your money. This kind of stuff happens all the time. First time I heard of Heavenly Days, though."

"What you mean?" Smitty says. "What happens all the time?"

"Oh, these tourists from up north, they pack up their tents and canned goods and come down to see Florida. Some of 'em like it so much that when they get back up in the snow, they decide to move down here. They get mixed up with these flimflam men—binder boys, they call 'em—work for the real estate companies, runnin' around cheatin' folks outta every penny they've got."

"What?" Smitty says, turnin' pale. "What?"

I feel like I'm gonna faint. I knew it! I just knew it!

"Sorry, sir, but there ain't no place around these parts called Heavenly Days."

"But I've got it right here," Smitty says, pullin' out all the papers Duke had give us. He hands a paper to the policeman. "Here's the deed provin' we own it." Then he shows him the map and points to a spot on it.

The policeman looks at the papers and hands them all back. "Sorry, bud, that's Seminole land. Belongs to the Indians. Ain't nothin' out there but swamps and gators." He shakes his head like he's feelin' sorry for us.

"But," I say. "But . . . but we gave 'em all our money."

"I know, ma'am. You ain't the first folks this has happened to. There's a whole passel of con men out there doin' this to people."

I'm breakin' into a cold sweat. "But ain't that against the law?"

"Yes, ma'am, it sure is. And I can take your complaint if you want, but the insurance companies got these big, fancy lawyers, and most all of 'em get off free as a bird and you end up with a big lawyer bill."

Smitty goes to a chair and sits down hard, then leans over and puts his head in his hands.

I'm cryin', and when Lillie and Travis notice, they start tuning up again, and we're all in tears. I glare down at my husband. "Goddammit, Smitty. I told you that guy was lyin'."

He don't even look up.

"Oh, dear Lord," I say. "Heaven help us. We've got nothin'. Down here with none of our people around. Nobody to help us." I glare at him.

He looks confused. "Duke seemed like such an honest fella . . . "

"I told you, Smitty Mallet. I told you." I snatch Travis up and stomp to the door, and Smitty follows along with Lillie, who goes back to whinin' soon as she steps outside.

When we get back in the car, I say, "We're gonna have to head back home. Ain't nowhere else to go. Cousin Ellis is gonna have a good laugh about all this, ain't he?"

Smitty starts the car up and we head back the way we come. By now I'm so mad that even the kids are quiet. I know Smitty feels bad about the whole mess, but that don't change a damn thing. We got nothin' left. We're gonna wind up in the poor house!

We open all the windows real wide but the air's so hot and damp that it don't help one bit. You could pull a baked potato right out of the ground. When we stop for gas, some folks give us directions and say it might be better drivin' up the West Coast near the Gulf of Mexico, so we decide to head back that way. The roads are so full of potholes that we nearly get jounced to death, and I swear I see gators lyin' everywhere up in the brush, waitin' to run out and eat us up.

I get real sick of lookin' at flat land covered with palmettos and cypress trees and listening to the kids fightin' over who gets to sit where and who's lookin' at who. At least Smitty's quiet, which is good, 'cause if he says a word, I just might have to throttle him. The hotter I get, the more I think about what Smitty's done to us. Now we're poor as old Job's turkey. Smitty should'a listened to me.

We're about twenty miles from Tampa when we come up on a road that's washed out, so we either got to go twenty miles outta the way to get there on a paved road or take a dirt road. I told Smitty we need to stick to the paved road, but no, he says he looked at the map and this dirt road looks like a good shortcut. Well, that shortcut gets us our fourth flat tire. Thank the good Lord we're right near a lake.

We've just passed a sign that says *Toad Springs 3 Miles*, but we're all so tired and frazzled we don't try to walk there. Just set up the tent out by the lake and call it a day. As the sun goes down a little breeze comes up. It's cooler, but the skeeters nearly eat us alive. At least we all get to take a bath in the lake—keepin' an eye out for gators, of course.

The next mornin' we walk into Toad Springs. Ain't much there but some houses, a buildin' that needed a coat of paint, the Toad Springs General Store with a gas pump out front. And an alligator ranch, whatever that is.

We go in the store and meet the owner, Halt Brisco. He's kind of scrawny lookin' and his hair stands up funny in the back, but he seems real glad to see some new faces. He's tellin' us how all politicians are crooks when another feller walks in. He has a purple blotch on his face and says his name is Hank Plenty. He's kinda shy, real nice though, and when Smitty tells him he used to have a hardware store, Hank says Toad Springs needs one in the worst way and maybe we oughta stay. Says a hardware store would bring more folks into town. When I hear that, I feel a little bit of hope for the first time in weeks. At least somebody wants us around.

But Smitty says, "Oh, I ain't plannin' to run no more hardwares. I been lookin' for somethin' different. Somethin' more interestin'."

"That's too bad," Hank says. "We been wantin' to find a way to help the town grow."

I speak up. "Movin' here is the first good idea I've heard in a long time," I say. "That just might could work."

Smitty shakes his head. "Like I already said, I ain't runnin' no more hardwares."

I look him straight in the eye. "We can talk about this later." I go over to the counter and say to Halt, "Y'all happen to have whatever we'd need to fix a flat tire?"

"Why, sure, ma'am," he says, headin' toward the back room. "I'll get you a patch kit."

I also buy some flour and salt and then Halt gives us a ride back to the lake. After he leaves I remind Smitty that he wanted a change in his life, and here the good Lord give it to him, plopped it right into his lap.

"Aw, come on, Midgie," he says. "The whole reason we're down here's 'cause I don't want to be stuck standin' around in a store all day."

"Seems to me you was willin' to do exactly that, long as it was down in Heavenly Days." I say Heavenly Days in a sing-songy voice, just to spite him.

"That was different. And anyways, I hadn't said nothin' to you yet, but I was really thinkin' of openin' a swanky restaurant instead of a hardware. Maybe over on the beach. I was thinkin' we'd be livin' in a real nice place with interestin' people, not like some little podunk hole-in-the-wall town out in the middle of nowhere."

"Oh, you don't say!" I put my hands on my hips. "Well, ain't you smart!"

"I thought we'd be where them millionaires from up north go on a vacation, the ones with money to burn."

"Smitty," I say, shakin' my finger at him, "that's just what got us in this mess. We got no money, no home, two kids to feed." I take the kids inside the tent to help me clean up, and when I look outside, Smitty's workin' on the car. He's stompin' around and cussin' so bad when he can't get the tire off that I take the kids for a nice long walk, tell 'em we're lookin' for a turtle. The more I think about this mess, the madder I get. By the time we get back, I'm ready to kill him.

Looks like he's got the tire fixed, and he's sittin' at the card table. I don't say nothin' to him while I fix supper and the kids play with some little bugs they found. We don't talk for the whole meal. After I get the young'uns to sleep, I sit down at the table and say, "Smitty, you got family responsibilities. You got to put food on the table and clothes on our backs."

He just gives me a dirty look.

"Here, we got a chance to start over. With folks who want us, not like in Nashville. This kind of luck don't happen very often. I think God's got a hand in this, myself."

He stares out at the cypress trees, but the only answer I get is the crickets singin'.

"Now, if you want to go on back to Nashville, I reckon we could get there. But we won't have no place to stay and you won't have a job. And you already looked for other work up there and didn't come up with nothin'. Remember that?"

He don't answer.

"And Ellis would have a great time teasin' you about losin' everything. Come on, Smitty." I'm so mad, I could spit. I go in the tent and try to slam the door flap behind me, but, of course, that don't work. I throw his sleepin' bag outside and holler, "You're sleepin' out there tonight!"

"But there's gators—"

"I don't care."

Early the next mornin', I fix coffee on the little stove and don't take no pains to be quiet about it. When the kids start fightin' in the tent, I just let 'em go at it 'til Smitty finally drags himself up out of his sleepin' bag and hollers for 'em to stop, then sits down on one of the foldin' chairs. I slam his coffee cup on the card table, spillin' hot coffee everywhere, even burn my hand, but I try not to show it.

I say, "Smitty, we're stayin' here. We got no place else to go."

"Aw, Midge," he says, "I'm sorry about gettin' us into this mess."

"Yeah, I know. I'm sorry you did it too. But that don't solve nothin'."

"All I ever wanted was—"

I put both hands on the card table and lean in 'til we're nose to nose. "We're stayin'. And that's that."

"Aw, Midgie . . . "

"You take the kids down to the lake and clean up while I fix breakfast. Then we're goin' into town."

He gets up real slow, lookin' like a little boy who's just been told his mama's gonna cook his pet pig for Sunday dinner, and calls the kids to go down with him.

By the time we get to town, it's almost noon, and we head back to the general store. When we walk in, a lady's talkin' to Halt. He looks up at us and says, "Here's the folks who're thinkin' of movin' to town."

Smitty don't answer, but I say to her, "Hi there. I'm Midge Mallet. And this here's my husband, Smitty."

"I'm Sorrey May Only," she says. "I was just tellin' Halt it would be good to have some new folks here. My granddaddy's the one who started Toad Springs, and my daddy was the first preacher of the Church of Everlasting Liability. And if they was still alive, I'm sure they'd welcome any souls the Lord sends our way."

"Smitty here had a hardware store up in Nashville," Halt says. "I been tellin' 'em we could use one right here."

"We ain't decided on nothin' yet," Smitty says, not lookin' at me. "Just been talkin' about it."

"You seen that little old barn just up the road a piece? It would be a good place for a hardware," Sorrey May says. "Nobody's used it in years. And Hank Plenty's got a house on his property y'all could probably rent 'til you get your own place."

I look at Smitty, but he ain't lookin' back. "So nice of you folks to offer all this," I say.

"You'd be right welcome here," Halt says.

"We'll see," I say. "Right now, I need to get some coffee."

Smitty don't talk all the way back to the tent, and I just leave him alone. I'd promised the kids they could go swimmin' in the afternoon, so I take 'em down to the lake while he just keeps sittin' at the card table, starin' off into the cypress trees. After supper, I put the kids to bed, then come out and sit down with him.

"Well?" I say.

"Hrummph."

"I know it ain't what you had in mind, Smitty, but we've got to have some way of makin' money. No way we can do it back home. The only thing I want from there is the blueberry glop recipe, and ain't no way I'll ever get that."

"Just hold the fort," he says. "I got somethin' I want to tell you."

"It better be good," I say.

He leans back in the chair, crosses his arms in front of him, and looks at me. "I only got one life to live," he says. "And I don't aim to spend the rest of it doin' somethin' I hate."

"So what you—"

"Just listen to me, Midge. Like I said, I ain't gonna spend the rest of it workin' in some damn hardware store. But I'm willin' to do it for a while."

My heart skips a beat. "What's that supposed to mean?"

"That means, I'll do it for a while. I don't rightly know how long. Maybe a few years."

"Then what?"

"I don't know. I just can't stand to think that I'll spend the rest of my life sellin' crowbars and washtubs and fertilizer. Maybe we'll stay here long enough to build up the business and sell it for a profit. Or who knows, maybe someday Travis would want to take over runnin' the store."

I don't say nothin' about him soundin' just like his daddy. "That sounds good. I'd like that."

"So, we got a deal?"

"A deal."

I go over and give him a big hug, thinkin' to myself that I'll worry about everything later.

When we go back into town the next mornin' we tell Halt we're thinkin' to stay and want to look into what they was talkin' about. He calls Hank, who comes over after lunch, and the men go look at the barn together to see what they'll need to do to turn it into a store. Turns out it'll cost a pretty penny, but Hank says he'll buy the lumber and even have a few of his ranch hands help fix it up. And he'll loan Smitty money to get up and runnin', and Smitty can pay it back. That's how bad Hank wants a hardware store here, and he's the only one around with the money to do it.

A week later we're livin' in that little house out at Hank's and Smitty's off to Tampa to buy stuff to sell in the store. At the same time Halt's wife, Hester, is goin' around to the post offices in some of the towns that are close by and puttin' up notices that Smitty's Hardware and Feed will soon be open.

Turns out that about that time the folks at the Church of Everlasting Liability get enough money to fix up an old house to use for their meetin's, and they buy supplies from Smitty's store to do it. After that, of course, we kind of have to go hear the preacher every Sunday. I even went to the Ladies' Circle meetin' 'til I couldn't stand it no more. Them gals was always playin' the "ain't it awfuls" 'til it'd make you feel all antsy just to be in the same room with 'em.

The first fella Smitty hires to work for him is Mort Thinly. He just comes to help out in the mornin's but it seems to me he ain't hardly got the energy it takes to blink his eyes. He can find you anything in the store you want, but he ends up quittin' 'cause the work's too hard—meanin' he has to stand up and walk around once in a while rather than just sittin' in one spot all day.

I have to say, it's been a few years now, and Smitty's kept up his end of the bargain. I haven't heard no talk of leavin'. He goes to work smilin' every day and he's made good friends here. I think it helps that he keeps readin' up on all the latest inventions and helpin' the farmers get stuff for the best price. Folks come from miles around just to talk to him.

You know, sometimes I wonder where we'd be if Smitty hadn't decided he just had to do somethin' more interestin' and dragged us down here all them years ago. I still miss seein' Nashville in the fall with all the leaves changin' colors, and in the spring with the trees growin' new leaves and the flowers bloomin'. And I never did get that blueberry glop recipe.

But down here we got warm weather and nice folks, and Toad Springs is a good place to raise kids. Reckon if you look hard enough, you can find lots of *interestin'* stuff right under your nose.

Miracles Can Happen
by Smitty Mallet

Back in 1920, me and Midge packed up the kids and moved down from Nashville. Toad Springs ain't where we headed out for, but it's where we ended up. But then, that's another story. Back then, the town had its own little grocery store—even had a gas pump—but you still had to go to Turkey Creek for your feed and lumber and nails and such.

I opened up Smitty Mallet's Hardware and Feed and wasn't long before folks start comin' from Turkey Creek and Mango, even Lithia Springs, 'cause I know about some newfangled things farmers are usin' around Nashville that they don't know about down here. I tell 'em about the new rubber tires they got for tractors and the tractor guide that makes it easy to keep the rows goin' straight and all different kinds of new fertilizers. Word gets around pretty fast that I give good advice.

I carry all sorts of other stuff—seeds, arsenic of lead to kill the bugs and varmints, fertilizers, saws and axes, lumber and nails, and feed for livestock and chickens. I got kerosene lanterns, buckets and tubs, post hole diggers, paint, fishin' and huntin' gear, and things like that. Keep all the lumber out back. Lucky for me, it turned out I knew about some new kinds of farmin' equipment they'd been usin' up in Tennessee that folks down here didn't know about, so farmers come from all around lookin' for advice, and that brought more people into town.

I set up a couple of tables and chairs out front of the store where the old-timers hang around playin' checkers and swappin' lies—a couple even play chess. Ain't never had the brains for that myself, but havin' them old guys around is good for business, except when they get at each other's throats over what some crazy politician's gonna do next.

I bought a wood stove for inside that keeps the place nice and cozy in the winter. Even if it don't snow here in Florida, the damp cold we get down here goes right to the marrow of your bones.

When folks ain't got the cash to pay me, I'll trade supplies for work, like paintin' the store or cleanin' up. Or I'll take whatever they come up with—eggs or vegetables or blankets, stuff like that. Have to say, I've took in some real strange things over the years, like the bustle off a lady's dress from a hundred years ago, an old player piano with a bunch of keys missin', and an old printin' press. Now, I couldn't use none of that junk, but lots of folks around here are too proud to take charity, and you can't let people go without things they need to earn a livin'. I do my best to keep Midge from findin' out and some folks say I'm henpecked. But I call it keepin' the peace.

Through the years, I've gotten to where I just let things slide with Midge, 'cause fussin' ain't hardly worth the trouble. I just let her think she won the argument, then do whatever I was gonna do in the first place. Like when she started naggin' at me to give up my chaw.

Now, I been chewin' Red Man since I was thirteen years old, and Midge ain't never liked it—calls it the black nasty. I never said I'd quit, but I just do it at the store or when she's not around. I spit in an old coffee can I keep hid down under the cash register, but if I know Midge is comin' in, I spit out the chaw and hide the can. Sometimes I think she knows what I'm doin', but she don't say nothin'.

Another thing she didn't like from the start was me takin' a little drink of shine once in a while. Now, wasn't but a few times in my whole life that I overdone it and got wobbly, but she always says it makes me stink like the devil, and anyways, God didn't intend us to drink—or dance neither, for that matter. Well, givin' up the dancin' wasn't no trouble, 'cause I never could dance in the first place, so she got her way on that one. But not on the other. A man needs to be able to have a little drink now and again.

I recall this one night . . . it'd been rainin' all day and I come home from the store feelin' real good. Me and a couple of the boys been sittin' around playin' cards all afternoon, 'cause there wasn't hardly any customers. They'd brought some moonshine along, and we had us a good old time. Lookin' back now, I don't know what I was thinkin, but when I got home that evenin', I went in the kitchen and said, "Hello there, sugar dumplin'."

She's stirrin' a pot of somethin' on the stove, turns and gives me that sideways turtle eye, then clanks the spoon on the side of the pot. "What's the matter with you?" she says.

"Ain't nothin' wrong, sweet pea. I'm just feelin' fine tonight."

She turns down the heat and looks up. "What you got to feel so good about?"

That's when I know for sure that I ain't gonna get lucky tonight. "Um . . . nothin'. Just crossed my mind how glad I am to be married to you."

"What's that I smell?"

"Aw, honey, come on . . . "

She comes over and gives me a sniff. "Where you been, Smitty Mallet?"

"Just down to the store. It's been rainin' all day."

"I know it's been rainin'. What you been doin?"

"Aw, honey, can't I just say somethin' nice once in a while?"

"Could. But you don't never. Who all was at the store?"

"Aw, Midge, sweet pea. Why you always got to be so . . . "

"You been with hangin' out with some of those lowlifes, ain't you? You been drinkin'."

"Midge, honey, they ain't lowlifes . . . We just have a few once in a while. I'm always workin—"

"Don't you 'Midge, honey' me! Why do you do that, Smitty? You just tell me."

I sit down on the sofa, lean forward with my elbows on my knees, and look at her. "Well, tell you the God's honest truth, Midge, everything looks a lot better after a couple of drinks. I don't worry about makin' ends meet at the store or who's gonna bring back their feed, fussin' that it don't make their cows give more milk or their chickens lay bigger eggs like it says on the bags. I'm just happy I don't got to worry about nothin' for a little while. Makes me want to be nice to folks."

"You're already too nice to folks, givin' things away for free or takin' trash in trade for stuff. It's a wonder we make it from one year to the next."

"Come on, Midge. We always get by. You know, it wouldn't hurt you none to try a drink yourself. Seems like you could use some cheerin' up."

Well now, *that* was a big mistake. She shakes her finger in my face. "Smitty Mallet, alcohol is an abomination unto the Lord! So help me, Moses, don't you never say nothin' like that to me again, you hear?"

I sit there and hang my head, thinkin' I must have been crazy to talk to her like that. She goes off to bed, and I sleep on the couch for the next three nights. Every time I'm anywhere near her, she sighs real deep and rolls her eyes or clatters the dishes and slams doors and drawers. After what feels like a month of Sundays, she cools down to her usual simmer, and things get back to normal.

You know, I'd always thought that maybe if I could just get her to try a sip of moonshine, she might like it and maybe be a little happier. But after they made it against the law, I knew I didn't have no hope of makin' that happen. She's always sayin', "Lips that touch liquor ain't gonna touch mine," and, "If God wanted us to drink shine, he'd have put it here for us like he did the water."

When business got good enough that I needed a little help around the store, I hired Mort Thinly to work every mornin' till noon, 'cause that's the busiest time. Now, Mort could find anything in the store that you wanted, like some funny little cotter pin or wire hose that had fell off your tractor or a screw for a lantern that your great-aunt Bixie's grandma brought over from the old country. But he couldn't tell you what to do with 'em after he found 'em. When somebody come in askin' how to dig a well or lay out a plan to add on a back porch, Mort wasn't worth a tinker's damn. 'Course, he thought he knew how to do things. Why, he'd sit there and give you advice as long as you'd listen, but nothin' would ever work like he said.

He started courtin' Pollie Pryer, who was runnin' the town's first post office that we'd set up in the back of the store here. She's a real sweet girl—pretty too—but after a few months she run into some trouble with the US Post Office big shots—somethin' about readin' other folks' mail. She said she never done it, except for the post cards, but she quit anyways and went back to washin' and iron-in' clothes. She said they'd taken all the fun out of the job. After a while, her and Mort got married.

A few years after that, one afternoon Mort come wanderin' into the store carryin' a paper bag. He was actin' all sneaky-like and said he wanted to talk private. Mort always was a little on the odd side, so I didn't think nothin' of it and we went out back. We stopped behind one of the piles of lumber and sat down on a stack of two-by-eights.

Mort sets the bag down between us and looks around to make sure nobody's watchin'. "Lookie here what I got," he says.

I look into the sack, thinkin' I'm gonna see a snake or some-thin', but alls I see is the top of a Mason jar. I grin at him and slap him on the shoulder. "You makin' strawberry preserves?"

He shakes his head and looks around real serious. Then he pulls down the sides of the bag. It looks like murky water. "It's shine," he whispers.

"Moonshine?" I say.

"Shhhh," he says, closin' the bag back up.

"Where'd you get it at?" I ask.

"Made it," he says.

Now, I have to say, it's hard to believe that Mort could make anything. "You and who else?" I say.

"Just me. Alls you need is sugar and yeast and some mash."

"You? You done this by yourself? Pollie didn't help?"

"No, sirree!" he says, puffin' up his chest, proud as the president of the United States standin' on a bear. "She don't want nothin' to do with it."

"You sure it ain't gonna kill nobody?"

"Yes, sir. I been real careful. And besides, I tried it out myself."

"So, why you showin' it to me?"

"Well, I was thinkin' you might want to get in on sellin' it," he says. "I figured if folks knew they could buy shine right here when they come in for their chicken feed and fertilizer, it might stir up a little business for you. And I'll give you somethin' for your trouble, besides."

"Aw, Mort," I say, shakin' my head. "I might buy a few jars from you now and again just for my ownself, but . . . you know, I ain't got no plans to go off to jail."

"You don't have to sell it yourself if you don't want to," he says. "I could just hang around in the back room and folks could come there. It's just that we live so far outside town . . . "

"Now, I'd like to help you, Mort, but I ain't gonna be breakin' no law. Constable Grogan comes by all the time, you know, and he could go nosin' around. And besides, Midge'd kill me. Kill you too, I reckon."

"But . . . but . . . you ain't gonna be breakin' no law," he says. "I'll be the one makin' and sellin' it."

"Naw, Mort," I say, shakin' my head. "I don't think it's a good idea."

"Come on, Smitty. You gotta help me. Please. If I don't come up with the tax money for the house, the county's gonna take it away. Granddaddy left it to me free and clear, but I just never got around to payin' no taxes."

"Oh, good Lord. You got the tax man after you?"

"Yeah. Them fellers ain't too friendly, neither. They don't give a damn what happens to you, long as they get your money."

"What about findin' work? I hear Hank Plenty's been lookin' for some hands."

"Aw, I can't do that. I need a job where I can mostly be sittin' down."

"Now, just why is that, Mort?" 'Til that very minute, I hadn't never thought about how when he worked here, if he wasn't lookin' for somethin, he was always sittin' somewhere.

"I don't like runnin' around like I had to do here. It's too damn hot."

"Don't none of us like the heat, Mort."

"Yeah, but look at you. You're at the counter all day under that electric fan."

I can see he's got a point there, but I keep on talkin'. "Mort, you're a young feller. A hard day's work would be good for you."

He frowns. "If you won't help me," he says, "we're gonna be out on the streets. We ain't got no place to go—ain't got one relation with a pot to piss in."

"Mort, I'm sorry . . . "

"Yeah," he says, grabbin' up his moonshine and givin' me a dirty look. "Thanks a whole lot."

I watch him stomp off, carryin' the bag under his arm. Then I go indoors and try to forget about it but two weeks later he's back, all droopy and hangdog. He sits down hard in one of the chairs on the porch and holds his head in his hands. Ain't nobody else at the store but me. "What's the matter, Mort?"

He looks up and his voice is all wobbly, like he's tuning up to cry. "We're gonna have to move and ain't got nowhere to go."

"Uh, oh. The tax man?"

"Yeah. The tax man."

"How much you owe?"

"Sixty-seven dollars and fourteen cents."

"Damn, man! How'd it get so high?"

"Told you. I forgot to pay it . . . for a while now."

"Je-sus Lord. Will they let you pay it off a little at a time?"

He sniffs and wipes his nose with a big old grey hankie, then says, "Didn't ask."

"How much you got that you could pay right now?"

"Twelve dollars and some."

"Thought you was gonna be bringin' in all kinds of money from that . . . your . . . new business. What happened?"

"I can't find a way to let folks know what I got to sell, and Pollie's scared to death that Constable Grogan's gonna hear about it. She won't even let me say the word 'still' inside the house, and there ain't but the two of us in there. When I go to tend to it, I have to say I'm goin' out to hunt rabbits."

"What about that job with Hank Plenty? Did you go see him?"

"Yeah, but he give the job to some other fella. I couldn't have done it anyways. But if you'll just let me hang around out back so folks in town can buy from me . . . I got a whole lot already made up, and I think I could pull in enough money in a week or so to pay the taxes. Come on. I'll give you part of the money."

I just stare at him while he sits there, and then he puts his head back in his hands. I spit in the coffee can and stuff another plug of Red Man in my cheek. "I don't want no trouble, Mort. Man oh man—if Midge ever found out, I'd be livin' under the porch with the dogs for the rest of my life."

Mort, he just sets there lookin' real pitiful, and I start thinkin' that it would be a damn shame for him and Pollie to lose that old place. And he'd only be here a week or so . . .

After ten minutes of goin' back and forth, I decide I can't just let the tax man take the house. That sweet Pollie deserves better. And, truth be told, I'm probably the only one who's gonna be willin' to help. Pollie works so hard . . . and they still barely got enough to get by.

"All right, Mort," I say. "You can do it right on the edge of the property, all the way back to the lot line under them scrub oaks. But you got to make sure nobody sees what you're doin'."

Mort stands up and I'm afraid he's about to come over and hug me. I take a few steps back and hold up my hand.

He grins and shakes it. "You won't be sorry. I promise you won't."

"And if somebody wants to know what you're doin, what you gonna say?"

"Um, I dunno . . . "

"You say, 'Smitty's payin' me to clean out the brush,' that's what you say. And you gotta do it too. And don't forget to tell 'em I'm payin' you for the work."

"Okay, okay," he says, noddin' his head. "I'll start lettin' a few folks know today. But I'll be careful, Smitty. Promise. I won't get you into no trouble. Thanks. Thanks so much."

"That's only for one week, now. And I don't know nothin' about all this. Understand? I'm just hirin' you to clear brush. You hear me? You get caught and you're on your own."

"Yes, sir."

"You don't get the money by then, it's too damn bad. And you ain't payin' me nothin' for this. I'm payin' you for clearin' out the brush."

He's grinnin' ear to ear. "Yes, sir! You told me. Thank you, Smitty. You won't be sorry!"

Soon as he runs out the door, I'm thinkin' I shouldn't have give in like that, but I'm more worried about Midge than the law. I grab the broom and start sweepin' out the store, tryin' to get back to my regular job of worryin' about farmers tryin' to return feed they only used half of and the ones that say they just forgot to pay the last bill after I'd heard they'd been over in Turkey Creek livin' it up at Schnitickers.

That was the longest week of my life. Constable Grogan kept droppin' by and hung around for two hours on Wednesday. Said he didn't have nothin' to do. Even sat there part of the time watchin' Mort out back clearin' out the brush. He told me I oughta make Mort work faster, 'cause when folks come by, he'd just stop what he was doin' and talk to 'em. Once or twice, they'd even go sit down for a spell. I tried to get Grogan to play checkers out front with some of the old fellers, but he thought it might look bad to play a game while he was supposed to be workin'. Didn't want to ruin his reputation, he said.

Mort made a big show of workin' out back, but he did it so slow (not too hard for him) that it took the whole seven days, and nobody thought a thing of it. He said he'd got enough money to pay the taxes with a little left over. Him and Pollie even went to Tampa and bought her a new dress, then saw a movie.

After that, he had his customers all lined up. He told me they was more than happy to meet him at a clearin' just east of Grasshopper Lake Road to pick up their shine.

Must have been about a year later that Constable Grogan caught up with him and put him out of business. I was sweatin' blood while all that was goin' on, scared to death Mort was gonna give 'em my name, but he never did.

Found out later that Mort had a whole bunch of shine he'd hid way out in the woods that the law never found, and he gave me a box full for my trouble. I have to say, it was the very best hooch I ever had, and I was sorry to think he wouldn't be makin' no more—saved me some under the back steps for when somethin' special come along.

Not too long after that, Mort found a job he could do sittin' down—took up knittin', of all things. He still sells sweaters with pictures of gators on 'em down at the gator ranch. Like I always say, that Mort's one of a kind.

One nice, cool spring evenin' a few years after that prohibition law got repealed, me and Midge were sittin' on the porch after supper. Right out of the clear blue, she says to me, "Smitty," she says, "I want to ask you a question."

"Huh?" I say. "What?"

She looks down at her hands in her lap. "Never Riley was talkin' about how good Lydia Pinkham's Vegetable Compound is. It's supposed to give you lots of energy and she says it makes her feel better. Said she takes some three times a day." She looks over at me, then away. "I tried it, and you know, it don't taste all that good, but it did make me feel better."

I can't believe my ears. Everybody knows that stuff is full of alcohol. If I wasn't already sittin' down, I'd have flopped over like a dead mullet. But I try to act calm. "Is that so?"

She leans toward me. "Now, you can't tell anybody what I'm gonna say next, you understand?"

"Sure," I say, feelin' like I must be losin' my mind. I cross my heart. "I won't tell."

She settles back in her rocker. "Well, Never Riley said there's just a teensy drop of alcohol in that compound, just one drop in every bottle, and a few years back she found out she could get some shine from Mort Thinly cheaper than she could buy Lydia Pinkham's stuff and that it does the same thing, only better."

I try to stay calm. "Hmmm."

"I been feelin' a little rundown lately, myself," she says, "and I just thought . . . well . . . I was thinkin' that it might be good for me to try it." She looks over at me.

I can't believe my ears! After all these years of preachin' about the evils of drink, that crazy old Never Riley's convinced her it's okay? I say, "Why, sure, Midge. I'll see can I find some."

"I remember you sayin' how good it made you feel, how you didn't worry so much and all, and I just thought, you know . . . "

"Sure."

"And now that it's legal . . . "

"Think I might have an old jar of Mort's out back somewhere. I'll fix you a little toddie, Midge, and fix one for me, too." I make her a drink with orange juice and set a strawberry on the top. When I hand it to her, she looks at it, sniffs it, sticks her finger in it, then twirls the ice around. I remember the clinkin' sound. She licks her finger, then looks back down to the glass.

"All right," she says, her eyes open wide. "Here goes." She leans over and takes the littlest sip you ever seen, kind of twitches some, then sets the glass down. She don't say nothin'.

I wait as long as I can. "Well? What do you think?"

"I can feel it all cold on my lips after I swallow it."

"Good, huh?" I say, smilin'.

She looks at me, then takes another sip. A bigger one this time. "That ain't too bad," she says. "It sure tastes better than Lydia Pinkham's."

I take a swig of my drink, and she gives me a big smile. Within half an hour, she's talkin' and laughin' like she did when we was courtin', and before long she scoots over next to me on the swing and snuggles up real close. I can't remember her doin' that since our youngest was born. I have to say that was one fine evenin'. Fact is, to this very day, we still have a nice drink or two every Saturday afternoon. And if you ask me, we don't argue near as much as we used to.

'Course, all Mort's old moonshine is long gone, so now we buy our alcohol at the liquor store over in Turkey Creek. Ain't none of it good as his, though.

You know, I've always been glad I helped him and Pollie earn that money for the tax man so they could keep their house. And I have to laugh every time I think about him usin' the money he made outside the law to pay them property taxes. Serves the government right.

On top of that, I have to say, Mort sure enough made my life a whole lot better.

Do the Best You Can and Let the Low Side Drag

by Constable Lester Grogan

I never thought I'd wind up livin' in a little town like Toad Springs, much less be a constable there. Me? In charge of enforcin' the law? For years, I'd been the manager of the receivin' department in the Maas Brothers store in Tampa. When I first got there the place was a real mess, but I had it runnin' smooth in no time. Then, when the nephew of one of the big shots needed a job, they up and fired me. Right out of the blue. For no reason at all. And there you are.

To make a long story short, the only job I could find was as a night watchman at one of the cigar factories in Ybor City. It was around the time of them big strikes when tempers was high and people like Charlie Wall—big man in the Mafia—would have somebody killed just 'cause he didn't like the way a guy wore his hat. And I sure didn't like bein' in a dangerous neighborhood like that all by myself at two or three in the mornin', but at the time, I didn't have no other choice.

I'm a peaceful man, a lot better at managin' folks than chasin' dangerous criminals around in the middle of the night. Anyway, I was takin' a break around two o'clock one mornin' when I seen a couple of fellas slinkin' down an alley, actin' like they was up to no good, so I followed 'em. When I seen they was breakin' into Santino's Cigar Store, I ran a couple of blocks to where I knew a real policeman was on duty—I sure wasn't gonna do nothin' by myself. Anyway, the cop come back with me, big man named Jack Johnson. He pulled out his gun, and we headed down that same alley where I'd seen the fellas.

We could see a flashlight wavin' around inside the store, and it sounded like they was throwin' stuff around in there. My heart was beatin' like a son of a gun. The door was cracked open just a little, and I made sure to stay behind Jack when he sneaked in. We tiptoed over and peeked into the office where one of the fellers was kneelin' down, lookin' into an open safe, and the other one was standin' over to the side holdin' a bag.

All of a sudden, out of nowhere, Jack holds his gun up in front of him and yells, "Stop! Police! Put your hands up!" He scared the livin' daylights out of me!

The flashlight clicks off, and the fella holdin' the bag hollers, "Don't shoot! Don't shoot!" while the other one runs out the front door. Jack flips on the light, then chases after the guy, even shoots at him a couple of times. I just stare at the other fella and try to act tough, but he never so much as glances at me. He's watchin' the floor, lookin' like he might cry. Jack comes back a few minutes later all out of breath and says the feller got away but he got a good look at him. It was Gunny Grunchon, some tramp who lives in a boxcar over in the railroad yard.

He grabs the other fella by the scruff of the neck, and the guy hands over the bag. While Jack's lookin' into it, he says, "What's your name, buddy?"

"Blander. Buck Blander. But I—"

"Does that Grunchon fella have a gun?"

"No, sir. I don't think so."

"So you wanna tell me why you're breakin' in here and stealin' money?"

"Well, um . . . he said his mama was real sick and he wanted to go see her. He told me the fella that owns this place stole his money in a poker game, and I was just tryin' to help him—"

"Help him? Help him? By breakin' the law? You think that's a good idea?"

"Well, er, um, no sir," the Buck fella told him. "I reckon not. I mean—this ain't what you think. I was just tryin' to help him go see his mama."

"You standin' there with a bag of somebody else's cash, tellin' me you ain't doin' nothin' wrong?" Jack shakes his head. "Ain't no way you're gettin' out of this."

"Please," Buck said, holdin' up his hands like he's prayin'. "I'm a God-fearin' man. I'm a fireman on the Seaboard Air Line Railroad. I don't hardly know the man, just made a deal with him. I'd help him get his money, if he'd promised to get saved. That's all I ever wanted, was to lead him to the Lord and save his soul."

"Well, looks to me like he's the one been doin' the leadin'. And it ain't to the Lord."

"God as my witness—"

"You're goin' to the hoosegow, buddy," Jack says, handcuffin' him. "Caught you red-handed." Then they head out to call the paddy wagon.

I couldn't get out of there fast enough, and by the time I got home I'd decided to quit that job before I got killed. If the only job I could find around Tampa was one where I might get shot, well, I'd just have to look in some other town.

While my wife, Ethel, was fixin' breakfast for me the next mornin', she said, like she always did, "How was work?"

"Well, other than almost gettin' my head shot off, it wasn't too bad."

She looked up, her eyes wide. "Shot? Who'd be shootin' at you?"

"Wasn't nobody shootin' right at me. A policeman was chasin' a robber and was shootin' everywhere."

She put her hands over her mouth. "Oh, no. Did he kill anybody?"

"Nope. Lost him. But I'm here to tell you I'm done with this job. I quit."

She put her hands on her hips. "Quit? You can't quit. You ain't been there but a few months."

"Already did. I ain't gonna take a chance on gettin' shot, my ownself."

"And what'll we do for money?"

"If we have to move, we'll just do that. I ain't riskin' my neck no more."

I knew Ethel wouldn't like the idea, so I spent the next week stayin' out of her way so she could whine and complain to all her friends about how irresponsible I was. I been married to that woman for almost ten years, but she ain't never been what you'd call a happy, contented person, maybe 'cause we never had no young'uns. I'd finally decided there wasn't no pleasin' her, so I just quit tryin'.

When I heard they was lookin' for a constable over in Toad Springs, I thought my time as a night watchman might help me get hired on. I figured it would be easier than workin' in Ybor City, no problems with all them dangerous criminals and cigar factory strikes. Found out all's I'd have to do is study up on the law and I'd be all set.

And glory be! By the time I got hired, Ethel had gotten into a big squabble with her best friend after she caught her copyin' a dress pattern Ethel had made. Then Ethel was ready to move too. She still grumbled a good bit, though, sayin' I'm too soft to be a constable, that I wouldn't try hard enough to make sure the bad guys went to jail. Reckon I'd say she had a point there.

Turned out I was right about this little town. There ain't much excitement here, and that's just fine with me. The first case I got was when an old lady called Never Riley stopped by the office sayin' a peepin' Tom had been hangin' around her place.

"I'm tellin' you, Constable," she says, "I'm scared half out of my wits. I even started lockin' the door. Don't know what this world is comin' to."

"When did you first see him?" I ask.

She looks up at the ceiling like she's thinkin'. "Oh, about two weeks ago."

"Two weeks? You waited that long?"

She harrumphs. "I just wanted to be sure. And now I am. He's been there every single night."

"What's he look like?"

"Well, of course, it's dark, and he's in the shadows. Big old fella, but I can't see him real good."

"And you're sure he's there? Every night?"

"That's right. Every night. Between eight and nine o'clock. Right around the time I'm changin' into my nightgown, he's outside my bedroom—that's on the left side when you come in the front door. Oh, I hope you can catch him, that awful man. He's scarin' me to death!"

Now, I didn't say nothin' to her, but it goes through my mind that a peepin' Tom could find somebody better to peep at than a sixty-year-old lady, and I figured it was probably just trees movin' in the wind or somethin'. Folks had told me Miss Riley was a little strange, and I figured there probably wasn't anybody in her yard, but she nagged me day in and day out until I promised to investigate. For three nights in a row, between eight and nine o'clock, I hung out in the woods behind her house and didn't nobody ever show up. And I sure didn't try to do no peepin' myself.

I went to see her on a Friday mornin', and she sat down with me on the porch. "Did you find that no-good pervert?" she asked.

"Well, matter of fact, all I seen back there was a possum and a couple of raccoons amblin' around."

"What? He was there. I seen him out there last night! At eight thirty. And the night before, too! Why, didn't you even—"

"No, ma'am. Wasn't nobody else out there last night. If you seen anybody, it was me."

"No, no. It wasn't you. He's lots bigger than you." She looks at me sideways. "Better lookin' too."

Said she couldn't hardly see him, but somehow he's better lookin' than me? "Well, ma'am," I say, "I'm tellin' you there wasn't nobody out there but me. It was just a shadow from a tree or maybe the tree movin' in the wind."

She grabbed onto the arms of her rockin' chair and leaned toward me. "I'm *tellin'* you there's some pervert watchin' me, and you got to catch him."

Things went on like that for three weeks, her callin' and complainin' and whinin' and hollerin' that somebody was out to kill her 'til I was ready to kill her myself. Finally, it come to me there wasn't no way she was ever gonna believe me. Didn't matter that there wasn't nobody there. Took me back to what my daddy used to say: "When you can't fix somethin' right, just do the best you can and let the low side drag." And I sure couldn't fix things for this crazy lady.

So around three o'clock one Thursday afternoon, I knocked on her door. She was frownin' when she saw me.

"Got a minute I can talk to you?" I say.

"Catch him, did ya?" she says comin' out on the porch and closin' the door behind her.

"Yes, ma'am. I think we got our man. There's been a fast-talkin', beady-eyed stranger hangin' around town the last couple of weeks and I run him off today. Now you shouldn't have no more trouble. He looked real scared, and he won't be comin' back around here."

"Oh, thank you, Constable Grogan," she said, huggin' herself. "Thank you so much." Then she turned around, went back in the house and closed the door behind her without even sayin' goodbye. A few days later, she called to let me know that she hadn't seen the peepin' Tom since I talked to her and thanked me again for bein' such a good constable.

Stuff like that was small potatoes, but with that prohibition law that all the ladies was so hell-bent to get done, things got worse. Sure, you didn't see folks drinkin' much, but they were—only they were hidin' it. If you think you can stop people from drinkin' whiskey, well, fella, you got another thing comin'. The woods and swamps around here were full of stills. I even caught me a few bootleggers, and a couple of times a revenooer man nabbed somebody and turned 'em over to me rather than botherin' to take 'em in theirselves. I didn't think that was right, but I didn't argue. Instead, I come up with my own punishments.

First, I'd tell them fellers about all the awful things I'd heard could be done to bootleggers, but I didn't say that the idiots who come up with this stuff was a helluva lot worse than the drinkers. Why, there was folks who thought anybody who made whiskey oughta be beaten to a bloody pulp by the police or have tattoos put all over 'em or make 'em get gelded so they couldn't have no young'uns. The craziest was that they'd hang 'em by the tongue underneath an airplane and fly 'em all over the country. I ask you, what in God's name is wrong with folks? Makes you wonder, don't it?

Anyhow, then I'd lock 'em up in the only cell we got and let 'em set a few hours and worry. You know how when it's all nice and quiet, your mind can sneak up behind you and drive you nuts? Scarin' the livin' daylights out of 'em is what I was tryin' to do.

A while back, right after I got saved and was still thinkin' the good Lord was finally on my side, I started givin' 'em a nice, long sermon every single day instead of just a speech about why they should obey the law. I'd tell 'em what God would have to say about what they'd done, and I'd keep 'em there 'til I figured they'd learned their lesson.

'Course, I'm not talkin' about lettin' a murderer get off scot free here or nothin' like that. Why, killin' somebody, that deserves real punishment, like goin' to jail for years . . . a few years, anyway, unless, say, they had a real good reason to do it. Actually, the only murder case I ever had was when Sorrey May Only said her husband Lucas was killed by Gladys Heppner, a schoolmarm who lived next door to 'em. Well, I done a thorough investigation, and it was plain to see that Sorrey May's husband just had a heart attack while Gladys was yellin' at him about his dog, Dirty Sally. That don't count as murder in my book. That ain't nothin' but an accident.

Anyway, gettin' back to my wife . . . even though Ethel had decided she wanted to move to Toad Springs, after about five years, she changed her mind and wanted to go back to Tampa. Said the house was too small and too far away from the neighbors, the grocery store was too little and didn't have all the stuff she wanted, and the folks here weren't friendly enough for her likin'. But most of all, she didn't like Harold Mayfield, the preacher at the Fiery Freedom Holiness Baptized Church.

Truth be told, Ethel was whinin' most all the time 'til I wouldn't have minded one little bit if she did move back to Tampa. It wasn't 'til we switched over to the Church of Everlasting Liability that she finally started settlin' in. We went to church every week and while I didn't think Preacher Outlaw was sayin' nothin' special, Ethel thought he was "just wonderful," and she got real friendly with him and his wife, Gloria. She said the three of 'em was always havin' big important meetin's about church business, like raisin' money for the leaky roof, gettin' new Sunday school supplies for the young'uns, or what to do when one of the parishioners was fallin' away from God. Sounded like Ethel and Gloria didn't agree on much, 'cause, accordin' to Ethel, Gloria was picky and sarcastic and mean to everybody, especially her poor husband.

Got to where Ethel was at church more than she was home, and when I come in at night there wouldn't be no supper ready—or even on the stove. Sometimes I wondered what was really goin' on. Bein' a constable and havin' to make investigations and all tends to make a body kind of suspicious, but I was willin' to put up with whatever she was doin', 'cause for once in her life, Ethel finally seemed content. I'd even heard her singin' hymns while she worked around the house, and she kept the place extra clean and shiny, just in case Preacher Outlaw came by, she said, but he never dropped in while I was there. She tells me they're workin' together real hard on somethin' for Jesus, but she can't tell nobody about it. It's a big secret.

Then, all of a sudden, Preacher's wife up and leaves him, moves back home to her mama's in Zolfo Springs. After that,

Ethel talks even more about what a fine man Preacher is and how he deserves better than that hateful woman he'd married. And, of course, he needs Ethel there to help him at every turn.

That's when I start hearin' stories about Preacher havin' an eye for the ladies, and I started payin' more attention. It turns out him and Ethel was workin' together, but it sure as hell wasn't for Jesus. One evenin', I come home for supper and find a house key along with a note lyin' at my place at the kitchen table that says, *"Dear Lester, I'm leavin' town with Preacher Outlaw. Me and him are in love and we're movin' away to start over on a clean slate. We both prayed over it a lot and we're sure this is the Lord's will. P. S. There's some cold beef stew in the ice box. Ethel"*

While I'm still readin' the note, Sorrey May Only, the church secretary, calls. "Lester," she says in this real sad voice, "Got some real bad news for you."

"Is that so?" I say.

"I just come by the church office to pick up a few things. I know this is gonna be a terrible shock and I hope you don't pass out when I tell you this . . . but . . . " then I hear a real deep sigh and a little sob. "I found this note—"

"Ethel run off with Preacher Outlaw," I say like it happened every day.

"Oh, you dear man, you poor thing. I'm just so sorry to be the one—"

"You ain't the one, Sorrey May. I know all about it."

"But . . . well . . . if there's anything you ever need help with . . . I don't know how she could do this to you. You're such a fine man. Why, you've always been the salt—"

"Thanks for callin', Sorrey May. I'm just fine." I hang up the phone and sit down on the nearest chair. It's a surprise, I guess, but not a big one. It bothered me some but not nearly so much as I would have thought. And after a few weeks of not havin' to hear Ethel singin' the praises of that man, I'm feelin' pretty good.

It took the church a while to find a new preacher, and when I heard the new guy was named Buck Blander, that fella I helped arrest in Ybor City, you could have knocked me over. I remembered seein' in the Tampa paper before we moved here that he'd got sent up to Raiford. When I realized who he was, I didn't say nothin' to nobody, but I did go to the church to see if it was the same feller. It was, but he didn't seem to recognize me. The second time I went, I shook his hand and talked to him, but he still didn't act like he remembered me.

In the end, I decided that even though Blander got sent to prison, he probably really had been tellin' the truth and was just tryin' to help that Gunny Grunchon fella find the Lord, like he'd claimed. What do I know? Maybe he'll end up gettin' his reward in heaven.

So now we got an ex-convict preachin' to folks, and I'm guessin' I'm the only one who knows it. He seemed nice enough, so I figured there wasn't no reason to mention it to anybody. I learned a long time ago that it don't never hurt to have somethin' tucked away that nobody else knows about.

These days, I go to church every Sunday, and even though it ain't perfect, I'm still constable here and I'm makin' do with the bachelor life. It's been over ten years now, and most folks think I do a good job, that I'm fair. Still, when I get me a prisoner, even though I don't believe like I used to, I'll give 'em a good dose of what God would be sayin' to 'em while they're sittin' in that jail cell. If God could talk, that is.

And you know, it's too bad, but as hard as me and all the other lawmen try to set things straight, it don't always turn out the right way. That's when I think about my daddy sayin', "Son, sometimes you just got to do the best you can and let the low side drag."

The Wine Stain

by Hank Plenty

To hear some people talk, I was born a freak of nature. It wouldn't have been so bad if it wasn't the first thing folks saw when they met me or if I could hide it under somethin', but you can't go around wearin' a mask all the time. My mama would tell me to straighten up and be proud of myself, that I was a good boy and I didn't have nothin' to be ashamed of. Easy for her to say. She wasn't born with a purple blotch coverin' half her face.

Mama said when she first saw me she thought she must have eaten too many strawberries, 'cause she craved 'em before I was born. But Doc said it was just somethin' that happened sometimes, called it a port wine stain. Wasn't no rhyme or reason to it, wasn't nobody's fault, and it didn't mean I wouldn't be normal. And so that's how her and daddy always treated me. Like I was normal. Even though I never felt like I was.

They told me that the Sunday I got christened, everybody in town was there so they could take a look. A few of 'em said they'd heard I had horns and a tail, so I guess they was disappointed. But from the time I can remember, the other kids were always teasin' me, callin' me Purple Monster Face or askin' why I was wearin' a mask 'cause it wasn't Halloween yet. One of the girls called me Hankie and said I should wear one on my face. If I had a nickel for every time I ran home cryin' . . .

Once in a while I'd get so mad I'd go after somebody, but I'm usually the one who got beat up. Since fightin' didn't work too good for me, I tried ignorin' 'em like Mama and Daddy always said I should, but that hardly ever worked either.

I kept to myself a lot and got to where what I really liked to do was to figure things out. I'd just turned eleven when I put together the first short-wave radio in Toad Springs, set up a big antenna so our signal was clear most all the time. Give me a problem to figure out and I'm happy as a clam at high tide.

Might seem funny, but my best friend was a girl my age who lived just down the road, Marie Brewster. She never ever teased me even once and we were always together. She played cowboys with me, runnin' around outside, shootin' and yellin, and then I had tea parties with her where I had to sit real still and be careful to put my cup down just right on the saucer and not clink my spoon when I stirred the tea. When she was in charge, everything had to be just perfect.

If we went somewhere and some kid started teasin' me, she'd jump all over 'em and put 'em to shame. That worked when we were little, but when we got older, I was embarrassed. I should'a been the one protectin' her, not the other way around. But it felt good to have somebody stand up for me.

I remember the day I fell in love with her. We were twelve or thirteen, and by then she had long blonde hair that she mostly wore pulled back with a pretty colored ribbon, and her eyes were a green color that made you want to look at her forever. And she had this way of walkin' just a little slew-foot, with her toes turned out a little. That got me right in the heart. It was summertime and Daddy'd let me off from workin' in the fields that day, 'cause he had to go to Turkey Creek. I reckon Mama wanted Marie and me out of her hair for a while so she gave us each a peanut butter and jelly sandwich and a Mason jar of orange juice and said we could go have a picnic by a little river not far from the house.

Before we left, she said, "I don't want you two goin' down into the water. Last time your daddy was there, he saw a big old rattlesnake. You got to be real careful."

"Yes, ma'am," we both said.

As we were leavin, she called out, "Catch us some supper while you're down there, Hank!"

I thought that was a great idea, so I dug up some worms and grabbed my cane pole, and off we went. When we got to my favorite fishin' spot, I baited my hook and threw out the line. I have to admit I was tryin' to show off, wanted to catch the biggest fish out there just for Marie. When I didn't get any bites, I put the pole down, then sat beside her on the edge of the bank.

She gave me my sandwich and said, "What do you want to be when you grow up?"

"Not a farmer, that's for sure. Daddy wants me to take over the truck farm, but I ain't gonna do it."

She looks at me and smiles. "Why not? Your daddy grows the best vegetables around. That's what Mama says. Sweetest green beans she's ever tasted."

"Yeah, well, I just want to do somethin' different." I take a bite of my sandwich. "I've had enough of pullin' weeds and chasin' bugs. I might try raisin' cattle or somethin', but what I really like is figurin' out new ways to do things."

"You're sure smart enough to do whatever you want," she says.

I'm too embarrassed to look at her. "Aw, Marie," I say.

Then, all of a sudden, my pole jumps into the water all by itself. I scramble down to the water's edge and grab hold of it. Then I see the gator with my fishin' cork in his mouth. He come up out of the water, seemed like out of nowhere. Must have been ten feet long.

"Hank!" Marie yells.

"Shhh," I whisper, settin' the pole down real careful. "Be still."

We stare at the gator and the gator stares back. Then it starts swimmin' right at us. He looks hungry to me.

"Don't make any quick moves," I say in a low voice. I take her hand, put down my sandwich, and we get up real slow. I say, "Leave the food here in case he wants it. If he starts after us, we got to run. Either run or climb up a tree."

"Okay," she whispers.

We start backin' up real slow, but I never take my eyes off the gator.

When we're far enough away that it don't look like he's gonna chase us, we turn and run like the devil's on our heels. We slow down when we get to the road. Then she starts cryin'.

"That . . . that was so scary!" she says. "I never been that close to a gator before." Then she hugs me like she never wants to stop, and I hug her right back. It seems like a long time before she lets go, but not long enough for me. When we start walkin' home, she says, "I've never been so scared. But you knew just what to do. Wait 'til I tell everybody how brave you are!"

Really, all I did was get her to run away, but I was a hero for a week or so. Then everything went back to normal. But that was the day I knew Marie was the only girl for me. I was gonna marry her. For sure.

After that, as far as I was concerned, the world went along fine until, overnight, when we were sixteen, Marie changed.

"Hank," she said on the way home from school one day, "you know Claude Wilson, that new kid that just came to town a few weeks ago?"

"Um, yeah. I guess so."

"He's cute! Don't you think?"

I'm not sure I heard her right. "Huh?"

"Claude. Have you seen him makin' eyes at any of the girls?"

My heart drops down to my toes. "Not so's I'd noticed."

"I saw him at church last week. Wish he'd ask me to go out."

My stomach is clenched in a knot. "Why you want to go out with him?" I ask.

She grins, lookin' embarrassed. "'Cause he's cute, that's why."

"Oh," I say, my heart draggin' along in the dust behind us. "Well, I don't know nothin' about him. Sorry."

That was the first time, but before long, she was askin' about other fellas too. That's when I knew that I was good enough to be her best friend but not her boyfriend.

It took me a long time work up the nerve to ask somebody else to go out, but when I did, all I could think about was that she wasn't Marie. The other girls were nice and all, but I couldn't shake the thought that they were just feelin' sorry for me . . . or they went 'cause their mamas made 'em. They'd never want to marry me. Marie had been my only chance.

After we graduated, she started goin' out with Landis Perkins, and my heart just broke into a million pieces. He was a good lookin' feller—didn't have no port wine stain on *his* face, that's for sure. The story was, he'd come here when he was thirteen after runnin' away from home over somewhere on the East Coast, and he never went back. With good reason, so I heard. I don't know how he ended up in Toad Springs, but everybody said he was smart and a real hard worker, determined to make somethin' of himself. He started out graftin' trees and said he was gonna own his own citrus grove someday. And he did it too. Won prizes at the state fair almost every year there for a long time.

When they got married, Landis said everybody had to call Marie "Ree" instead of her real name 'cause his mama was named Marie and he couldn't stand the sound of it. After that, I made sure to call her Marie every time I talked to her, which wasn't a lot. I tried not to hate him for marryin' her, 'cause that's not a Christian thing to do. But . . . well, you know how that goes.

As time went on, I decided that since I wasn't gonna be gettin' married, I'd make myself lots of money. My daddy had a few cattle and a big truck farm. We grew corn, collards, tomatoes, potatoes, onions, green beans, sugar cane, peanuts, anything you could think of. When stuff was ready for market, we'd throw a big load of it in our wagon. Then, early the next mornin', we'd hook up our oxen, Redden and George, and go to Tampa. Since oxen ain't known for breakin' no speed records, it was a real long day. We'd leave home before the sun came up and get back way after dark. For sure, it wasn't no easy life and wasn't no way to make lots of money.

"Daddy," I said a million times, "there has to be an easier way to make a livin'."

"Maybe so, but this farm's all I got," he'd always say. "Just keep up with things one step at a time, and make sure you don't never expect to be done with it all."

"But we could make it easier. I've got lots of ideas. If you'd just try 'em."

"You ain't come up with nothin' worth doin' yet. And you know we ain't got money for one of them fancy tractors."

"But Daddy, it would pay for itself in the long run. We could plow more land and grow more crops—earn more money and make things easier at the same time."

"Cost too much."

"And folks are tryin' new weed killers and fertilizers—"

"Cost too much."

But I didn't give up. Instead, I come up with a new way to irrigate the crops. There was a ditch that run along the north side of our biggest field, so we had water close to the plants, but we still had to haul it out to the rows. It come to me one day that if the whole field sloped downhill, just a little bit, we could dredge us some little canals at the highest point near the ditch, and it'd flow down all by itself. But Daddy said movin' all that dirt was way too much work.

I didn't think it was fair that he wouldn't even try it, so I made up a wooden box about five feet by five feet, propped it up so it sloped downward a little and filled it up with dirt. Then I made some furrows and added a hose at the top with holes poked in it. Worked just perfect, watered the whole thing. But it didn't convince Daddy.

Now, he was a good man. He was a good father too. But he sure wasn't what you'd call a forward thinker. If it was good enough for his great-granddaddy, it was good enough for him.

Not long after, I told one of the farmers about my idea, and he set up a few acres that way. Had some problems gettin' the slope just right, but he liked it. Made me feel good, but it didn't earn me any money.

In my twenties, I started thinkin' about goin' off to Tampa and doin' somethin' totally different, maybe work in an office or the like, but just the thought of leavin' Toad Springs with this damn mark on my face stopped me cold. Folks around here had got used to me, but the fact is, I'm different from everybody else, kind of a loner. To this day, it still don't seem right that I can't even decide to move off somewhere without havin' to worry about my damn face. The thought of all them strangers starin' at me is just too much. Call me a coward. Maybe I am. But I stayed right here.

Anyway, me and Daddy kept plowin' the fields with Redden and George, plantin' all our seeds by hand and haulin' water out to the fields when it didn't rain. I got to where I hated bein' a farmer with every single bone in my body.

In my thirties, I finally come up with an idea that made money. I figured out an easier way to clean up all the citrus before it got shipped off. Called it Plenty's Citrus Washer. First, you toss the fruit into a big old vat filled with soapy water and swish it around with a wooden rake. Then you pull the citrus onto a special-made conveyor belt (which is where I made the money). It goes down the line where folks are waitin' to toss the bad fruit out, and when the good ones hit the end of the belt, they just fall into the wooden crates you've made to ship 'em in. I'm still workin' on a better way to make them boxes or a way to get 'em back after they've been shipped off so we can use 'em again. It's a lot of trouble to make all them crates.

Anyway, once word got out about the conveyor belt, it wasn't long before folks were askin' me to come set up citrus washers all around central Florida. And I found out if you can save a farmer money, he don't care what you look like—made me lots of new friends. I was right proud I was doin' so good, even fixed up the house and got Mama the new furniture she'd been wantin' for ten years. Then, when everything was lookin' real good, the worst thing in the world happened, right out of the blue.

For their thirty-ninth weddin' anniversary, my folks went over to Plant City to see a movie, and on the way home a drunk fella ran into 'em head-on. I still don't like to talk about it. Mama died right there, and Daddy was hurt bad. I think he might have been okay if she'd lived, but after losin' her he just didn't have the heart to go on.

For the first time in my life, I was entirely alone. 'Course, people were nice to me, but there ain't nothin' like a family. It took me a long time to get used to walkin' through the back door into a kitchen that didn't have the smell of fried chicken or beef stew cookin'. Most times I'd heat up some soup and eat sittin' at the kitchen table listenin' to the radio. I hired some men to help on the farm, but I still hated every minute of it.

I'd been livin' alone for a long time when this scraggly mutt shows up in the yard. He was just skin and bones, dirty old grey color with reddish brown patches on him, and you could tell he hadn't been eatin' too good. Wasn't the best-lookin' dog around, but that just made it seem like he was meant to be with me. I named him Buddy, and sometimes I got to feelin' like Mama and Daddy'd sent him down from heaven. He'd go with me when I went around settin' up new citrus washers and wait on the front seat of the truck 'til I was done. I even let him sleep in the house, which Mama wouldn't never have allowed. As time went by, I saved my money 'til I had enough to give up farmin' and finally start raisin' dairy cattle. Before too long, I was one of the richest fellas in Toad Springs. But I was still all alone.

By the time I was gettin' into my late forties, Landis had taken to the drink real bad and I'd heard Marie wasn't happy with him. I went over to Schniticker's Tavern one Saturday afternoon, which I hardly ever did, and Landis was there and took me on in a game of pool. I was about to beat him too when I sneezed just as he was makin' a shot and his cue ball went crooked. It cost him the game and he was fit to be tied, said I'd done it on purpose. I told him I did not either, and he backed me up against the wall. When he pulled back to hit me with his fist, I ducked and he slammed his hand into the door jamb. That fella let out a holler you could have heard in Okeechobee and I got the hell outta there. Made me feel good, I have to say, that he's the one ended up gettin' hurt instead of me. I wonder if he ever told Marie about that.

Every time I saw her and Landis around town, I felt sick. She was always nice, but Landis wouldn't even look me in the eye. He'd quit comin' to church a long time ago, so she'd sit with Sorrey May, 'cause *her* husband never come to church either. I always sat a few rows behind 'em just so I could look at her. Instead of listenin' to the sermon, I'd daydream about what it would be like to be married to her, to go to bed with her every night and wake up next to her every mornin'. I wondered if we'd have had kids if she'd married me. I wondered if she'd been mostly happy, what her life was really like from one day to the next. But I never let anybody know what I was thinkin'.

Pretty much all I ever said to her was, "Good mornin', Marie. You're lookin' nice today," even though she mostly just looked tired.

Some days, she'd look up at me and say, "Well, hello there, Hank. It's good to see you." Other times she'd hardly notice me on her way out the church door.

After Landis had that stroke, he couldn't walk or talk or nothin, and she was takin' care of him and runnin' the citrus business too. Got to where she hardly ever smiled anymore. He died a few years later, and a month or two after his funeral, I decided to drop in on her. I'd always seen her at church, but I hadn't really sat down and talked to her since before she got married. Now, I know it's not Christian to think like I did, but I couldn't help it. I'd loved her for so many years. Way, way in the back of my mind, I wondered if it could be possible that she'd always loved me like I had her, if she'd ever been sorry she'd married Landis.

It seems silly now, even to me, but I was nervous when I knocked on her front door early that winter afternoon. When she opened it, she looked worn out. Her hair was all stringy and she was wearin' a dirty apron.

"Why, hello, Hank," she said, pullin' her hair back from her face. "What are you doin' here?"

I'm holdin' my hat in my hands, feelin' around the rim. "How you doin, Marie? I was out this way and thought I'd say hello."

"You wanna come in?"

"Why, sure. That'd be nice."

She steps back and says, "Place is a mess. Sorry. Ain't been myself lately."

"That's all right," I said.

She points to the couch. "Sit down. Want some tea?"

"That sounds real good."

When she leaves to fix it, I look around the room. There's a pile of dirty clothes in the overstuffed chair, a moldy towel crumpled on the floor, and the dinin' room table is covered with crumbs and dirty dishes. My heart gets tight. She used to always have everything just perfect. This sure ain't the Marie I used to know. But then, I remind myself, she's been through hard times.

I'm surprised when she comes back in with teacups on a tray instead of glasses of sweet tea. I hadn't drunk out of a teacup since we was kids, and I find myself bein' careful not to clink the spoon when I stir it, like I did at our tea parties. But I notice she clinks hers a little, 'cause her hand's shakin' some.

Then she starts talkin' fast, lookin' around the room or out the window, not at me. "What you been doin' lately? Stayin' busy, I bet. You know, my Ginger's gonna have another baby. Hope that's the last one. Her and Grady's sayin' I can move in with them now that Landis is gone, but I'm gonna stay right here. Last thing I need is to be livin' with a bunch of squallin' young 'uns. And besides, Ginger ain't the housekeeper I taught her to be. I don't need to be around all that clutter." She looks at me and shakes her head.

I say, "It's been a long time—"

"And my boy, Worthy. You heard he won that big prize over in Bartow? He's come up with some new kind of fertilizer they say is gonna make him famous all over the world."

"Yeah, I heard—"

"That boy . . . I'm right proud of him."

I nod, wonderin' why she's talkin' so much. "We're all proud of him. The whole town."

She looks at me and smiles a little. "Smartest person ever born in Toad Springs."

"Yes, ma'am. He sure is."

It's quiet while we each take a sip of our tea and put the cups down real careful in the saucers. She glances at me, then down at her hands. "That was too bad about losin' your folks all them years ago, Hank. Don't think I ever even told you that. Couldn't go to the funeral and all . . . "

"That's okay."

She stares at the floor.

I clear my throat. "Got me a good old dog. Buddy's his name, and he goes everywhere with me. But I have to say that sometimes through the years, I been kind of lonesome . . . "

She gives me a hard look. "You don't know nothin' about bein' lonesome."

It's too quiet. I say, "You know, I give up farmin'. Doin' real good with the cattle now."

"Yeah. I heard about that." She pauses, then leans back in her chair and looks right at me. "Um, Hank, you remember back when we was kids? How we used to be best friends?"

"Sure do." I take a deep breath and screw up all my courage. "You know, Marie, I know I didn't ever tell you this, but—"

She speaks up. "I've missed havin' you around all these years, Hank. Ain't never had another friend like you." She glances down at her hands in her lap. "But Landis . . . well, he had some funny ideas. Didn't like me talkin' to other fellas for some reason. But you were the best friend I ever had."

I smile at her. "You were my best friend too, Marie. You know—"

"Marie. You're the only one who ever calls me that . . . Everybody else says Ree."

"That's all I've *ever* called you. It's your name, after all."

It's quiet.

"Well, what's done is done," she says. "All water under the bridge now, I reckon." She sighs.

The more we talk, the more I see how she's changed through the years. The Marie I remembered, laughin' and bein' silly, so young and full of life, always determined to make sure everything was just so. That Marie wasn't there no more.

Then it comes to me. This is all that's left of the girl I've been in love with all these years. I been sittin' here talkin' to Ree. Not my Marie.

When I get back to the truck, Buddy's waitin' in the front seat, waggin' his tail. I reach over and pet him. Drivin' home, I can't help but wonder how different it might have been if I hadn't had the wine stain. If she'd have married me then instead of him. If she'd have ended up any happier than she has.

But I'll never know the answer to that. And I guess it don't matter anyways.

I Never Fit In

by Bob Only

Back when I was a little girl, sometimes I felt a lot like that old man, Hank Plenty, who had a wine stain on his face. I never fit in either. I didn't have no marks on me, but it ain't easy when you're livin' in a little town like Toad Springs and you're different from everybody else.

When I was a kid, I always helped Daddy fix the truck when it broke down and patch the roof when it leaked. He'd say, "Ya, know, honey, sometimes I feel like I got me a son after all. You work as hard as any man I know."

I liked that he said that. Made me different from my stupid sisters. Made me feel like Daddy loved me best.

I'm the third oldest of four girls, and I was the town's tomboy. Daddy always said I can catch a black bass when there ain't even one there and shoot a twenty-two better than Rusty and Little Mike Heppner who lived next door. They were always over at our house playin' cowboys or tag or dodgeball or somethin'.

I was six or seven when one day, I said to Mama, "I'm gonna change my name."

"What?" she said. "What's wrong with Barbara Jean?"

"I hate it. I'm gonna change it to Bob."

She frowned. "Bob? You can't do that. That's a boy's name. Girls can't be named Bob."

I knew it'd make her mad, but I said, "I'm gonna do it anyway."

Then she puts her hands on her hips. "Oh, no, you ain't. I ain't havin' no girl with a boy's name."

I knew I was probably riskin' my life, but I turned and ran out of the room, yellin' over my shoulder, "You already got one!"

She finally caved in a little and started calling me Barb, instead of Barbara Jean. That way she could pretend nothin' had changed and I could pretend she was sayin' Bob. Or maybe it was 'cause I reminded her that she had a cousin named Roberta—like a girl's name for Robert—and sometimes they called her Bobbie, but with an *ie*.

My sisters, though, were another story. We were all out on the front porch one afternoon, watchin' the rain and arguin' over whose night it was to wash the dishes when I told 'em.

Dancy Lynn's the oldest. She looks at me like I'm a fool and says, "That's stupid. You're a girl named Barbara Jean, and that's what I'm callin' you."

"Barbara Jean is somebody else, not me. Call me that, and I ain't gonna answer you."

Elsie Lou pipes up. "Your name's better than mine. Mine's got too many Ls in it."

"Better than mine too," Mindy Sue says. "Mindy. Ugh."

"Oh, hush up," Dancy says. "Mine come from one of Daddy's old girlfriends, remember? Mama said if she'd found out when I was a baby, she could have changed it, but I was four years old, and by then, it was too late to call me Elizabeth like she wanted. And since you're older than four, you can't change your name either, Barbara Jean."

I stand up and put my hands on my hips and lean into her face. "Just watch me."

When our neighbors, the Heppners, first moved in next door, Mama took 'em some banana bread. She said she was tryin' to make 'em feel welcome, but we all knew she just wanted to find out what sort of furniture they had and what kind of people they were. When she got home, she said Mrs. Heppner had told her, in no uncertain terms, that she did *not* want to live in Toad Springs around so many uneducated country bumpkins, 'cause she'd gone to college for a year and was used to more refined people.

Now, it ain't unusual for my mama to rub folks the wrong way, but normally it takes more than one meetin' to get 'em so uppity. I don't know what Mama said, but she only left the banana bread there, she told us, because it was *the Christian thing to do.* She brought her dish home 'cause she was sure Mrs. Heppner would never give it back. Within a couple of weeks, everybody at church knew you didn't want to put Mama and Gladys Heppner in the same room if you could help it.

Funny thing is, the Heppner boys, Rusty and Little Mike, turned out to be my best friends. And their mama was my school teacher startin' in the sixth grade. I think, deep down in her heart (if she even had a heart), she hated kids. When I got to her class, that's when my trouble really started. Everybody was callin' me Bob by then, but she decided that at school, the kids had to call me by my given name. Barbara Jean. If anybody slipped up and called me Bob, she made 'em stand up by their desk and look me in the eye and say, "Barbara Jean," which was supposed to make me feel bad. And it did.

She was always sayin' things like, "Barbara Jean, it's too bad you're such a plain Jane. If you'd act more ladylike and stop cuttin' your hair so short, you might be able to find yourself a beau someday."

"I don't want no beau," I'd say to her. "Don't want no boy bossin' me around."

"Well, you certainly won't find a man the way you behave. Your comportment is abominable. The whole world knows that every decent young lady sits with her knees together or her legs crossed, not the way you sit all sprawled out. Why, you sit like a boy!"

I'd just give her a dirty look and try to act like I didn't care what she said, but inside I was really, really mad. And after a while I decided to do somethin' about it. So one day I sneaked a pair of Rusty's overalls off the clothesline and wore 'em to school the next day—behind Mama's back, of course. I sneaked in the classroom real quiet and sat in my seat while Mrs. Heppner was writin' on the blackboard. I was scared half to death, but I was gonna show her she couldn't tell me what to do. She must have felt it, 'cause when she turned back to the class, her eyes went straight to me.

"Barbara Jean Only!" she growled in the meanest voice I ever heard. "Stand up, young lady."

My heart was beatin' fast, but I got up real slow, lookin' right at her. There wasn't a sound in the room. All the kids turned to look back at me, and you could have heard a pin drop. First they looked at her, then at me, then back to her. Rusty and Little Mike were both tryin' not to smile.

She walked over my way . . . I can still hear her shoes clompin' on the wood floor. She stood in front of me with her hands on her hips. Her face was beet red, and her eyes were all squinty. "Barbara Jean Only," she snarled like an old yeller hound dog, "you march yourself home this instant."

I stared at her like I hated her.

"And you dress properly before you come back to school," she says. "Do not *ever* come here dressed like that again. If you do, you'll be expelled." Then she harrumphs herself up to her desk while I just stand there. She sits down, snatches a piece of paper from the drawer, and her hand's shakin' while she writes a note to Mama. When she's done, she holds it out to me. "Give this to your mother immediately, and tell her I expect her to do a better job of supervising her children."

I was glad to get out of there, but I was still shakin' a little too. Somehow, I managed to keep myself from cryin' 'til I got home and Mama lit into me. She was fit to be tied, mad at me for wearin' the overalls and at Mrs. Heppner for sendin' me home.

That afternoon, soon as Mrs. Heppner got home from school, Mama went next door and gave that woman a piece of her mind. I don't know what she said, but it just made the old witch hate me all the more.

Except for havin' to be around Mrs. Heppner, things went along pretty good for a few years. For some reason, my sisters just started ignorin' me. By the time I hit fifteen, all three of 'em were spendin' all their time gigglin' over boys and fightin' over each other's clothes. They'd pinch their cheeks to make 'em pink and roll their hair in rags every night so they'd have curls, then talk all afternoon about who said what to who and who was in love with who and the like. All they wanted to do was get married and have babies.

"You don't like Daddy tellin' you what to do all the time," I'd tell 'em, "but you start moonin' over some boy who's just gonna do the same thing. What makes you think you're gonna be happy with that?" But they didn't pay me no mind.

I don't know what started it, but it seemed like one day my mama and my sisters all ganged up together and decided they had to change me. I wanted Daddy to stand up for me and make Mama leave me alone, but he wasn't never one to get into an argument with her if he could help it. "Just try and do what your mama says once in a while," he'd say. "She means well."

One day, me and Dancy were in the kitchen helpin' Mama bake a pecan pie. For no reason at all, Mama stops and looks at me, then says, "Barbara Jean, honey, you got to start fixin' yourself up in some nice clothes." She winks at Dancy, then looks back at me. "And your sister's got some really pretty hand-me-downs would fit you, don't you, Dancy?"

"Sure do. You could have that green—"

"No! I *hate* Dancy's clothes."

"Well, honey, folks might call you Bob, but it's still a fact you're a girl, like it or not."

"I *like* bein' a girl," I say. "I just don't want to wear those stupid dresses."

"You damn well better like bein' a girl, 'cause you're stuck with it," Mama says. "And it's high time you started actin' like one."

I put my hands on my hips. "If I'm a girl, any way I act is like a girl acts. 'Cause I *am* a girl."

Mama says, "You know what I mean, Barbara Jean. Don't sass. Now, you wait right here. I got somethin' to show you." She goes into the bedroom and comes back in holdin' up the most god-awful blue dress I ever seen. It has white lace around the neck and a ruffle on the bottom of the skirt. "Now, look here what I made for you. I been workin' on it for almost two weeks, and you're gonna look so pretty in it, honey. We'll put some ribbons in your hair, and you'll turn every head in church."

I'm so mad, I'm ready to explode, but I try to look calm. "Mama," I say, "you know I hate all them ribbons and frilly stuff."

"Well, you're gonna wear 'em, like it or not," she says. "That's what girls do."

"Mama, I ain't wearin' ruffles."

"Come on now, baby. You're as pretty as any girl in town, and you should be proud of yourself."

"I *am* proud of myself," I say. "And you can give that dress to one of the others. Give it to Dancy."

Mama shoves the dress in my face. "Just stop it right this minute. You're wearin' it on Easter Sunday, come hell or high water. Show everybody what a pretty girl you are."

I'm gettin' mad now. I take a deep breath. "Come on, Mama. Give it to Dancy. She'll like it."

"No, I won't," Dancy says.

Mama gets that look on her face like she's gonna cry and starts whinin' like she does when things ain't goin' her way. "But I made it especially for you, honey. I got the cloth from Carrie June and it's the same color blue as your eyes. I worked so hard on it. And you'll look so pretty—"

"Please, Mama," I whine back. "No. Please."

But that just makes Mama switch back to bein' mad. "All right, miss smarty pants. You just stop sassin' me, young lady. I ain't talkin' about this no more. Try it on. Right now."

I wore the damn dress to church on Easter Sunday, and Mama was right. People did notice me, especially the boys. Even Little Mike looked at me like he'd never really seen me before and told me I was beautiful.

I just wish I'd liked hearin' it.

Mason Jar Treasures

by Rusty Heppner

One summer when my brother, Little Mike, was nine or ten, we went fishing with Worthy Perkins, and a gator bit Little Mike pretty bad on his legs. The doc patched him up, but it took him a long time to heal, so he was moving slow for a while there. That's when he first started collecting things, just to give him something to do. In the beginning, it was whatever he could find near the house, things that were easy to catch—inchworms and ladybugs and grasshoppers and the like.

He'd sit out front with his legs all bandaged up, and while he was looking for bugs, every morning around ten o'clock the Sheeley's sweet old yellow hound dog named Flora would come strolling down the street, minding her own business. And every day she'd run into Dirty Sally, a bad-tempered old mongrel, ugly as homemade sin, that belonged to the Onlys who lived next door. Dirty Sally wasn't ever what you'd call friendly, but Flora was everybody's best pal. Little Mike said that every day was the same. Dirty Sally would come running up to Flora, snarling and growling and dancing around like she was about to attack. Then she'd turn around and run off, yipping like she'd got hurt, while Flora just kept on walking down the road.

Now, Little Mike and I wanted a dog in the worst way, but our mama was a school teacher and was real persnickety, so she wouldn't ever let us have one. Said they drooled all over everything and carried fleas and God knows what else, and she wasn't having any filthy animal hanging around. She didn't even want me and Little Mike inside our house during the daytime because we might make a mess. And we had to be careful not to start talking like the people from here—she thought they were uneducated and unsophisticated and she didn't want us to be seen that way. She wouldn't let us say *y'all* or *nothin'* or talk like our friends.

One day, while Little Mike was having his lunch on the front porch, Flora came up wagging her tail and sat down beside him. She was licking his cheek when Mama saw and yelled out the front door for him not to let that nasty dog get slobber all over his face and to get it off the porch. After that, Little Mike sat under the oak tree out front where Mama couldn't see him, and it got to where every day, after Dirty Sally did her dance and left, Flora'd come sit with him. Seemed to me that Little Mike healed a lot faster after Flora showed up. From then on, she was with us most all the time.

After his legs got well, Little Mike kept on collecting things out in the woods, like old bones and arrowheads and little pieces of pottery and the like. Some days, he and I would go next door to see our friend Bob. Her real name was Barbara Jean, but she wanted everybody to call her Bob. She played with Flora as much as we did, even though Dirty Sally was her dog. Well, hers and her sisters'. Since kids *were* allowed to go into Bob's house, we'd sneak in the kitchen and get Flora a piece of bacon or some leftover soup bones when Bob's mama wasn't looking. Once in a while, Bob would give Dirty Sally a treat too, but she really liked Flora better.

After the sun came out one rainy afternoon, we were splashing around in the puddles and got so dirty we decided to hose ourselves down. And we hosed Flora down too. That's when we noticed that she had a lot of ticks.

"Ugh," Little Mike said. "I saw some on her before, but not this many. We've got to do something."

"They're everywhere," Bob said, parting the hair on Flora's coat. "I'll hold the hair back, and you can pull 'em off, Little Mike."

"I don't have any tweezers," Little Mike whined.

Bob just stared at him. "Well, how about your mama? She's got some."

"You trying to get me killed?" he said. "No way."

"Just use your fingers, then."

He folded his arms across his chest. "Oh, no. I did that once, and it popped and got blood all over me. It was so squishy and nasty." He shivered. "I'm not doing that."

"We need some matches," I said. "Touch 'em with a lit match and they'll let go."

"But if you slip, you'll burn Flora instead of the tick," Bob said. "How about lard? You put that all over the ticks, and they'll smother. They can't breathe through that stuff."

"Won't work," I said. "Dogs love lard. Flora'll just lick it off before the ticks die."

Little Mike piped up. "How about kerosene? That kills head lice."

"No," I said. "She might lick that off too. Then *she'll* die. But I heard you can freeze 'em out, chip off some little pieces of ice from the icebox, and mash the tick down with it. They wouldn't like that."

Bob stood back and crossed her arms. "So, what are we gonna do?"

"I bet your mama's got tweezers," Little Mike said to her.

I rolled my eyes. "Her mama won't let us use her tweezers."

Bob grinned. "She will if she don't know about it."

She sneaked in and got the tweezers, and we went out in the backyard and took turns pulling the ticks off. We were all surprised how patient Flora was. She'd just make a peep once in a while when we pinched her instead of the tick. She had a ton of them too. We didn't want to just drop them on the ground because then they could get right back on Flora, so I went to the garage and got a jar that Daddy used to keep old nails in. When we were done, we'd just about filled it to the top with big, fat, ugly, nasty, grey ticks full of Flora's blood.

"I'm going to collect them," Little Mike said, smiling while he screwed the lid on tight after we finished.

"What for?" Bob asked.

"I don't know. I just want to."

"You'll have to hide them in the garage," I said. "If Mama ever saw them, you'd be able to hear her yelling in Tallahassee."

Little Mike had been storing his collections in the garage all along because Mama wouldn't let him keep them inside, so we put the ticks out there with the animal skulls and snake skins and boxes and jars full of little tiny bird bones. One time, he'd glued some of those bones onto a piece of cardboard and made a real pretty eagle design. Another time, he found what looked like a person's arm bone, but couldn't think who it might have belonged to, maybe some Indian from a hundred years ago or a monster who could still be haunting the woods, looking for it. He didn't bring that one home.

He got really interested in arrowheads and found some pottery that was left by the Indians that had designs like zigzag lines or rows of little dots. He'd talk about how it had been a real person who'd made what he was holding in his hand, and he wondered who they'd been and what they'd looked like. He felt like they were connected in some way.

Mama got him a book called *The Lure and Lore of Archeology*, which was way too hard for a kid to read, but she went all through it with him. After that, Little Mike was hooked, and Mama kept talking about how we were gonna have a real archeologist in the family. She even let him keep the pottery in the house, but everything else had to stay in the garage.

For a while, they let Little Mike set up a sort of museum area in the Toad Springs Library. He studied the best he could about the things he'd found and made up little cards he put beside each piece, telling what it was along with when and where he'd found it, because that's what real archeologists do. Lots of folks came to see it.

Mama wanted him to go to archeology school, but it cost too much. Instead, when we grew up, he moved to Tampa and went to work in a bank. He thought that way, he could be sitting at a desk all day so that when it rained and his leg acted up from the gator bite, he wouldn't have to be walking around on it.

A good while later, after we'd both been married for a while, Mama invited us and our wives over for supper one Friday night. Sweetie and I brought a cherry pie for dessert and Little Mike and Judy brought some store-bought flowers from Tampa. While the ladies got the pork chops and green bean casserole on the table, us men were sitting on the porch talking, when Little Mike slapped his knee and looked over at me. "Hey, Rusty, remember all the bones and arrowheads and pottery I collected that we kept out in the garage?"

"Yeah, sure I do."

"I was telling them at work about my collections, and they want to see them. Especially the bones. Man, I loved finding all that stuff. I should start doing it again. Remember the cards I made when I set it all up in the library? Wonder if it's still out there." He turned to Daddy. "Did you throw that stuff out?"

"I don't know what you're talking about. What stuff?"

"There was a big poster along with a lot of cigar boxes that I kept in old orange crates."

"Doesn't ring a bell. I can't remember seeing anything like that."

Just then, the ladies called us in to eat.

"Let's look after supper," Little Mike said to me.

After the blessing, Mama sat up straight, cleared her throat, and picked up her fork. She looked at me, then at Little Mike, and said, "I'm so glad you boys could come tonight. I know you young people don't have a lot of time to waste on your parents."

"Oh, Mama, please," I said. "Being with you isn't wasting time."

"I just hope you can all come to the big supper a week from Sunday at the Church of Everlasting Liability. They're holding a cooking contest, and I'm submitting something. It's different from the usual, though, because now they assign the dishes. That way, they can see how skilled a cook you really are."

Little Mike and I looked at each other and Sweetie said, "We wouldn't miss it." (That was back when Sweetie was still trying to be nice to Mama.)

Little Mike said, "Okay."

"In that case, I have a favor to ask you," Mama said, looking at Little Mike. "One of the ear pieces broke off my glasses last night, and I was wondering if you could take them back to Tampa and have them repaired."

"Sure, I will," he said. "And I'll bring them back next Sunday."

She took a sip of sweet tea, then said, "Thank you, son."

"Do you know yet what dish you're going to fix?" Judy asked.

"Well, they have four categories: desserts, breads, meats, and vegetables. I'd rather bake my famous red velvet cake. Everyone knows it's my specialty. But the committee assigned me to bake muffins." She rolled her eyes. "I shouldn't have to bake muffins. Any idiot can bake muffins."

"Yours will be good," Judy said. "You'll think of some way to make them special."

Mama wiped her mouth with a napkin, then said, "Actually, I heard that Sorrey May's bringing a red velvet cake."

"Well, hers won't be good as yours," Sweetie said. "It'll be their loss."

We all nodded in agreement.

"Anyway, Edna Sheeley said she has some extra special kind of raisins I can use that her daughter sent her from California. She said she'd drop them off sometime in the morning on her way to the grocery. If I'm not here, I told her to just leave them on the porch."

"Um, hmm," Daddy said.

Mama took a deep breath and let it out slowly. "I've decided to put some special cream cheese icing on the muffins, just to dress them up a little."

"You're a good cook, Mom," Little Mike says. "I'm sure you'll win first prize."

She looked around the table and smiled at each one of us. "Now that you mention it, that's exactly what I intend to do."

After we finished our pork chops and applesauce, all the men went to the porch like always. "Got a flashlight I could use?" I asked Daddy. "Little Mike and I want to see if we can find those old Indian arrowheads."

"Right by the back door," he said. "On the top shelf."

The garage was full of cobwebs and bugs, and the flashlight wasn't all that bright. But behind some lumber that was stacked against the wall, it was all there, that big old poster, all stained and faded, beside three dusty orange crates full of cigar boxes that were all covered with cobwebs.

Little Mike started going through it. "Look at this," he said, wiping the dirt off a Mason jar. "Look! These damn things are still here." He held it up, and I could see all those nasty little shriveled-up brown ticks still inside, dead as doornails. He opened the jar and stirred them around with a screwdriver, and they all separated. It's been so many years, they don't even smell bad.

"What you gonna do with them?" I asked.

"Throw them out. Yuck. Why did I ever keep them in the first place?"

We picked up the jar, along with a box of arrowheads, one of bones, and one with a snakeskin in it, and walked back around to the front porch just as they were calling us inside for dessert. Little Mike put everything down on the porch floor next to the door as we went in. Mama would have a fit if he took any of it inside. We told the ladies about the arrowheads and bird bones while we had dessert, and Mama reminded us how impressed everybody was with Little Mike's archeology display years ago. After the ladies cleaned up the kitchen, they joined us in the living room to talk for a while with the radio on real low. About eight o'clock, we all headed for home.

When we came back the next Sunday afternoon, Mama was glad to get her glasses and really proud to show us the muffins that she'd layered with two different kinds of icing—lemon and cream cheese—to impress the judges.

When we got to the church, we saw they were holding the contest outside, with tables and chairs already set up for folks to sit down and eat supper. I thought to myself that they'd better hurry up. It was a little cloudy and the sun was getting low. I could see it would be dark before we finished eating. At least they had a few lights around.

Up front was a table covered with a fancy blue tablecloth, and that's where the food sat. Three men were standing behind it talking, and one of them announced, "It's six-thirty! Time for the judging to start."

Everybody sat down at the tables as the judges went to the blue table and started to work.

As luck would have it, Mama's muffins were the last in line, and she was a wreck by the time they got to her. She watched every move the judges made, the expressions on their faces, the way they held their heads, and whether they licked their fingers. When they got to the muffins, they each picked one up, took a bite, looked at each other and nodded their heads, then put the rest of their muffins back on the plate. After that they went off to consult with each other while one of them made notes on a piece of paper.

Mama almost cried when they announced that she'd only won second place in the bread section, and I felt bad for her. But she tried to put on a good face. Hester Brisco's cornbread won first, and Carrie June Neal's biscuits were third.

After it was over, Mrs. Sheeley ran up to Mama and gave her a hug. I saw them talking for a few minutes, with Mama shaking her head. Then she came back over to us, looking confused.

"It wasn't Edna," she said. "She didn't leave me the raisins."

"What raisins?" Little Mike said.

"She was supposed to leave me a jar of raisins for the muffins. I told you that at dinner the other night. She just told me that she forgot. Well, if she didn't leave them, somebody else did, because I found them sitting on the porch. In a Mason jar. Just like she'd said hers were, in an old Mason jar. And I used them to make the muffins."

I looked at Little Mike, and he looked at me. My stomach knotted up. "Just where on the porch did you find the jar?" I asked her.

"Right by the front door. Just where I told her to leave them. They were near the cigar boxes you forgot to take home."

"Mama," I said, "are you sure they were raisins?"

"Of course! Just don't know where they could have come from. You know, I remember the jar was a little hard to open. And I did wonder why Edna would keep them in such an old jar."

"But you didn't have your glasses . . . Mama, go and get me one of the muffins the judges tasted. They're still on the table."

"Why? What's the matter with you?"

"Mama, just do it, please. I think the raisins might be something else."

"Oh, don't be silly," she said but she went and got two muffins.

Little Mike and I each took one, and Mama followed us over to one of the lights so we could see better. We broke them open and looked at them closely. Then we looked at each other. Then we looked at Mama.

"What?" she said.

Little Mike said, "I'll go get the ones that are left. You tell her."

"Me?" I said as he trotted off. "Come back here, you! You tell her!" But he was gone.

Mama looked at me. "Tell me what?"

"Come over here for a minute," I said, walking her off to the side. "Remember back when Little Mike was collecting things?"

"Yes. But what does that have to do—"

"Well, remember Flora? That big old yellow dog?"

"I guess. Sort of."

"Well, she always had lots of ticks. And one day, well, this one day, we pulled them all off of her." I shook my head. "That poor dog."

"And?"

"And Little Mike saved them. In a Mason jar. He didn't want to throw them in the grass where they'd just get back on Flora again. When we were here on Thursday night, Little Mike took the jar out of the garage and was gonna toss it out . . . but I guess he forgot . . . and left it on the porch."

Even in the dark, I could tell she turned white as a sheet. She screamed, "Nooooooo!" Then she fainted dead away and fell down flat on her back.

People came rushing over. "What is it? What happened?"

I knelt down beside Mama and said to everybody, "Oh, she'll be okay. She just had a little surprise, that's all." I kind of gently slap her face, and she opened her eyes and looked around, surprised. Then she started crying.

Sorrey May Only knelt beside Mama across from me, leaned over and stared down at her. "What happened to you, honey?" Then she looked at me. "What's going on here?"

It seemed odd, Sorrey May being so interested in Mama. Those two have hated each other since the instant they met. "It's nothing," I said. "Something just caught her by surprise. She'll be fine."

Sorrey May looked deep into my eyes. "You have to tell me, Rusty. What is it? I need to know so I can help her."

"Really, Mrs. Only. Thanks for your help, but she's all right. We're gonna get her up and take her home now."

I don't know how word got out, but by the next day, everybody knew there were ticks in the muffins that won second place. (I felt especially bad for Carrie June, who came in third.) Anyway, I guess Sorrey May must have managed to get herself a muffin and found them. And once that woman knows something, the entire town knows it—but usually a worse version of the story than what really happened.

Mama had to confess because rumors were flying, but she made sure that everybody knew her side of things—the real truth. She told them about her broken eyeglasses and how Edna Sheeley forgot to deliver her the raisins like she'd promised and if Mama'd been able to make her regular red velvet cake that everybody knew was the best in six counties instead of that committee letting Sorrey May sneak in and do it, none of it would ever have happened.

Mama never entered another cooking competition.

And I heard that all three judges said they'd judged their last contest too.

Gator Cookin'

by Angus Hewitt

I know it ain't a manly thing, but I loved to cook from the time I was a little feller. My mama made it a point to stay out of the kitchen as much as she could. Her specialty, still today, is chipped beef on toast and it's most always burned. When I was a kid she made me help her fix supper every night, probably 'cause I don't have no sisters and I'm the youngest. Got to where I liked it—at first 'cause I got to take bites along the way and later 'cause the grownups told me I was good at it. My brothers always gave me a hard time, callin' me a sissy and a mama's boy, but they sure ate up my fried chicken and buttermilk biscuits. There was never a crumb left. And we all ate better, everybody could see that.

When I got out of school, my secret dream was to move to Tampa and be a chef in one of them big fancy restaurants, but instead I ended up countin' nails and haulin' fertilizer at Smitty's Hardware and Feed in Toad Springs. After me and Joetta got married, Smitty hired me on 'cause he knew my daddy, and I took the job 'cause I couldn't find nothin' else. After that, the only time I was in the kitchen was when I was teachin' Joetta how to fix things my way. Can't say she always appreciated my help, but she had to admit that my cookin' tasted better than hers. As time went along we had us two boys, Edgar and Ernie, who I love more than I ever thought I could love anybody.

Wasn't too long after Flavey Stroudamore opened his Rare Reptile Ranch here in Toad Springs that I first thought about openin' up a little restaurant. I figured the town was far enough off the main road that folks who come to see the gators might want to stop and get somethin' to eat afterwards. Now, the Reptile Ranch had lots of gators, but the most famous ones were Precious, who only had three legs and a mark on his side in the shape of Jesus; White Lightnin', who was an albino gator; and Sampson, who had these great big baby-blue eyes like nobody'd ever seen. Sampson's the one who'd come over to the crowd and look at 'em, sometimes open his mouth so you could see all his teeth. He's the one the little kids liked the best.

Now, some years back, my pop had bought a little piece of property in Toad Springs, thinkin' it might grow faster than Mango was growin' and he could make some money. But that sure didn't happen. So anyways, the land was next door to the gator ranch, and when I asked about buyin' it, Pop just give it to me along with the old buildin' that was sittin' on it. Then, all I had to do to open the restaurant was to fix it up and customers could just come over from Flavey's.

My first idea was to make it a drive-in, like that A&W Root Beer Stand in Tampa. Then pretty much all we'd need is a kitchen with a window to push the food out to the carhops. I figured that all the fellas around here would like havin' pretty young gals carryin' their meals out to their cars and settin' 'em up on the window trays.

When I told Joetta what I was thinkin, she said, "Angus Hewitt, we ain't in Tampa, and ain't no way you're hirin' a bunch of young gals to work for you. Over my dead body! You *know* what kinds of stories Aunt Never would start spreadin' around. I ain't gonna be puttin' up with nothin' like that."

"Aw, honey," I said, "Nobody pays any attention to that crazy old woman. We all know she's got a screw loose, havin' everybody in town call her Aunt Never. She sure ain't my aunt."

She puts her hand on my arm. "Don't try to change the subject. Just listen to me, now." Then she turns into somebody else, like she always does whenever she sets out to change my mind.

When she bats them big brown goo-goo-googley eyes at me, I lose every bit of sense I got. She says, "I already been thinkin' about how we could fix up a nice little restaurant, hang ruffled curtains and pictures of the town on the walls. Or maybe pictures of movie stars!" She pauses and tilts her head a little. "Or . . . I've been thinkin' about pictures of them silly dogs playin' cards. Somethin' kind of funny, you know, but in good taste. That'd be much more respectable than some old drive-in."

"But . . . it would be cheaper if . . . "

She gives me a big kiss. "Glad we got that straight," she says and goes out back to the garden.

In the end, I get a loan from the bank and fix up the old buildin' to make it a restaurant. It's big enough to hold a countertop with seven stools, five tables—each with four chairs—and it's got a front porch if we need more space. I plant a garden out back for the vegetables we'll need and hire Maggie Mooney to take the orders and bring the food to the tables. We paint the outside walls blue and the inside yellow, and Joetta makes blue and yellow tablecloths and gets alligator salt and pepper shakers from the Gator Gift Shop.

After I explain to her that them dogs in the pictures she wants to hang up ain't just playin' cards, they're playin' *poker*, she lets me put up pictures I took of alligators lyin' in the sun instead. Figured folks would think one of 'em was Sampson, Flavey's blue-eyed gator, but since there ain't no color in the pictures, nobody'd ever know it wasn't him. You see one picture of a gator, you've seen 'em all.

I work on a menu and even come up with "Gator Juice" for the kids by addin' a little green food colorin' to some limeade.

After we'd been workin' on the place for a couple of weeks, Flavey comes amblin' over from the gator ranch one day. "Angus," he says. "What you think you're doin' over here?"

"You know what I'm doin'. I'm buildin' me a little restaurant."

"You just need to make sure you don't put nothin' on my property. There's a property line right about here," he says, takin' a couple of steps towards his place. You just better make sure you stay on your side of it."

"I know where the line is," I say. "My daddy bought this property years back now. I know what I'm doin'."

"Just be sure you do. Don't want no trouble outta you." He spits on the ground and turns to leave.

"You know, Flavey," I say, "havin' a little restaurant right here'll be good for your business."

He looks back over his shoulder and says, "Harrumph," then keeps on walkin'. What an old grump. He didn't ask what I was gonna name it, and I didn't tell him. Lookin' back now, maybe I should have. But the truth is, he's just so ornery, I couldn't make myself do it. Didn't tell *nobody*. Decided that if I had 'em guessin', that would keep 'em interested, you know, to build up the business. I tacked up papers here and in the towns that was close by, sayin' that a new restaurant was startin' up business next to the gator ranch on Saturday, September 21, and for everybody to come by and have a free cup of coffee.

I bought a great big sign for the front of the buildin' that was made by a feller in Bartow, but to keep the name a surprise, I didn't put it up 'til late on the night before the big day. I baked some coffee cakes and pies and put the breakfast menu on a little blackboard: Coffee—5¢, Eggs—5¢, Regular Bacon—5¢, Gator Bacon—6¢, Hotcakes—10¢.

The first day, we opened at seven in the morning and the old retired fellas who play checkers at Smitty's Hardware was the first ones there, along with Aunt Never and her sister, Sorrey May. Maggie took all the orders, and things was goin' along good for about an hour.

Then Flavey comes tearin' through the door, mad as a hornet. Storms right back to the kitchen, shakin' his fist at me, hollerin', "What the hell you think you're doin', Angus? Just who do you think you are?"

I look up from the fryin' pan, where I'm turnin' over some onions and gator bacon I got sizzlin', and just smile. "Me? I'm Angus Hewitt, that's who I am. And watch your language! I got customers in here."

"You can't name this place after one of my gators!"

Makin' out I'm real surprised, I say, "Well, Flavey, I didn't!"

"You're callin' it the Blue-Eyed Gator Restaurant!" He's shakin' his fist at me now. "You're tryin' to make money off my Sampson. That gator's mine and he's the only blue-eyed gator in the world. You're just tryin' to get rich off of me."

"Calm down, Flavey. I *told* you, I figure more folks'll come to the gator ranch if there's some place in town to eat. That'll *help* you!"

"But *I'm* the one should be runnin' a restaurant," he says, stabbin' himself in the chest with his finger. "I was just gettin' ready to start workin' on it."

"Now, Flavey. You knew I was openin' this place up, and you never said one word about it."

"And *you* never said one word about the name! Was real careful to keep it secret, wasn't you? You are one low-down, no-good, sneaky devil. Well, you got the restaurant, but you can't have that name. Sampson's *my* gator."

I hold my palms up to him. "Well, you're right. Sampson's your gator. That's true enough. And if I'd named the place Sampson's Restaurant, you might have a leg to stand on. But, first of all, you don't *know* there ain't another blue-eyed gator in the world. There could be lots of 'em, just not around here."

"Nope. Sampson's the only one. I looked it up in the encyclopedia."

I flip over the slice of gator bacon before it burns.

He puts his hands on his hips. "And you know damn well that anybody around here who's talkin' about a blue-eyed gator would be talkin' about Sampson."

I just shake my head and stir the pot of grits. "I ain't changin' it, Flavey."

"We'll see about that," he says. "I'm gonna sue your ass."

He stomps off in a snit, hollerin' that I'll be hearin' from his lawyer Monday mornin', and as soon as the door slams, all the folks clap for me. Except for Aunt Never, of course, who's sittin' there with a frown on her face. I can just see those wobbly wheels turnin' inside her head.

By the next afternoon, Joetta hears that on the big openin' day, me and Flavey had a big fight, rollin' around on the floor and he's hollerin' he's gonna kill me, and Aunt Never just happens to know personally that Flavey's already called a lawyer. Then, when they win the lawsuit, Flavey's gonna take over my restaurant and run it his way and everybody can just stand back and watch. Aunt Never's plum nuts. The stories she comes up with . . . I swear she's livin' in a whole different world from the rest of us. At least most folks know not to believe hardly anything that comes out of her mouth. And I guess really, when I think about it, Toad Springs would be borin' without Aunt Never always stirrin' the pot.

I don't hear no more about the lawyer, but a week later, Flavey catches me as I'm walkin' up the front steps of the Blue-Eyed Gator one mornin'. "Angus," he calls out.

I stop and turn around.

"I know about them gator pictures you got hung up in there, and you never got no permission to take pictures of my gators and use 'em in a place like this. You ain't gonna use my Sampson to make money for yourself."

"That ain't Sampson in them pictures."

"You're gonna have to pay me if you want to keep 'em up on the wall."

"Flavey, I ain't payin' you nothin'. That ain't Sampson. That's some gator I found out in the swamp. We already ate him."

"You're lyin'."

"Them's my pictures I took myself and they're my private property and you can't do nothin' about it." I stomp inside the restaurant and leave him standin' there.

For the first few months, when I start runnin' low on gator meat, me and a couple of my buddies from Mango would go out and shoot a gator, drag the carcass back home through miles of swamp, clean it, and put the meat in one of them storage freezers over in

Turkey Creek. When it come to runnin' the restaurant, huntin' them gators down took the most time of anything—a whole day at the least, sometimes two. Every time we had to go out, I'd come home mad enough to make a preacher cuss.

Finally, I swallowed my pride and went over to the gator ranch. Flavey was sittin' in the office drinkin' coffee and complainin' to one of his hired hands about some citrus commission. "God only knows what'll happen if the government sticks its nose into . . . " He looks up at me. "What you want, Angus?"

"Just want to talk to you a minute. Got a money-makin' deal for you."

He frowns. "Is that right?"

"Yep. Thought you might be interested."

"Now, what makes you think I'd ever want to go in on a deal with the likes of you?"

"Just listen. You can make money on this."

He rolls his eyes, then shoos off the hired hand. "What you got in mind?"

"Okay if I sit down?" I say.

"All right. But I'm a busy man, now."

I take a seat. "I was thinkin' maybe I could pay you a little somethin' to shoot me some of them spare gators you got out back and serve 'em up at the restaurant."

He narrows his eyes at me. "Oh, you were, were ya?"

"You got a lot of 'em back there. Smart of you to put up that fence around your swampland and trap all them gators inside. You got big ones, little ones, all sizes."

"Yeah," he says, leanin' back and crossin' his arms across his chest. "So?"

"That was a smart move on your part," I say, wonderin' if I'm layin' it on too thick. "'Course I'd never take one of your good gators, the ones folks come to see. But them other ones out back don't cost you a penny. They take care of theirselves. Now, that's where I come in. They ain't costin' you nothin', and I'd be willin' to pay you a little somethin' if you'll let me shoot one every once in a while. For the restaurant, you know."

"Ain't no way in hell . . . "

"Now just listen, Flavey. I'm just tryin' to help you out here. Help us both out."

He glares at me but doesn't say anything.

"I was thinkin' I could pay you . . . say five dollars a head."

He slams his hands down on the arms of his chair and yells, "Five dollars a head? You crazy? You know what cattle are sellin' for these days?"

"Last I heard, maybe ten dollars?"

"No sirree. Twenty-five's more like it."

"Twenty-five? Hell, man. That's for a big old cow. I'm talkin' about a gator. And all I want is the meat. You can have the hide, could get a pretty penny for that. And you might could even sell the bones to Halt Brisco. He's still makin' jewelry out of them bones."

"Twenty-five. That's as low as I'm goin'," he says, smilin'.

"I'll give you ten. And that's it."

"Make it fifteen and we got a deal."

I shake my head. "Come on, man. This can work out good for the both of us. Take ten. And the hides. And you don't have to do a damn thing to earn any of it."

He stares at me. "I'll have to think on it," he says. "Come back tomorrow."

I end up payin' him thirteen dollars a head, which was still too much, but I'd started out offerin' five 'cause I knew he'd try to raise my offer. Hell, if I'd offered him a hundred he'd have wanted a hundred and twenty. Anyways, I gave in on that one. It was lots easier than huntin' them nasty things down and draggin' 'em back through all that swampland. 'Course, I still had to clean 'em, but it all worked out. After we closed the deal and Flavey was finally takin' some money out of my pocket, he turned more agreeable. Sometimes he'd even shoot a gator for me.

I kept addin' to the menu, and as time went by, I made up brand new recipes for gator stew, gator steak, gator burgers, gator gumbo, gator stroganoff, and barbecued gator. Since we were so close to the gator ranch, I'd turn on the fan in the kitchen and blow the good cookin' smells toward them big gator jaws on the door where folks was comin' in and out of the ranch, and business was good. By then, Flavey'd mellowed out and even came in to have a gator burger now and again. But he always made sure to tell me that his wife's fried chicken tastes better.

Things was goin' pretty good for a while, and I was all settled in for the long haul. Some folks from Tampa even said they'd heard talk about the restaurant over there, so the word was gettin' around. I felt like the luckiest man in the world.

Everything was great 'til one day, this reporter for the *Tampa Tribune* came out to the gator ranch with his young'uns. Afterwards, they came by the restaurant for lunch. He ordered gator burgers for the kids and a gator steak for himself, and when they was all done eatin', he told Maggie he wanted to see me.

I figured there was a fly in his coffee or somethin' else was wrong, but he said that was the finest steak he'd had in years and he wanted to write an article about me for the paper. I was plum flabbergasted. The *Tampa Trib*! A week later they run a real fancy story with pictures and everything. I read it to Joetta that evening. *This rural atmosphere lends itself perfectly to the tasty Florida dishes, all made from scratch right on the premises. And the food, especially the gator steak, was beyond excellent.* After that, business picked up even more.

A couple of weeks later that same reporter comes back out and tells me that the owner of Madison's Restaurant, a big fancy "fine dining" place over on Bayshore Boulevard in Tampa, wants to talk to me about workin' there. I can't hardly believe it. It's what I always wanted, what I prayed for all these years. He gives me the phone number and I screw up all my nerve to call. Turns out that since gator's cheaper than beef they're thinkin' about addin' it to their menu. When he tells me that he's heard about my cookin' I just can't believe it. My head starts goin' lickety-split, all day every day, thinkin' how I might could work with a professional cook, maybe even wear one of them chef's hats and a white jacket.

Seems like as soon as I give up on my dream of workin' in a fancy restaurant and decide I like things just like they are, this pops up right under my nose. Now, I know I'm a good cook, but I never really thought I was *that* good.

The first thought that comes to mind is that I want to get out of this little podunk town and live in Tampa. The second thought is that Joetta ain't never gonna agree to go to Tampa. When we got married she wouldn't even move a couple of miles to where I was livin' in Mango, so she sure ain't goin' that far away.

It's a Sunday afternoon, and our young'uns are at her mama's when I work up the nerve to have a talk. You can't never have a serious conversation with a two-year-old and a three-year-old in the house.

We're in the livin' room drinkin' some of my special Gator Juice from the restaurant. I'm in the rockin' chair, and she's on the couch, knittin' with some yellow yarn. I screw up all the courage I can muster. "Hey, honey," I say, "remember the fella who wrote that nice piece in the paper about us?"

"Yeah. Helped us out, didn't he? The gator ranch too. Why, I—"

"Well, 'cause of that, somethin' else has come up," I say. "Somethin' that could make a real big difference to us. Might be able to get you that new cookstove you've been wantin'. Might could even get you an electric icebox. You deserve better than that thing you're usin' now."

She looks surprised. "Well, I'd like that! Just what's the 'somethin' else'?"

I know she ain't gonna be wild about this and I shouldn't act so excited, but I can't keep myself from grinnin' ear to ear. "Madison's Restaurant over in Tampa said they want to talk to me about goin' to work for 'em. It's a real fancy place too. I'd be a chef!"

She lowers her head and gives me one of her looks up from under her eyebrows. "Oh?"

"It's the chance of a lifetime, honey. You know that's the one thing I've always wanted. Nothin' like this is ever gonna come along again."

"Why do they want *you*?"

"'Cause of the way I cook. They been thinkin' about addin' gator to their menus, and I can cook 'em better than anybody around. It's my specialty."

"Aw, sweetheart," she says, battin' those eyes at me, "you don't want to go doin' that. Things are great right here in town. You don't want to throw away all the hard work you've done buildin' up the business."

"I know, I know, but this is somethin' I really want to try."

"Sweetie, this just ain't a good time."

"There ain't never gonna be a better time, honey. Won't ever be another offer like this, that's for sure."

She crosses her arms in front of her and stares at me. She bites her lip.

"Now, just listen, Joetta. Hear me out. We been gettin' by all right, I reckon, but—"

She squints those big brown eyes at me. "Don't you go tellin' me you want to move out of Toad Springs."

"Well, I don't *want* to move. But, baby, you know that since I was a kid, I wanted to work in a nice restaurant. And it sounds like I could be a real chef! A gator chef. *And* I'd be makin' more money."

Now she's jigglin' her foot *and* bitin' her lip. "But this is our home!"

"You can make a home anywhere, hon. Long as we're together, we got a home."

"You know what I mean."

"Tampa ain't all that far, really."

"It's too far to live here and work there. That old jalopy of ours won't go over fifteen miles an hour, and it's on its last legs anyway."

"Well, it would be a long drive. But I want to meet those folks face-to-face . . . see the restaurant. At least see what it could be like. Don't mean I'm gonna do it for sure."

She's quiet, but she's still jigglin' her foot a mile a minute. "I don't want to have to—"

"Listen to me, now. I won't know if I can even work there unless I talk to 'em. I'm at least gonna do that and see what happens."

She's shakin' her head. "But . . . "

My stomach's in a knot, but I ain't backin' down. "I have to, Joetta," I say in a quiet voice. "I don't have a choice."

She takes a deep breath and looks at me. "You know, Angus, it's a shame they couldn't have picked somebody who don't have the responsibility of a family." Her foot stops movin', and she looks at me hard. "Who don't have three young'uns to raise."

I frown at her. "Three? We only got two."

"Well, we got two and then some, that's what we got. You're gonna be a daddy again, and this one's gonna be a girl, I'm sure. I was waitin' to tell you 'til I was a hundred percent sure, but I'm up to ninety-nine percent. It's either that or I'm dyin'."

I lean forward, elbows on my knees, buryin' my face in my hands.

"Well, ain't you happy?" she says. "I thought you'd be happy."

I look up at her. "I don't know, Joetta. I just don't know."

Her eyes fill with tears. "You tellin' me you don't want no more babies? Is that what you're sayin'?"

I hold up both my hands. "No, no. 'Course not. You know I want more kids. And I'm happy about the baby. But it's just . . . well . . . right now . . . "

"Angus, I told you before we ever got married I wanted lots of kids."

"I want 'em too, honey. I do. And if I was makin' more money at a better job, we could afford to have more. I mean . . . and take good care of 'em."

She frowns at me. "You sayin' I don't take good care of my kids?" Her face turns red, and she stands up and comes toward me, shakin' her finger in my face. "Angus Hewitt, what's the matter with you?"

I stand up and look down at her. "Listen here to me, Joetta. I'm the head of this family. If you want to have a whole house full of young'uns, that's fine with me. But I'm the one has to earn enough money to buy 'em food and clothes and pay the doctor bills. I'm the one who—"

"And I'm the one who's tellin' you that I ain't movin'."

I'm about to bust a gut. I take a deep breath and try to settle down. "I'm not passin' up this chance. It's what I've always wanted and it'll bring in more money."

"Well, you're on your own, then. You just go right on ahead. I'm not leavin' here. And neither are the kids. We'll just move in with Mama and Daddy." She puts her hands on her hips and leans forward. "Me and all *three* of my babies!" She stomps off to the kitchen.

I go for a walk before I say somethin' I'll really be sorry for. I knew she wouldn't want to move, but I sure never seen her like that before.

Madison's is right on Bayshore Boulevard, and when I walk through the front door, my heart's beatin' fast. I never had to go lookin' for a job before. I almost feel like I'm livin' somebody else's life.

I'm wearin' my Sunday suit and got my hair slicked down, hopin' I don't look like the country bumpkin I am. The view out the front windows onto Tampa Bay is real pretty. You can sit there and see the water while you watch the cars go by. A young fella shows me back to an office where I meet the owner, Mr. Jacobs, who explains that their head chef—*chef*, he calls him, not *cook*—just left town. But he'll be back next week and he'll have the final say on who gets hired.

Then he shows me the kitchen. They got a great big electric refrigerator instead of the little one like I use and a giant stove with six burners instead of the regular old stove I cook on. And they got four times the workspace. Their sinks—they got three—are real deep. Mr. Jacobs says they got two fellas washin' dishes full-time. Me, at my place, I get Maggie to help me wash when it gets too busy. I don't think I could have come up with a better layout, myself. It's everything I've ever wanted.

Mr. Jacobs explains how lucky they are to have gotten Harrison McMains as their head chef. He has real high standards, and his cookin' has done a lot to help make them a big success. He'll be my boss.

I tell Mr. Jacobs about the Blue-Eyed Gator, which he says he's heard about and he's sorry he ain't never had the chance to come by. Before I leave he says he wants to hire me right away and to let him know when I can start.

On the ride home, the idea of workin' there really takes hold of me. Why, I could build myself a good reputation in a big town. Even though times ain't the best, rich folks still come and vacation in Tampa. Why, I might could even be famous one day.

All the way back, I'm thinkin' how I can make it work, and by the time I pull up in front of the house, I've figured everything out.

Joetta and the boys are sittin' at the kitchen table. Edgar's cryin', and Ernie's poundin' the highchair tray. I can tell by the look on Joetta's face that this ain't a good time to talk to her.

"Hey there, boys," I say. "You givin' your mama a hard time?" I lean over and kiss her on top of her head.

"He hit me," Ernie said.

I pretend to be shocked. "Well now, he hadn't oughta be doin' that, should he?"

Ernie hits the tray with his spoon. "Hit you! Hit you!"

Joetta looks up at me. "How'd it go?"

"Okay," I say with a big smile I know I shouldn't have on my face. "Had quite a day. I'll tell you all about it later."

"No," she says, turnin' to me with her hands on her hips. "Tell me about it now."

"Okay if I fix myself a plate first?"

She wipes Edgar's face and grabs the spoon from Ernie. "Stew's in the pot on the stove. Cornbread's on the table."

I pull out a chair and sit down with my dinner. "This looks good," I say.

She gives me a sour look. "Not as good as what you fix, but then, I'm used to that. Everybody ain't born to be a good cook, you know."

I take a big bite. It needs a little more garlic, but I ain't about to say nothin'. "This is real tasty, honey. I like it."

"So," she says, "tell me what happened."

"Well, Madison's is right on Bayshore Boulevard. Did you know that?"

"Yes," she says, soundin' sarcastic. "I knew that."

"Nice place." I look at her. "Could you pass me a piece of corn-bread, please? This is mighty good."

She passes it. "Are you gonna tell me what happened or not?"

"Well, honey, I just think that after the boys are in bed might be—"

"Well, I think this is just the exact right time," she says. "Tell me, dammit. Quit chasin' your tail."

I take another big spoonful of stew, and she gets the boys down from the table. When she sits back down, I know the jig is up. "I can start at Madison's in two weeks, but the head chef will have to approve me after he sees what I can do."

"I can't believe you're doin' this to us, Angus. It'll be the ru-ination—"

"Nobody has to move right now. Nothin's gonna change, at least not yet. Except I'll have to drive twenty miles to and from work in our old jalopy. At least as long as the old car holds out. And that way, I can see if it's really what I want before we get se-rious about movin' the whole family over there."

She's glarin' at me. "I already told you. I ain't movin'. No way."

"Just listen 'til I'm finished. I've figured it all out. It'll take time for me to show Maggie anything she don't already know about runnin' things at the Blue-Eyed Gator, but she's a fast learner, and I don't expect no problem there. And I was thinkin' that you can help her with waitin' the tables, at least 'til your bel-ly gets too big."

"What in the hell are you—"

"And your mama can watch the boys while you're workin'. That way, we'll have money comin' in from both restaurants, and there should be enough to buy us that ice box and stove I told you about. And maybe even a washin' machine."

She grabs the kids' dishes, and there's a loud clatter when she dumps 'em in the sink. "My stove and icebox are just fine." Then she scrapes out the stew pot and starts scrubbin' it.

"Want me to dry the dishes?" I ask.

"Get the hell out of my kitchen," she says. "Now."

"I'll take the boys out in the backyard and give you some peace and quiet," I say. "It's been a long day. We can talk more about it later."

"I ain't talkin' about it no more!" she hollers at me. "It don't matter what I think anyway. I can see that."

"Come on, hon. This is the only chance I'll ever have to make somethin' of myself. I'm just askin' for this one chance."

"You got another young'un comin'," she says, "and you expect for me to be on my feet all day, bringin' coffee to grumpy old men who don't never leave a tip. And the boys . . . I'm just supposed to leave 'em at Mama's all day? You know she's got the arthritis."

"But it's only for a while," I say. "Remember, the chef has to decide whether I get to be permanent."

"You ain't thinkin' about nobody but your own self. And that's all you're ever gonna think about."

I stop the boys from fightin' in the livin' room and take 'em for a long walk.

Me and Joetta don't say a word to each other the rest of the night, and after we're in bed, I lie there wonderin' if she could be right. Maybe I *am* bein' selfish. I know she's right that it ain't the best time to do somethin' like this, what with a new baby on the way.

But on the other hand, even if she doesn't like livin' in a big city at first, when more money starts comin' in she'll get used to it real fast. I know she will.

When I'm finally about to drift off to sleep it's time to get up, so I drag myself out of bed and go in the kitchen. She's already sittin' at the table so I pour myself some coffee and listen to the kids talkin' in the bedroom. I take a deep breath and sit down. "Joetta," I say. "Honey?"

She gets up and starts crackin' eggs into a bowl but don't answer.

"Just listen a minute," I say. "I been thinkin'. I agree with you that this ain't the best time to make a big change like this . . . what with the new baby and all."

She glares over her shoulder at me but don't say nothin'.

I clear my throat. "I been thinkin' about it all night. Couldn't hardly sleep."

She turns to look at me, then back to the bowl. "Me neither."

I take a sip of coffee. "And I know we been doin' okay right here in Toad Springs."

She don't say nothin', but her shoulders relax a little. She grabs a fork and starts beatin' the eggs.

"I love you, Joetta. And I wouldn't ever want to make you unhappy."

She adds some milk to the eggs. "Well, at least that's good to hear."

"But I'm real proud that I've got this chance to make somethin' of myself. And it's all 'cause of the Blue-Eyed Gator. I'm lucky I get to make a livin' doin' somethin' I like."

"Yep."

"But . . . "

She looks down at the eggs. "I knew there was a *but* comin'."

"Honey, you deserve better than we got out here in the backwoods. We could be livin' in a bigger town, where you could ride the streetcar to get around instead of walkin' so much, and the young'uns could go to really good schools when they're old enough. You'd have lots of churches to pick from, and we wouldn't be so far away that you couldn't come see your folks whenever you want."

She don't say a word.

"You know I'll never have another chance like this. And I'd hoped you'd want to do it as much as I do. After all, sweetie, I've been wantin' this since I was six years old, my whole life almost."

She turns around, red in the face, and puts her hands on her hips. "Well, I *don't* want it. Not even a little bit." Then she slams the fork into the sink, crosses her arms in front of her and stares at me.

"But think of all the good things you'll have. They got movie theaters, nice restaurants, and drive-ins. And you could shop at Maas Brothers more than twice a year."

"I ain't gonna change my mind about this, Angus Hewitt. No use even talkin' about it. That's that."

I hang my head as my hopes start circlin' the drain. "I understand. We don't have to move right now, but I *have* to try it out, at least for a few months."

"You *what?*"

"And who knows, I might even find out that I don't like it after all. Maybe even decide I want to stay right here in Toad Springs."

She sloshes the eggs into the fryin' pan, spillin' some on the stove, and the sizzlin' sound makes me think I've jumped out of the fryin' pan into the fire myself.

She turns and faces me with her hands on her hips.

"I ain't movin," she says. "And that's that."

"I know, I know. That's okay. I'll drive over there and back every day if that's what you want. At least *I'm* willin' to *give in* on somethin'. Now it's your turn to give a little." Then, knowin' good and well that I shouldn't, I say, "And by the way, Joetta, if you don't stir them eggs, they're gonna burn."

She dumps the half-cooked eggs onto a plate and bangs it on the table in front of me. "This *is* how you like 'em, ain't it?"

I get up and slam out the front door, more determined to go than ever.

Thank goodness Maggie says she's happy to run the restaurant for a while, that she gets tired of just waitin' tables and she'll get somebody to waitress. She promises me it won't be her daughter, Violet, who ain't the most reliable person you'll ever meet. I'll drive from here to Tampa every week, Tuesday through Sunday.

The first time I walk into Madison's as an employee, I'm real excited. Mr. Jacobs introduces me to the regular chef, Harrison McMains, who's back from his trip, but he don't seem all that happy to meet me. He's about my build but older, gettin' bald on top, with a little Charlie Chaplin mustache. He's wearin' a white jacket and tells me to call him *Chef McMains*, not Harrison or Mr. McMains.

"The first thing you're going to have to do, Angus," he says, "is learn how to prepare the food on our regular menu correctly. I'll supervise all the dishes you make the first few times, and, of course, I'll be the only one making the specialties. Then, when you're doing things to my satisfaction, you can tell me what you know about cooking alligator."

"All right," I say, a little surprised. I was hopin' he'd be glad to have a helpin' hand, but I swallow my pride and go along with him, thinkin' maybe this is what life is like in the big city. What do I know? He says until I develop a sense for food preparation, I have to measure everything exactly as he says, down to the last grain of salt.

It's two weeks before he's ready to watch me fix up some gator stew, but he gets his nose out of joint when I can't write down a recipe for my dishes 'cause I just fix it, don't never measure anything. That really sets him off and runnin', says I can't just toss ingredients in willy nilly, I have to figure out exactly how much of each ingredient and such I'm addin'.

"You know, *Chef McMains*," I say, "the problem is, I never measured it out, myself, so I don't know. Like you don't measure all *your* stuff."

He turns to me and puts his hands on his hips. "The impudence! Young man, I am a chef. I have the formal education, the skills, and the talents required to be a chef. I prepared food at the Hotel Pennsylvania. People came to New York just to taste my cooking. Now, you're starting here as a line cook, and if you ever want to become a chef, you'll do as you're told."

Later, when I asked him why he left there, he says the hotel management got a new head chef from France who was jealous of all the attention he got and wouldn't let him fix the dishes that were his specialty. He said, "That man didn't recognize superb cooking when it was right under his nose. So, I come to Florida to change the palate of the entire area with my fine food," whatever that means.

I honestly do try to come up with the recipes for the gator dishes, but he says when he follows 'em that I've left somethin' out 'cause the taste is different, and he ain't puttin' up with that. And, of course, *McMains* don't like the way I do the other dishes we serve, so he has to taste everything before it's taken out to the customers. A couple of times, he tosses it in the trash and makes the whole thing over. Just to make sure I don't ruin his reputation, he says.

Finally, he decides I can cook all the gator meat, and lots of folks try it. By the end of the second month, when I walk in the kitchen, every day his eyes are shootin' daggers at me. I can feel 'em even when I'm lookin' the other way.

Even though the waiters all tell me how much folks like the gator, McMains never has a good word to say about me. Not even one time.

I get to the place where every mornin', I have to drag myself out of bed. While I'm gettin' dressed, Joetta gets up, grumbles while she makes coffee, then puts some in a thermos for me to drink on the way to the restaurant. Have to say, she's bein' nicer to me about all this than I ever thought she'd be.

I'm workin' at least twelve hours a day—sometimes more—and that means I hardly ever even see her and the boys. And McMains has his eye on me the whole time, don't trust me to pour a glass of water without him tellin' me how.

I spend my day off at the Blue-Eyed Gator and come to find out that Maggie's run into some problems with the cash register. She's doin' all the cookin' and hired a girl to help her out who hadn't ever worked before, and somehow the books and the money have gotten all screwed up. Sure hope that new gal ain't tryin' to steal from me. Then the stove went on the fritz, and only one of the burners was workin'. And there's a leak in the water pipes under the floor. I swear, if it ain't one thing, it's six or seven others.

But all in all, the sales of the gator dishes at the Madison is goin' great. Gator meat's all the rage 'cause folks want to try somethin' new once in a while. They even advertised it in the *Tampa Trib* and put a picture of me in it, which Chef McMains didn't like worth a damn. That made me like it even more. But it made him treat me even worse.

After I'd been there almost three months, the day finally come when I'd had enough. It was a Saturday evenin' and the place was real busy. We had a big table full of hotshots from City Hall who all wanted to try the gator. They was gonna order one of every gator dish on the menu. So, of course, McMains says he's gonna fix all their dishes and I'm supposed to just do the regular customers.

"Hey," I say to him, "Gator cookin' is the reason I come to work here. I oughta be the one to fix those and you do the others."

He's standing over the stove, red-faced, hot, and sweaty. He turns around and waves his spatula at me, splattering greasy minced onions everywhere. "I'm in charge of this kitchen, you impertinent hillbilly, and you will do as I say."

I'm mad enough to spit nails. "That don't make no sense," I say. "That's why Mr. Jacobs hired me—to cook the gator."

"Jacobs also hired me to run this kitchen, and that's exactly what I'm doing. You listen to me or I'll fire you."

I'm standin' there thinkin' that them big shots out there will figure I'm cookin' the gator, and if McMains does it with his recipes, it ain't gonna be as good as mine. And all them important people I want to impress will think I don't know what I'm doin'. Then it come to me in a flash. He can serve his damn gator to them folks, but they'll know I didn't do it, 'cause they're gonna see me leave.

"I quit," I say to McMains.

"Don't be ridiculous. You're acting like a child."

"I'm leavin' here and never comin' back."

"You can't! Not now!"

I take off my apron and fling it on the counter. "Watch me!" Then I make a big deal of walkin' into the dinin' area. I go over to the hotshots' table and say, "Hello, gentlemen. I understand you folks ordered gator for dinner. I'm Angus Hewitt, the gator chef, and I just want you to know that I'm sorry, but I ain't gonna be fixin' gator tonight. If you want some that I've cooked, just come on over to the Blue-Eyed Gator in Toad Springs. We're right next to the gator ranch, and I'll be real happy to give you just what you want." Then I turn and walk out the front door.

I felt real good drivin' home that night for the last time. I was proud of myself that I'd taken the job and done somethin' I'd always wanted to do. I wished it could have turned out different, but if that's what life is like in a big city restaurant, I don't want no part of it. I'll be happy runnin' my own little place.

Joetta was surprised to see me when I walked in early. "Angus!" she said. "Are you sick?"

"No," I said. "Just changed my mind about somethin'. I figured Maggie could use a little help at the restaurant, and I could use a little more time with my wife and my kids."

"What happened? You get fired? You quit?"

"Walked right out the door durin' the busiest part of the night. McMains can have the whole place to himself, that grumpy old bastard. I don't need it. I did learn a few cookin' tricks along the way, but most of 'em are too fancy to use here. Except maybe at Christmas."

Mr. Jacobs called me the next day askin' what happened. I told him that Chef McMains really didn't want me there and made that real clear, and since I had a choice, I was choosin' to come back here to my own place.

"I know he can be difficult," Mr. Jacobs says. "But he is the best. I was hoping you could learn from him."

"Tell you the truth, I did learn a lot from him. But most of it wasn't about cookin'."

"Well, I'm sorry to lose you, Angus."

"Thank you, Mr. Jacobs. I'm glad I came, even if things didn't work out. And if you'd like to come out to Toad Springs one day, we'll give you a real treat. On the house."

Still, to this day, Mr. Jacobs and some of the big shots in Tampa come over once in a while, and I always fix 'em up somethin' special. And Maggie's happy 'cause they leave big tips. Flavey Stroudamore's stopped complainin' about us bein' right next door, and he even admits that more folks started comin' to the gator ranch after the restaurant opened.

I'm glad to be home where I belong, cookin' my own recipes in my own restaurant and listenin' to my neighbors argue about politics and spread rumors about each other. Makes me smile just to think about 'em.

Instead of the girl Joetta was plannin' on, we got us twin boys. Maybe she'll get her girl next time.

Have to say, though, even if it didn't last long, I ain't sorry I went to work in Tampa. But I have to admit that Joetta was right about movin' to the big city.

And she don't let me forget it, neither.

Three Marys is Enough
by Bubba Stroudamore

Me and my big brother Willard grew up workin' in our daddy's strawberry fields here in Toad Springs, and that convinced us both that we wasn't gonna farm for a livin'. We both hated it, but then, Pop hated it too. He got stuck with it when Mama's daddy died and left the place to 'em not long after they got married—wasn't ever somethin' Pop chose.

As the years went by and he could tell for sure neither one of us boys would ever take it over, he leased the land out to other farmers and opened up Stroudamore's Rare Reptile Ranch. He'd found this three-legged gator out in the swamp with a scar on his side that looked just like Jesus, and that was all he needed to get started. Mama named that gator Precious 'cause that's the first thing she said when she saw the Jesus picture. "Precious Jesus!" The gator ranch turned out to be real good for Toad Springs, even though lots of folks was against him openin' it up at first. Then, when Pop had had enough of it, he wanted me to take it over but I wasn't gonna do it.

Pop said that since I'd lost one of my legs in an accident when I was a kid and Precious was missin' a leg too that we had somethin' in common and I'd be the perfect man to run the place. That didn't make no sense to me. Wasn't no way I was gonna spend my days talkin' about some stupid alligator or tryin' to get folks to buy stuff from the gift shop. I didn't want no part of it. Problem was I didn't know what I wanted to do instead, so I tried out some other ways to earn a livin'.

Growin' up in a place like Toad Springs just naturally makes a man want to move off somewhere else, somewhere far away if he can, but the farthest I ever made it was to Tampa. Went right after I got out of school. Figured I could find work over there, big healthy fella like me, even if I had a wooden leg, and, you know, seek my fortune.

Took a while, but I finally got hired on at a restaurant in Ybor City, mostly washin' dishes, and that's where I met my first wife, Maria (that's Cuban for Mary). She was from Cuba and didn't speak a lot of English, but I didn't care. She was a pretty little thing, with long black hair and big dark eyes that would grab your heart and run off with it. Anyways, one night at work I hear all this hollerin' in Cuban. Turned around to look, and the head waiter was yellin' at Maria, but she was givin' back as good as she got. 'Course, I couldn't tell what they was sayin', but after she threw a bowl of yellow rice at him, then picked up all her stuff and stormed out the back door, I knew she wasn't gonna be workin' there no more.

I followed her out into the alley and she was standin' there, smokin' a cigarette. When I asked what happened, she didn't tell me, just said she didn't do nothin' wrong and they didn't have no reason to fire her. Then she started cryin' and said she was afraid to go home 'cause her daddy would beat her 'cause she'd gotten fired. Well, right away I knew I couldn't let this sweet little girl get beat up by her own daddy, so I took her home with me. Ended up we got married two weeks later and stayed married for five long months.

That gal could cuss me up one side and down the other and I knew just exactly what she was sayin' even though it was all in Cuban. Finally, she found another fella who *could* understand her, and off she went. Can't say I was sorry to see her go, either. I didn't even tell Mama and Pop about her, 'cause I was afraid Mama would have had the apoplexy, me marryin' somebody I couldn't hardly talk to, and from Cuba to boot. But she heard about it in the end and blessed me out real good for not tellin' her. It ain't easy to keep secrets in Toad Springs.

After the divorce, me and one of the other guys who was washin' dishes at the restaurant got fed up with kitchen work and found us real good payin' jobs at a phosphate mine over in Mulberry. That's where I got a job I loved, runnin' one of them big old dragline cranes. At first they didn't think I could do it with my wooden leg and all, but a couple of fellas rigged up a pedal so I could drive it. Man oh man, that rig was somethin'. With one swipe of the bucket, I could dig us a hole fifteen feet deep to get down to the phosphate. Then I'd transfer it to these hopper railroad cars that had big funnels in the bottom so it was easy to empty 'em out when they got where they was goin'. Worked with some tough characters and learned some real good cuss words that I can only say when I'm all by my lonesome.

While I was there, I met Mary Margaret at Berryman's Grocery Store. I walked in one day, and there she was, yellow hair in a braid down her back, big blue eyes, and pretty as a movie star. She was puttin' stuff up on the shelves, and looked over and gave me a smile. Then she tried to pick up this box filled with cans of peas, and when I seen it was too heavy, I walked over and told her that a fine young lady like her shouldn't be liftin' such heavy stuff. That's when she looked down at my leg and I knew she'd seen me limp. 'Course everybody always notices I walk a little funny, but back then the shoe I had to wear on that foot was different from the other one, and it was easy to see my problem was more than just a sandspur. "A wooden leg don't make you a weakling, you know," I said, pickin' up the box.

Then she turned all shy and said, "Oh, I'm sorry . . . I didn't mean to stare."

"Lost it in a horseshoe accident when I was a kid," I said. "It ain't nothin'. To tell you the truth, I'll never figure out why people think a wooden leg is such a big deal. Don't keep me from doin' what I want."

"Oh, my," she said with a grin. "And thank you for your help. I'm Mary Margaret." Later on, I found out she made everybody call her both names, Mary and Margaret, not just one name or the other, 'cause that's the way she was christened in the Catholic Church, and she was real holy when it come to that.

We got to talkin' about one thing and another and ended up courtin'. She wouldn't let me kiss her anywhere but on the cheek 'less we was married, so there you go. Neither one of our families were too happy about it, but we tied the knot anyway.

Lookin' back now, I could have saved myself a peck of trouble if I'd told her about Maria, 'cause Mary Margaret wouldn't have had nothin' to do with a divorced man. You know, it's still hard for me to believe that I ended up with a Catholic. God knows Mama tried to talk me out of it, even warned me that they had this law that you had to eat fish on Fridays, and if you didn't, you'd go to hell. And sure enough, we had tuna fish casserole every Friday night.

We was married for about six months when Mary Margaret decided she couldn't stand livin' with a heathen. She'd thought she could switch me over to bein' a Catholic, even though I told her right up front that I wasn't gonna do it, but when she seen the naggin' wasn't gonna work, she give up. Said she couldn't get divorced, but she could get the pope to fix it so we wasn't ever really married at all. And she did too. And I guess he made her a virgin again, but I didn't ask her about that.

My third wife was named Mary too. Mary Ethaline was her whole name, but she just went by Ethaline. Now, she wanted kids real bad and after a few years it was beginnin' to look like I wasn't never gonna be a daddy, so she found some new feller at the church and that was the end of that. She's got her four young'uns now, just what she wanted. That's what I heard, anyhow.

After that, I decided I'd had enough of bein' married. I like the ladies just fine, but I sure wasn't good at livin' with 'em. I couldn't see how Mama and Pop stayed together all those years. Nowadays, they get along pretty good, but they sure didn't used to. Figured I just wasn't cut out to go through all the bad stuff you have to put up with, like goin' to church and not drinkin' more than one beer and havin' to be home by six every night, just so I could have the good parts of bein' married, you know, like home-cooked food and a clean house and somebody to sleep with at night.

After I got divorced from Ethaline, I left the phosphate company and moved to Turkey Creek 'cause I'd lucked into a real good deal and bought me a dairy farm. Now I got more than fifty head of cattle.

About a year after I had the dairy farm up and runnin', Mama called me one day. She'd been talkin' to Sorrey May Only, who said that my brother Willard, over in Fort Pierce, had taken to the drink real bad. Since Sorrey May's daughter, Mindy Sue, was married to him, she thought Mama should know. She said Mindy Sue didn't know what was gonna become of her and the kids 'cause Willard couldn't hold down a job. Mama was so worried about him that she talked me into drivin' over to the other coast to see if all that was true—you couldn't ever be real sure about what Sorrey May said. Still can't.

I hadn't seen Willard in a few years and even though I was glad to have a reason to visit I didn't have no intention of talkin' to him about his drinkin'. I wrote him and Mindy Sue a letter sayin' that I was comin' over to go fishin' over there, and Mindy Sue wrote back and invited me to spend the night, said she'd fix a nice supper. After I got some of the cowhands to fill in for me at milkin' time, I packed up my fishin' gear and took off.

It was real good to see Mindy Sue and the kids. I was surprised at how big Jolinda and Deloyd were. She was almost six and he was almost four, as I recall. Willard was pretty much drunk the whole time I was there. Just about the only thing he said to me was, "You wanna beer?" Even though he didn't talk much, Mindy Sue sure did. She told me their troubles, and there were plenty. When I got back home there sure wasn't no good news for Mama.

Not too long after that, Mindy Sue called and told me that Willard had moved off to Vero Beach and left her and the kids and could I maybe come and get 'em and bring 'em back to Toad Springs to stay at her mama's house. "'Course," I said. "Sure, I'll do it. I'd always had a soft spot for Mindy Sue. For a while there, I was even sorry that she'd got hitched up with Willard instead of me. But that water'd passed under the bridge a long time ago.

I left before sunup the next Saturday and got to Fort Pierce around two. Mindy Sue and the kids was all ready when I pulled into the driveway. She told the young'uns they'd have to ride in the bed of my old pickup 'cause she wanted the dishes and such in the front with us so's they wouldn't rattle around and get broke. I didn't think that was right myself, what with the roads bein' real bumpy, and I thought the kids should be up front and put the dishes in the back even if they did get broke. I told her maybe she should unpack some pillows and put 'em back there along with the blanket she'd folded up for 'em to sit on, that it would make their ride easier. But she said she was in a hurry and wasn't gonna stay in that godforsaken place one minute longer than she had to, so I kept my mouth shut and got in the truck.

When we start off, she tells me all about the kids. Jolinda will be startin' school in the fall, and Deloyd is a pretty quiet kid but busy and into everything. Then we talk about the gator ranch and how Toad Springs has changed since she left, and I fill her in on the gossip I've heard. Every twenty miles or so, one or the other of the kids hollers out from the truck bed so we know they're fightin' but I can tell Mindy Sue is doin' her best to ignore it. Finally, she asks me to stop so she can talk to 'em. I pull over and we both get out of the truck and head to the back at the same time, but after I hear her lightin' into them kids, I just turn around and get back in the cab.

When she gets in, she slams the door and says, "Hope you don't think nothin' bad about me and the young'uns, Bubba."

"No, no."

She clears her throat, then says, "I didn't mean to sound so ugly to 'em. Sometimes my nerves get all tangled up and I get short with 'em. Don't mean to, though."

"It's okay."

"Willard ain't been no help for a long time, now. I've had to be both mama and daddy."

I don't answer. I ain't sayin' nothin' bad about my brother.

"It ain't been easy, Bubba, but I do my best."

"I'm sure you're doin' a good job."

"Well, tell me what's been happenin' since I seen you last," she says. "When you came over to visit us, I'm afraid I did all the talkin'. Didn't even ask about you."

"Well, nothin' new, really. Had some trouble with mastitis in the milk cows there for a while. Then one of the cowhands sneaked off with a week's payroll. Other than that . . . "

She turns toward me in the seat. "I heard you got married a few times."

I glance at her, then back to the road and think to myself that it's gonna be a long ride. "Yeah, I did. But I'm done with all that. Took me a while to figure out I just ain't the marryin' kind."

"Any kids?"

"Nope."

"Do I know any of your wives?"

"Naw."

She leans back and looks straight ahead. "Well, I reckon you're right. I guess bein' married ain't for everybody. Maybe it ain't for me neither." She glances through the rear window at the kids, then turns back. "You must be livin' pretty high on the hog now, with your own dairy farm and just yourself to take care of. Must be makin' pretty good money."

"I do okay. It ain't so much the money comin' in that matters. It's what's left after you pay all the bills."

"Mama says you've got a nice house."

"Ain't nothin' fancy, but it's enough for me."

"How can you manage all alone? Don't you need a woman there to take care of you?"

Uh oh, I think to myself. Why do the ladies always think men can't get along without 'em? "Oh, I do just fine. There's a lady down the road who comes every Monday and cleans up.

Cooks me a big old pot roast or somethin' I can eat off of for the rest of the week. It works out okay."

"That's good, Bubba," she says, but her voice don't sound like she means it.

The rest of the drive is quieter. By the time we get to Toad Springs, we're all tired and hungry. Her mama has a real good supper ready for us—fried chicken, collard greens, and home-made applesauce. As soon as we're finished, I head for home.

Within the week, Mindy Sue calls sayin' she can't find a job in town and do I need any help over here at the dairy. Said she'd tried at the Blue-Eyed Gator Restaurant and talked to my mama and pop about workin' at the gator ranch, but no luck. Seems to me they should have been able to find somethin' for her to do in the gift shop since she's their daughter-in-law and the mother of the only grandkids they're ever gonna have, but they didn't. Mindy Sue said she's sunk down so low as tryin' to get on cleanin' rooms at the Green Gator Hotel, even though that's one job she always swore she'd never do, clean up after other folks. She said in a way it's a blessin' they didn't hire her.

I feel bad for her, and the truth is I probably could find work for her at the dairy, but she wouldn't have no way of gettin' here every day 'less I drove over to Toad Springs and picked her up, and then I'd have to be worryin' about one thing leadin' to another and her married to my brother and all like that, not to mention that I don't need some woman tryin' to get a hold on me. So I tell her I'm sorry, with the way things are right now, I ain't got nothin' for her neither.

A few weeks after that, she invites me over to have supper at her mama's, and I say sure. Ain't never one to pass up a good home-cooked meal. Before I go, though, I joke to myself that even if she gives me the eye it won't turn out to be a problem 'cause her name ain't got no *Marys* in it. Ain't nothin' gonna happen there.

It's a real nice meal, and after I'm full of pork chops, mashed potatoes with gravy, and sweet peas, topped off with key lime pie, me and Mindy Sue go sit on the front porch. Then she starts askin' questions about Willard and why he always said he wouldn't ever set foot in Toad Springs again. Now, it seemed to me it wasn't my place to go tellin' family secrets that wasn't mine to tell, and anyways, I'd figured Willard had already told her about all that long ago, them bein' married and all.

I said that it wasn't nothin' good to talk about, but she kept on 'til she wormed it out of me. When I told her about the big fight Willard and Pop had after Willard found out that Pop wasn't his real daddy, she was surprised but said that explained a lot. It was like findin' the missin' piece of the puzzle. She wiped away a tear and said if she'd known about all that sooner, maybe things could have worked out better with them. But she also said there ain't no point in beatin' a dead horse. What's done is done. She'd never go back to him. I felt bad, bein' the one who told the secret, but I reckon in the end, it's better when the truth comes out.

A month or two later she invites me to come to supper again. That time, when we're sittin' out on the porch after dessert, she says, "Bubba, I got a favor to ask you."

"What's that?" I say, thinkin' she wants to borrow some money or she's gonna ask me for a job again or somethin'.

"You don't have to do it if you don't want to."

"Okay."

"I was just wonderin' if maybe you could take Deloyd fishin' sometime. Willard took him once, but other than that he didn't ever spend much time with him. I think he needs to be around men."

"Well, sure, I can do that," I say, hopin' she's not plannin' to come along with us. "You know, Deloyd reminds me of Willard back when we was little, the way he's mostly kind of quiet. And he's got that same crazy cowlick, all cattywampus on the back of his head."

"I know," she says, smilin'. "Have to say, I worry about him, not havin' a daddy around to teach him how to do boy stuff. My daddy died years ago, and Flavey, he don't show no real interest in his only grandson."

"Well, Pop wasn't never all that interested in Willard and me neither," I say, laughin', "so Deloyd shouldn't take it personal."

Mindy Sue leans toward me, puts her hand on my arm, and says, "It would mean the world to me, Bubba, if you could. It wouldn't have to be fishin'. Maybe take him over to the dairy and show him the cows and all. Do man things."

"Sure, I'd like that, Mindy Sue," I say. "Looks like I ain't gonna have no young'uns of my own. Too bad, 'cause I like kids."

"Well, you never know what the future holds, Bubba. You ain't too old to be a daddy yet."

"Yeah, but I'm never gettin' married again. I decided that a long time ago."

She smiles at me. "Like I said, you never know what might be hidin' just around the corner."

She's makin' me nervous. I laugh. "Oh, yes I do," I say, thinkin' to myself that I ain't gonna get caught again, by Mindy Sue or nobody else. "Bein' single is what's waitin' for me."

She shakes her head. "Maybe. If that's what you want."

That next Saturday is Deloyd's birthday and after his party I take him home with me for the weekend. I show him how to milk a cow but his hands are too little to draw out much milk. But when he helped feed the livestock and the chickens, that kid was happy as a tick on a fat dog and could hardly wait to tell his mama. And he loved it that I didn't make him go to church the next mornin' with his grandma.

The next weekend, when we went fishin' on Grasshopper Lake, he caught a bream—and he got so excited, he almost fell out of the boat. I really like havin' him around. He's smart, always ready to try somethin' new. But fishin' is what that boy loves best. Says when he grows up he wants to be a fisherman who catches great big fish, maybe out in the ocean. Said Mindy Sue told him he can do whatever he sets his mind to. The only one who can stop him is him.

Hearin' that makes me think about when I got my leg cut off and folks was tellin' me all the stuff I'd never be able to do again instead of pushin' me to do my best. And that makes me like her more than I want to.

Now, I have to admit that I was kind of thinkin' that Mindy Sue might start makin' eyes at me, but she didn't, not really. Like I said before, I always had a little soft spot for her, but whenever I think about gettin' hooked up with another gal I get a big knot in my stomach. Of course, I miss havin' the ladies around, and sometimes I go over to Schniticker's Tavern and spend some time talkin' pretty to some of the girls over there, but I wasn't gonna get tangled with another woman, no sirree.

I'd see Mindy Sue when I went to pick up Deloyd on the weekends, and she was always nice, but I guess she believed me when I told her I was done with gettin' married. She just acted like a sister or somethin'.

She finally found a job at the Toad Springs General Store and Mama told me she was goin' out with a fella from Mango. Of course, Mama had to go on and on, sayin' it was a real scandal that Mindy Sue didn't even wait until her divorce was final before she started lookin' for another husband. Mama thought it didn't matter that she'd sworn she'd never have nothin' to do with Willard for the rest of her life. Seemed to me, though, that if she wasn't gonna stay married to Willard, why shouldn't she go out? Still, I have to admit, I didn't much like hearin' about her seein' that other fella. But I kept remindin' myself that it wasn't none of my business.

But an odd thing's been happenin'. When I'm at home by my lonesome, some crazy ideas about her sneak into my head. I know what Mindy Sue's doin' ain't none of my beeswax, especially since I don't want her comin' after me. At least I think I don't want her after me. But I . . . well, I just don't like her seein' that fella. Not one little bit.

So, I say to myself, Bubba, if you like her so much, maybe you should let her know instead of tryin' so hard not to get caught.

But on the other hand, I tell myself, I'm better off all by my lonesome. I should just spend time with Deloyd and be happy with that. I don't need to cause her any more misery than she's already been through.

Then it crosses my mind that maybe I'm the one who's been through enough misery.

Me and Deloyd, we get into a routine. Every weekend or so, I set it up with Mindy Sue to get him on Saturday mornin'. I pack us a picnic lunch, and we head out to go fishin' or take a hike in the woods and look for animals and such. I show him how moss grows on the north side of the trees—so you can tell which direction you're headed—and how to follow the sun to keep track of what time it is. When I help him make a trap to catch a possum, I think back to years ago when Willard taught me how to do it. I also show him how to tie different kinds of knots so they won't come undone, and we make a little shelter from dead oak tree branches and palm fronds. I teach Deloyd which berries to pick, what plants will make you sick if you eat 'em, and sometimes we pick flowers for him to take home to his mama.

After we've been doin' this for a good while, I'm pretty sure Deloyd could take care of himself if he ever got lost out in the woods. I guess he's been braggin' and showin' off at home, 'cause he says Jolinda wants to come along. I tell him sure, that's fine, and she catches on fast just like her little brother. After a few weekends, she has so much fun that she wants to bring her mama.

At first, I wonder if her mama put her up to it, but then I remind myself that I'd long ago got my head straight about how Mindy Sue's goin' her way and I'm goin' mine. And anyways, Mama tells me that Mindy Sue's still seein' that fella over in Mango, and now that the divorce is all done, him and Mindy Sue'll probably be gettin' married soon. That's good, I think to myself. That'll keep any of them crazy ideas outta my head.

Mindy Sue brings along a picnic lunch, and when we get to a spot by the river, she puts the food out on a little white table-cloth. Instead of the peanut butter sandwiches I always bring, we have ham and cheese on homemade bread, pickles, hard-boiled eggs, and sugar cookies. After we eat, the kids sit on an old log down by the water and throw out their fishin' lines, ho-pin' for a big old trout. Deloyd keeps tellin' Jolinda they have to be quiet or they'll scare the fish away, but they're havin' way too much fun to keep the noise down. I'm leanin' back against a tree with my hands behind my head, lookin' out at the peaceful water, thinkin' how lucky I am to be here.

While Mindy Sue puts the leftovers away, she says, "Well, tell me what you been doin' lately, other than takin' the young'uns out on hikes."

"Aw, let's see. Not too much. Had to go into Tampa the oth-er day to pick up some stuff for the new water troughs. Smitty didn't have what we need at the hardware. Said he'd order 'em for me, but I like goin' to the big city once in a while. It gets too quiet out here."

"Yeah, I know what you mean," she says, sittin' down near me. "I like Tampa too. Especially the big department stores. When we lived in Fort Pierce, there wasn't nothin' to do that you hadn't already done a million times and no place close by that was any better."

"You been back over there since you left?"

"To Fort Pierce? Never. It'll be a cold day in hell . . . "

"Ever hear from Willard? Or is it all right to ask that?"

"Yeah. It's okay to ask. And no. I ain't heard from him since we left. You'd think he'd want to find out about his kids, even if he never wanted to see me again."

"Reckon he's still over there?"

She shakes her head real slow. "Don't know. He said he was gonna stay in Vero Beach, but I don't know if he did." It's quiet for a while, and then she says, "You know, Bubba, sometimes I feel bad about how things ended up. When I think about what Wil-lard was like when we were all kids, you remember, sweet and kind of shy . . . sometimes I still miss *that* Willard. The old one. I thought he was gonna make such a good daddy."

"I miss him too," I say. "Maybe I should go over there and find him. See what he's doin'."

"You don't have to do that. I can tell you what he's doin'. He's drinkin'. And he told me a million times that there wasn't no way he was ever gonna quit."

"Well, maybe. Maybe not."

"It wouldn't matter to me if he did. The Willard I fell in love with is dead and gone. And that man's never comin' back. And even if he did, I'd spend the rest of my life alone before I'd live with him again."

Then, about that time, she looks over at the kids, and I can't help but notice how her hair is pullin' loose from her ponytail and the calm, peaceful look on her face . . . then, all of a sudden, she stands up and yells out to the young'uns, "Hey, you two! Come back this way! You're gettin' in too deep! There could be gators around here."

"Aw, Mama," Deloyd calls over. "I already looked for 'em. Uncle Bubba taught me how to find 'em."

She glances at me, then back to the young'uns. "Out! Now!" she hollers. "You can fish from the log."

Deloyd looks over at me to be rescued, but I say, "Go on, now. Do what your mama tells you."

He frowns right at me but follows his sister back to the log.

Mindy Sue sits back down, looks my way and says, "Now, where were we? Oh yeah. We were talkin' about Willard. So now, let's talk about you. Met any nice girls lately?"

"Naw. I told you. I give up on the ladies. Three wives is enough for any man."

"You shouldn't do that, Bubba. You're too young to spend the rest of your life all by yourself."

"Well, then, I guess you could just say the right one ain't come along. I hear tell you been seein' a fella over in Mango. How's that goin'?"

She looks down and blushes, pretty as a speckled pup, then glances back at me. "Oh, you mean Harold. He's a nice fella. He likes the kids, and they like him."

"You been seein' him for a while now, accordin' to Mama."

"Yeah. And like I said, he's real nice. He asked me to marry him, and I'm thinkin' about it, but I just don't . . . "

That's when I look up and see the head of a water moccasin pokin' out of the water, and he's aimin' straight for the kids. I'm on my feet before I know it and start walkin' toward the log where they're still sittin' with their feet in the water. I call over to 'em and say, not too loud, "*Kids! Don't Move!*" They both freeze, then look my way and I point to the snake and say, "Moccasin!"

In a flash, Mindy Sue's beside me, grabs my arm tight, and puts her other hand over her mouth. I pull away from her and start walkin' towards the kids sayin, "Real slow now, pull your feet out of the water. Slow . . . real slow."

They both do, and Jolinda starts cryin'.

"Just sit tight," I say in a softer voice. "I'll draw his attention over here."

I pick up a dead palm frond and hold it out over the water between the snake and the kids. I know when a water moccasin feels threatened on land, it'll fight back before it'll run off, but since it's in the water it ought to just ease away. And it does. Thank the good Lord.

When it's gone, Mindy Sue runs over to the kids and hugs 'em hard. "All right," she says, wipin' her face. "That's enough excitement for one day. Let's go home."

"Aw, Mama, it's okay," Deloyd whines. "It's gone."

Jolinda pipes up. "Yeah. It won't bother us anymore."

Mindy Sue looks at me, and I shrug my shoulders. "Whatever you want," I say.

"Oh, I guess if you think it's all right," she says, lookin' at me with a shy smile like I'm a hero. "But let's move down the river some."

"You're the boss," I say. "Pack it up, kids."

When I get 'em back home that evenin', the young'uns run in the house and we follow with the picnic stuff.

"That was fun," Mindy Sue says, settin' things down on the porch. "Except for that damn moccasin. Maybe we can do it again sometime."

I'm surprised. "Yeah. Sure. Maybe we can."

Then she looks up at me, real serious, tears in her eyes. "I want to thank you, Bubba, for what you done today. You saved the kids' lives, chasin' off that snake."

"Aw, it's just lucky I saw it in time."

"I know," she says, wipin' a tear away and givin' me a hug. I put my arms around her and hug her back. "I was scared to death," she says, leanin' back and lookin' up at me. "Like I said, you saved their lives, Bubba. You did!"

I want to kiss her so bad, I can taste it. Instead, I say, "I don't know about that."

"Well, I do." She gives me another big hug, then reaches up on tiptoe and gives me a little peck on the cheek.

I'm so surprised that I pull back, which ain't what I really want to do. "Oh!" I say, and I know my ears are bright red. "Well, thank you, Mindy Sue. That was real sweet of you." Then I hightail it outta there. What the hell is she doin'? She was my brother's wife. And that Harold fella wants to marry her. Forget it, I tell myself. You're bein' a fool. She's just glad you're helpin' her with the young'uns.

I don't ask to take the kids the next week, and the week after that I go fishin' with a buddy of mine over on the Hillsborough River in Tampa. By the third weekend, Deloyd's askin' when we can go hikin' again, just me and him, and I tell him to get permission from his mama and I'll pick him up around eight o'clock on Saturday mornin'.

When I pull up to the house in my truck, right on time, Mindy Sue comes out with Deloyd. She has a serious look on her face, but all she says is, "Y'all have fun," then turns and goes back inside right away. Guess she's sorry about that kiss. Ain't no other reason for her to act like that.

I turn to Deloyd, who's sittin' next to me in the cab. "Your mama okay?" I ask.

"Yeah. Yes, sir. Daddy called a little while ago. He's comin' to see us."

I feel like somebody hit the back of my head with a brick. "Your daddy?"

"Yes, sir."

"When's he comin?"

"Tomorrow afternoon."

"Do your grandma and grandpa know about this?"

"I don't know. He just called Mama a little bit ago."

"They'll want to see him too. Your grandma will, anyway. Where's he been?"

"I don't know."

"What's he want?"

"I heard Mama tellin' Grandma Sorrey May he wants to come back home to Toad Springs."

"What do you think about that?"

He looks confused. "Well, I don't know. I ain't seen him since I was four. And now I'm six."

"That's a long time."

"Yes, sir. I don't remember him too good."

"Well, I want to see him too," I say. "He's my big brother, you know."

Deloyd looks at me. "That's right. I forgot."

"Yeah. I grew up with him."

He cocks his head and says, "Was he nice to you when you were little?"

I give him a big smile. "Yes, sir. Nice as they come."

"Y'all didn't fight all the time, like him and Mama did?"

"Nope."

"Think he might could be nice again? Like you?"

"I don't know, Deloyd. Maybe. I hope so."

We fish for an hour, but the whole time I'm thinkin' about when me and Willard was kids—we were so different from each other but still got on real good. I remember how he changed af-

ter he threw that horseshoe that accidently hurt my leg so bad
they had to take it off. I always thought he felt worse about it
than I did. And then after that fight he had with Pop . . . he was
really a different person.

Then Mindy Sue crosses my mind, how I'd been thinkin' she
was maybe settin' her hook for me. And when it seemed like she
wasn't, it took me a while to figure out that I wanted her to.

Since neither me or Deloyd have our hearts in fishin', and
the fish aren't bitin' anyway, we come back early. When I drop
him off, I said, "You be sure to tell your daddy I want to see him."

"Ok. I will."

When I get home, I call Mama. She says Mindy Sue had told
her that Willard's taken the pledge not to drink no more and he's
comin' to Toad Springs. Mama's already fixin' up our old room for
him.

I go over to Mama and Pop's for supper on Sunday night, and
Willard gives me a big hug at the front door. "It's good to see you,
Bubba. I've missed you, you old son of a gun."

I can't hardly believe he's the same fella I seen in Fort Pierce,
that smelly, drunken old fool staggerin' around askin' me if I
want a beer 'cause he wants another one. He's dressed nice, in
a blue plaid shirt and grey slacks, all clean and neat, standin' up
straight, and he looks me in the eye when he talks to me.

"You look great. The last time I seen you . . . " I shake my
head. "What happened?"

"I give up the booze. Ain't had a drink in almost a year."

"You're kiddin'."

"Nope. Can't hardly believe it myself. Let's sit out here on the
porch and I'll tell you about it while Mama finishes fixin' supper."

We settle down in the rockin' chairs, and I can't stop lookin'
at him. I say, "Man, you're lookin' good."

"Thanks. I feel good too. I've changed my ways, and I swear
on the Good Book I won't go back to the old life."

"So. Where the hell you been?"

"Well now, let's see. When I left Fort Pierce, I went up to Vero Beach, heard there was work up there. I found a cheap room in a boardinghouse and dug ditches for a while 'til the job ran out. Have to tell you that was the worst time of my life. I'd thought it was bad in Fort Pierce, but in Vero I ended up out on the streets with no money even for food. I never thought I'd sink so low as to be a beggar. Lyin' in the gutter, that's what I done. Don't get no lower than that." He shakes his head. "And with nothin' to drink, I went crazy. I got the shakes real bad, was seein' bugs and stuff that wasn't there. It was hell, Bubba. Ain't no two ways about it. Hell couldn't be no worse than that."

"So, what did you do?"

"I ate out of folks' garbage cans and took food from their gardens. I begged and borrowed money from people, and when that run out, I stole from 'em. I thought about killin' myself, but I knew if I did that I'd go straight to hell for sure. For eternity. That's the only thing that stopped me. After a while I owed so many folks in Vero that they were tryin' to hunt me down. So I had to get outta there.

"I took out walkin', headin' north 'til I come to this little town called Melbourne. Folks there were real nice. A fella named Ambrose sat down next to me when I was real drunk one Sunday afternoon, sittin' under a tree in a park, sicker than a dog. He said he used to drink a lot but he quit. And if I wanted to quit, him and his wife would let me stay in this shack they had out back of their house, give me food to eat and a job pickin' fruit. All I had to do was promise 'em I wouldn't drink no alcohol. And 'course I said sure, I'd give it up, but I didn't mean it at the time. I knew it was wrong to lie but I didn't have no other choice. I was about to starve to death."

"And you just stopped drinkin'?"

"Well, no. Not exactly." He looks out towards the road, then down at the floor. "The folks who took me in—Ambrose and his wife, Bessie—they'd dedicated their lives to helpin' folks stop drinkin'. For a long time, Ambrose was a real bad drunk hisself, and he finally quit. They told me I could stay there and work with 'em out in the groves so long as I didn't go back on the booze. If I started drinkin' again, I'd have to leave. That man saved my life. If I hadn't run into him, I'd be dead by now. I know I would."

"I can't believe what I'm hearin'."

"Anyway, Ambrose and me, we'd sit up talkin' late into the night about the things we'd done—good and bad—and how we was both ready to end it all before we decided to give up the booze. Turns out Ambrose's life had been lots worse than mine, that's for sure. After listenin' to him, I figured that if he could quit, so could I.

"They took me to church with 'em every Sunday, and him and his wife prayed together every night. I got down on my knees with 'em sometimes 'cause he told me to, not 'cause I believed God was gonna save me, and I have to say, it didn't do me no harm. But real late one night, I was out in that shack all by myself with nothin' to do and felt like I was goin' crazy as a bat with the rabies, so I went out and got me some wine. When Ambrose caught me sneakin' a nip, he sat me down and talked for a long time about what I was doin' to myself and that I had to remember the deal: if I got drunk, I'd have to leave. I begged him not to make me go 'til he said he'd give me another chance. He made me pour out the rest of the bottle myself while he watched. A few weeks later, I drank some more wine. Then he said if I did it one more time, I'd have to leave.

"That's when I got real serious about things, 'cause I knew if I didn't stop, I'd end up dead. It ain't been easy, but I ain't had a drop since. After a while, I got cleaned up pretty good and found me a job sellin' used cars back in Vero Beach. Even got my own place. I was doin' pretty good. That's when I started thinkin' about things, like how it was my fault you only had the one leg, and—"

"Come on, Willard. That was an accident."

"And how I'd run off and left everybody. Not just Mindy Sue and the kids, but Mama and you, and Pop too, I guess. I'd treated everybody real bad and it come to me how much I missed y'all. That's when I decided I wanted my family back. I'm a daddy. I got kids to take care of." He looks at me with a big grin on his face. "So that's why I'm here."

"Wow," I say, noticin' that when he mentioned Mindy Sue, I got a knot in my gut. He's my brother, I remind myself. Mindy Sue was *his* wife. Deloyd and Jolinda are *his* kids, not mine. I take a deep breath and let it out slow. "I still can't believe you're here."

"Me neither."

"What does Mindy Sue say about all this?"

He cocks his head to the side and squeezes his eyes shut, then looks at me. "She's surprised, mostly. She told me we're divorced and all and that she never thought she'd see me again. But she gave me a hug. And so did the kids. I was afraid they wouldn't even talk to me."

"Well, the last time they seen you, things wasn't too good, from what I understand," I say. "After you went to Vero Beach, I drove over in the truck and picked 'em up and brought 'em back here."

"She told me. Said you been a big help with Deloyd."

"Yeah. He's a great kid."

"I appreciate all you done for him," Willard says. "You been a real good brother, steppin' up like you done."

"Well, they're family," I say.

"'Course, now that I'm back, I'll be wantin' to do all them things with him. Maybe you can come with us once in a while. We can all go together."

Part of me wants to sock him in the jaw. But instead I say, "Yeah, well. We'll see. And how's about Mama and Pop? After that big fight you and Pop got into, I didn't think you'd be wantin' to have nothin' to do with him."

"Yeah. I know. I didn't think I would either."

"What happened?"

"I don't rightly know. Just one day, it come to me that he'd been pretendin' I was his son when he knew I wasn't and that must have been hard on him. After that, it seemed like just out of the blue, I understood why he'd treated me so bad all those years. Like it wasn't me he hated, it was that I had a different daddy." He shakes his head. "All them years we spent arguin' . . . we didn't have to have all them bad times." He shakes his head again. "Well, sayin' it out loud, that don't make much sense, but then, well, I don't know. So I told him all that the first night I was here. And that I was sorry for the bad things I'd done to him. And, you won't believe this, Bubba, but he cried. He said he was wrong to treat me so different from the way he treated you, and he even give me a big hug."

I can't believe my ears. "Jesus, Lord! That's a real miracle."

Just then, Mama comes to the door and tells us supper's ready, so we go inside. She keeps talkin' about how glad she is that Willard's back and how good it'll be for the kids to have their daddy with 'em. Then Pop asks lots of questions about the groves over on the East Coast and how Willard got that car he drove over in. I don't say nothin'. I love my brother, and I'm glad he's back, but when it comes to Mindy Sue and the young'uns, well, I reckon I come to like bein' with 'em more than I knew. Sometimes it felt like they was more my family than Willard's.

Willard stays for two weeks, but about that same time the dairy had an outbreak of gut worms and I didn't get to see him as much as I wanted to. Mama tells me how she's real happy about him wantin' to move back and that she can't hug him enough. She also says him and Mindy Sue have been talkin' every day and that he sleeps in his old bedroom every night, which I ain't exactly sorry to hear. She's hopin' and prayin' Mindy Sue'll take him back and she'll have both her boys close by.

Mama invites me over for a Sunday dinner of fish and grits and hushpuppies with Willard and Mindy Sue and the kids, before Willard leaves on Monday.

When we all sit down at the table to eat, Deloyd says, "Me and Daddy caught all our dinner. And I caught more fish than Daddy did!" With that, he looks at Willard, who gives him a great big smile and nods at everybody.

"That's true," he says. "My boy is a damn good—oops, I mean a darn good fisherman."

Everybody laughs, and the happy look on Deloyd's face breaks my heart. After apple pie and vanilla ice cream, me and Pop and

Willard go out on the porch while the ladies clean up and the kids listen to the radio in the livin' room.

Pop looks at Willard and says, "Looks like things are goin' pretty good here, huh?"

"Yep. I'm thinkin' so."

"You and Mindy Sue decided anything?"

"Well," he says, "not yet. But I got my hopes up."

I look down at the floor.

Pop lights up a cigarette. "All that talkin' you been doin', and she ain't decided nothin'?"

"Well, I reckon she's got good reason to be careful, Pop. I put her and the young'uns through some bad times."

"Yeah, yeah," Pop says. "Women . . . So, you thought over what I said about the gator ranch? If you come back, you gonna take it over?"

Willard looks at me and grins. "Well, I thought Bubba should have first shot at it, since he's—"

I hold up both my hands and laugh at him. "Oh, no thanks, Willard. I got enough on my hands with the dairy."

Willard laughs back at me, but Pop don't seem to think it's so funny. "Well then," Willard says, "I reckon it'll depend on what Mindy Sue ends up sayin'. I mean, that'll decide whether I stay here or not. If she says no, I wouldn't be far away, just probably not here in Toad Springs. Maybe Bartow. Or Tampa. And I'll see the kids all the time."

"You got any idea when you'll get an answer?" I ask.

"She said she needs to think about it after I leave. Maybe in a couple of weeks."

It's quiet for a while, then Pop says, "I sure hope she says yes. We could use you at the gator ranch."

Willard smiles. "We'll see, Pop. We'll see."

Monday night, I get a call from Mindy Sue askin' if I can come over Tuesday evenin' for supper. She needs some advice. My heart jumps up in my throat when I hear that, but I remind myself that she probably just wants to talk about Willard 'cause I know him better than anybody. It'll be about him. Not about me.

She seems a little quiet and at supper, when the kids talk about how their daddy might be comin' back, I just smile and nod at 'em but don't say nothin'. She don't say nothin' either. When we go to sit in the livin' room, she takes the overstuffed chair and I sit on the couch. We listen to the radio and talk while we watch the kids play a game of checkers. I'm startin' to think their bedtime will never come when Mindy Sue finally shoos them off to go to sleep.

She fixes us each a glass of sweet tea, comes to sit beside me on the couch, and takes a deep breath. Then she turns to face me. "Well, Bubba, I just don't know what to do. One minute, I believe that Willard's a new man, and the next I remember how he used to treat us. I don't ever want to go through that again. I've told you lots of what went on over in Fort Pierce, but I didn't tell you everything." Her voice starts quiverin'. "And I ain't gonna tell you either. I don't know how I can ever trust him again. What if he falls off the wagon?" She wipes a tear from her cheek.

"I don't know what to tell you, Mindy Sue. He sure seems to mean what he says. Right now, anyway."

"I know he does. And I believe that right now he *does* mean everything he's sayin'. But how can I be sure he'll never go back to the bottle? How can I know he'll be like this for the rest of his life?"

"Well, you can't. Can't nobody be sure of nothin'. Life ain't like that."

"I know. I know. But it ain't just me. It's the kids. He's hurt them too. But now, when I watch Deloyd's face as his daddy walks into the room, I feel like I need to marry him again just to give the young'uns their father back. And then maybe everything would be perfect."

"Well, you can be pretty sure things wouldn't be perfect," I say, then laugh.

She smiles at me. "But, well, there's somethin' else too, Bubba. And it's kinda hard to talk about." She pauses, looks down at her lap, and then goes on. "But anyways, just before Willard came back, when I'd been goin' down to the river with you and the kids, it was . . . well, it was just real nice."

I grin. "I know. I liked it too." I think to myself, what is she sayin'? Could she want me to, um . . . But naw, she ain't thinkin' nothin' like that.

She clears her throat. "Bubba, what I mean is, you just got a way about you that . . . that, well, felt real good to me."

She's serious. She is! "I know what you're talkin' about, Mindy Sue. I mean, I feel the same way."

"Maybe the main thing is . . . you're so good with the kids. Just watchin' you with Deloyd and Jolinda, seems you really like bein' with 'em."

"I do, Mindy Sue. I love 'em."

"I know you do, Bubba. I can see it when you're together. They're the most important things in the world to me. They're more important than me or you or their daddy. I just want what's best for 'em."

I want to jump up and grab her and give her a long, hard kiss, but then it comes to me that she ain't talkin' about wantin' to be with me. She's talkin' about what's best for the kids. I take a deep breath. "I want what's best for 'em too. And if I knew what that was, I'd sure enough tell you, I swear. But I can tell you that I wish more than anythin' that I had a family like yours. I always felt like I'd make a good daddy, but it didn't never happen."

"But it still could."

"What are you sayin? Are you . . . are you . . . talkin' about you . . . and me?"

Her face turns bright red. "Could be. What if I was?"

I smile, then take a deep breath. "Well, I hate like the devil to say this, but I'd have to remind you that I been married three times already, and every single time I ended up gettin' divorced. I ain't worthy to marry you or anybody else. I proved three different times that I can't be a good husband."

"I'm not so sure about that," she says, givin' me this sweet, innocent look.

"Come on, Mindy Sue. I ain't got nothin' to be proud of in that department."

"But there's somethin' else that's important to me. And that is, I can't make myself believe that Willard's gonna be good to us. I know he wants to, but all it takes is for him to decide to have a beer one day. Then we're right back where we were when he left. I just don't think I'm willin' to take a chance."

"Ain't no guarantees either way."

She hesitates, then says, "Willard will always be Jolinda and Deloyd's daddy. Can't change that. And he said he's movin' over this way to be around the kids no matter whether or not him and me get back together."

It's quiet for a long time. Then I say, "You know, Mindy Sue, I've always thought a lot of you, even back when we was all still in school. But when you started seein' Willard, I backed away. My poor brother'd had a hard enough time puttin' up with the way Pop treated him and feelin' so guilty about hittin' me with that horseshoe without me tryin' to steal his girl away. He's my brother. I love him."

"I know you do. And I used to love him. But I just don't know if I can anymore. How do you love somebody you can't trust?"

"Well, like I said a while ago, if I knew the right thing for you to do, I'd sure enough tell you. But I also want to say that if you wanted to marry me, I'd sure like to give it a try. You're the only girl in the world I'd ever take a chance on marryin'."

Well, at first, Willard didn't take it too good that Mindy Sue wasn't gonna get back with him, but Ambrose convinced him that maybe it was God's will, and if it was, then it was all right. Willard moved over to Tampa and found him another good job sellin' new cars. Six months later, me and Mindy Sue started talkin' out loud about gettin' married, but by that time, of course, everybody in town had already figured it out.

True to his word, Willard saw the kids every weekend or so, and within a year he was married again too. At first, Mindy Sue and his wife didn't get on too good. Mindy Sue thought she was too strict on the kids when they went to visit, but little by little things got better.

Mindy Sue and me was married at the Church of Everlasting Liability, and lots of folks came 'cause it was all a scandal, me gettin' married for the fourth time, and to my own sister-in-law. The next week, her and the kids moved over to Turkey Creek with me, and while married life ain't been perfect, it's been damn close. Reckon it just takes findin' the right person. Who ain't named Mary.

A House Full of Girls
by Eustis Trydell

I was born in Georgia, the youngest of five boys, and was raised by my daddy. My mama run off with some fella before I was two, and we ain't seen her since. I got no memory of her, but I hear tell that she wasn't a happy person, always mad as a rattlesnake with poison ivy and for sure wasn't ever meant to be a mama. Since there wasn't no other family around to help, Daddy got stuck with us, but he wasn't no better than her when it come to raisin' us kids. That man ruled the house with a peach tree switch. Nobody got away with nothin', wasn't no two ways about that. And he couldn't cook, neither. I always promised myself that if I had young'uns of my own, I'd never treat 'em like he did us.

When I was nineteen, me and my big brother Ollie come down here to Florida lookin' for work. We started out in the groves around Toad Springs and decided to stay. After about a year, I hired on with Bubba Stroudamore, who run a dairy farm, but Ollie stayed with the groves. Today he's got his own spread. Me, I liked bein' around all those big old animals. I worked real hard and after six or seven years Bubba helped me get my own little dairy in Toad Springs. When I left, he gave me this little colt I named Rooster. I called him that 'cause when he whinnied he sounded just like a rooster. He was the best animal I ever run into. He'd know what I wanted him to do before I'd decided my-self. Sometimes I felt like if I turned him loose he could pretty much handle the cattle without me.

So things was goin' along good when I met Mazie. I was in Turkey Creek one day, pickin' up some supplies that Smitty's Hardware didn't have here in Toad Springs, and she was wor-kin' at her daddy's hardware over there. She had curly blonde hair down to her shoulders, big blue eyes, and was pretty as a goggle-eyed perch. She smiled a lot and it seemed like she took to me too. I started goin' over to Turkey Creek every chance I got, and after a while I took her to a cane-grindin' party. Man, how I love that sweet sugar cane. After that, I took her to some church singin' picnics and even to church every Sunday. I never went to church much myself, but she really loved it.

I bragged about how good things was goin' with my little dairy farm, and she said she loved cows. Said she always felt kind of peaceful when she milked 'em, leanin' over, restin' her head on that nice warm cow's side, listenin' to the milk plink down in the bottom of the pail. Said she even liked milkin' in the early mornin's, and that's what gave me the nerve to ask her to marry me. When she said yes, I couldn't hardly believe it. Look at me, I thought to myself. Got a job I love, my own place, and a pretty wife who likes to milk cows. Ain't no more I could ever ask for.

We got married at the Church of Everlasting Liability the Sunday before Christmas. Her folks seemed to like me and was glad she hadn't moved farther away, 'cause they said she'd al-ways wanted to get out of Turkey Creek. Told me I was just the man to settle her down, and I was proud to be the one to do it.

At first we was real happy. She was always smilin', had sup-per ready for me every night when I come in, and for a while there she helped with the milkin' every mornin' and evenin'. Then she started in on me to go to church with her on Sunday mornin's and Wednesday nights, which I never had no interest in, and even wanted me to get down on my knees by the bed and pray with her, but I wasn't of a mind to do any of them things. She said I'd been willin' to go to church all the time when we was courtin' and it wasn't fair of me to quit like that. Not to mention what I was doin' to my soul. I'd give in once in a while just to make her happy, but it was borin' and I got tired of bein' told what an awful sinner I am.

After we'd been married about a year, she started complainin' that she didn't feel good in the mornin's and she couldn't help with the milkin' no more. Turned out she was gonna have a baby. Also turned out she'd milked her last cow.

It was three o'clock one mornin' when she woke me up and told me it was time to call the midwife, 'cause the baby was comin'. I have to say, it made me real nervous knowin' it was her time. When the midwife got there, she was real calm and cheerful, like a baby gettin' born happened every day of the week and wasn't no big deal. Later on, Mazie's sister, Susie, come over too.

They all stayed in the bedroom, seemed like for two days, and wouldn't let me in—not that I was sure I wanted to see what was goin' on. With all the hollerin' and hullaballoo, I was ready to run out the front door. But I stuck it out. Then, when the midwife finally come and told me there was two little girls, not just one, I near about keeled over. Twins!

Mazie, bein' true to her religion, named the babies Patience and Harmony, and after she was up and around good she started naggin' me to go back to church with her again. I didn't want to, but finally I said I'd go for sure every Easter and Christmas.

Now, I'd never been around a newborn baby in my life. I'd seen 'em, of course, but I hadn't never touched one or nothin'. I didn't know they'd keep you awake half the night and make such a smelly mess of everything. And two was twice as bad as one. All that cryin's enough to make you crazy. Then, almost overnight, Mazie changed from bein' cute and flirty and fixin' me whatever I wanted for supper to fussin' all the time. She'd make a great big pot of soup or stew or somethin', and we'd have to eat it 'til it was gone. Then she'd make another pot.

Now, since Mazie was gonna be in the house all day, I figured she could keep strainin' all the milk I brought in from the cows, 'cause she didn't have nothin' else to do but tend to the young'uns, which is just natural for a mama. Anybody could see she had lots of extra time, could even take a nap if she wanted, and like I told her, a dairy farm don't run itself. Everybody has to pitch in.

I brought all our milkin' buckets inside the house and set a big pot near the back door where she could stretch some cheese-cloth across it and pour the fresh milk in. That way, she'd get rid of all the bugs and dirt and whatnot from the barn before she poured it into the gallon cans. Then I'd sell it to the neighbors and some to Halt Brisco at the General Store and to the grocery over in Mango. Folks was supposed to clean the cans out real good before they returned 'em, but ended up Mazie had to do most of the cleanin'.

For a while there, I offered to help her out some around the house, washin' dishes or sweepin' the floor, but seems like I never did anything right, the way she liked it. So in the end, I pretty much stayed as far away from her as I could. In the daytime anyway.

Then one night when the twins were about nine months old, I was sittin' in the livin' room listenin' to the radio. She'd just gotten the babies to bed, finished cleanin' up the kitchen, and swept off the porch when she came and sat down with me. I looked up and gave her a smile.

"Eustis," she says, "I need to talk to you."

I look over at her. "What's up, honey?"

She don't look happy. "We're gonna have another baby."

Uh, oh. That ain't what I want to hear. "But . . . but . . . we're just gettin' to where we can sleep through the night once in a while," I say. "And the cryin' . . . "

She sounds real tense. "I know all about that, Eustis. Better than you do. We'll just have to make the best of it."

I shrug my shoulders. "Well, maybe this time, I'll get me my boy."

"Thought you ought to know," she says. Then she goes to bed.

I sit there thinkin' how, from the day Patience and Harmony was born, the house has been full of screechin', yowlin' babies. Mazie's good with 'em, mostly, and I can see she's tryin' to be a good mama, but it seems to me like she ought to be doin' a better job of keepin' 'em quiet. But then, it don't look like this is the right time to say nothin' to her about that. I mean, come on, she's the mama. She's supposed to know what to do. When I get mad and yell at 'em, they just screech even louder, and then for sure there ain't no way to shut 'em up.

Wasn't that way when I was growin' up. We all behaved ourselves and minded our p's and q's, 'cause we knew what would happen if we didn't. My daddy thought we should act like grown men from the time we could walk. But since I had girls, I didn't feel like I could be so mean to 'em. I held the babies sometimes, mostly when they were asleep, though. I was always afraid I'd drop 'em. If they woke up, they went right back to their mama.

This time, I prayed for a boy. Like I said, I ain't a religious man and generally only go to church twice a year, but I went a few extra times just to show God I was serious. And then Faith was born.

By that time, Patience and Harmony was runnin' around all over the house, spillin' stuff and smearin' food all over the place, hittin' each other, and fightin' over blocks and baby dolls and stuffed toys. And with the new baby, we was back to bein' awake all night and havin' even more smelly diapers around. Whenever I tell Mazie to keep 'em quiet before I lose my mind, she tells me to do it my ownself. But I tell her that's the mama's job. I don't know nothin' about little kids.

Now, the only time Mazie went anywhere besides the grocery store was when one of the church ladies picked her and the babies up on Sundays and took 'em to church. After Faith was born, she started quotin' Bible verses and singin' hymns all day, every day, like "I Was Sinking Deep in Sin" and "Washed in the Blood of the Lamb" and "Onward, Christian Soldiers." I figure she done it to drown out the cryin'.

Then, just when I thought it couldn't get any worse, we had Innocence. By that time, I could tell that Mazie had more in her horse cart than she could carry, but I couldn't see no way to make it better for her. Then, when the next baby girl come four years later, Mazie gave up on the church names and called her Anna Jean. Said she'd run out of Bible names she liked, and besides, she figured that namin' the babies after words that are in the Bible wasn't earnin' her no big favors from the Lord. When Anna Jean was just a few months old, Mazie said that havin' five young'uns in seven years was more than she could stand and she wasn't havin' no more babies, if you get my meanin'. After that, I went around mad as a bear with a sore tail.

Now, you'd think the twins would grow up bein' best friends, the way they looked just alike, but them two never got along. Seemed to me it was like livin' with General Lee and General Grant under the same roof. Right after they turned twelve, things got so bad that I started a truck garden so I could sell vegetables for market and have an excuse to stay away from the house longer.

The younger kids wasn't so ornery, but we'd gotten burned out on them twins almost from their first breath. I couldn't tell 'em apart half the time, and to this day, I ain't sure they're goin' by their right names. But I reckon it don't make a whole lot of difference. They was both stealin' things from the least ones and teasin' the others. I'm tellin' you, I didn't know girls could be so mean. They was worse than me and my brothers! My daddy wouldn't have put up with all this fussin', but I sure wasn't gonna be like him. But then, at the same time, I didn't know how to make things better. I knew what *not* to do, but I didn't know what to do instead. Our house wasn't a happy place to be livin' in, that's for sure. By that time, Mazie hardly ever talked to me at all.

Now, I'd have kept on with the dairy farm if I hadn't hurt my back in that freak accident. One day, me and my horse Rooster was out checkin' the fences when he got spooked by a snake and I went flyin' off over his head and landed flat on my back. At first, I thought I just got the wind knocked out of me, but when I tried to get up, I seen I'd hurt my back pretty bad and couldn't hardly move. I hollered out for help for a long time, but didn't nobody come. Finally, I managed to stand up, and, holdin' on to Rooster, I hobbled back toward the house.

We made it to the nearest road, and after sittin' there for about an hour, Halt Brisco happened by in his old Model T. He helped me into the car, makin' real sure I didn't get the back seat dirty after I been lyin' in the field in agony half the day. He tied Rooster's reins onto the bumper, and we took him back home, then he drove me to see the doc over in Bartow. Ended up, Doc told me I wasn't gonna be ridin' horses no more 'cause of where I'd hurt my back. I hated it like the devil, but I didn't have no choice and finally decided to switch to raisin' chickens. We held back a few cows for ourselves but sold off the rest to Bubba Stroudamore. Have to say, Mazie thought it was a good idea.

I got some Leghorns and some Rhode Island Reds, and right off, the hens was layin' pretty good. In case you ever need to know, you can tell for sure what color eggs a hen's gonna lay by lookin' at her earlobes. The ones with white earlobes lay white eggs, and the ones with red earlobes lay brown eggs. Before I got into this I never even knew chickens *had* earlobes.

Now, chickens is somethin' altogether different from cows. You got a whole other set of problems with all the diseases that can sneak up on you and wipe out your whole coop before you can turn around twice and spit over your shoulder. And varmints can get 'em too. First time a coyote almost got in one of the coops, three of the chickens got so scared, they died. Then a bunch of 'em got the bumblefoot, and cuttin' all them nasty sores out ain't no picnic. Nothing's ever as simple as you think it's gonna be.

One evenin' after the kids was all in bed, me and Mazie was sittin' in the livin' room again, listenin' to the radio. She was knittin' a pink sweater for Anna Jean, and when I looked over at her it crossed my mind that she looked almost like a stranger. I remembered that first day I seen her behind the counter at her daddy's hardware store, so pretty and smilin' and happy. Now, her long blonde hair was pulled back hard into a tight knot at her neck, and she had all these frown lines and dark circles under her eyes. Her face was blotchy and those pretty hands were rough and red and all swole up. It hit me kind of sideways and made my heart sink down to my knees. It was like I hadn't really looked at her in years.

We never seemed to have a good word to say to each other anymore. I swear, there wasn't no way to make her happy. Didn't matter what I done, it wasn't good enough. She just seemed to naturally see the bad side of everything. The girls didn't do good enough in school, or folks at church was sayin' she was a bad mama 'cause the twins was always raisin' sand over somethin'. Mazie figured God must be punishin' her, but she couldn't figure out why, so she didn't know what she should change about herself.

One Saturday afternoon, it all come apart. She was sittin' at the kitchen table and outta nowhere said, "Eustis, I just can't live like this no more. I hate this place. I hate my life. And I don't know what to do." She started cryin'.

This come from outta the blue, but when I really took a good look at her, she seemed so sad and beat down that I didn't have no idea what to say. "Aw, honey. Do you think maybe the preacher—"

"That man don't know one thing about raisin' kids. Not families, neither. Ain't no point in even askin' him. All he knows to tell folks is to pray on it and things'll get better." She wipes her eyes. "But it don't ever get better. Just seems to get worse."

"How about your mama then? Maybe she could—"

"Come on, Eustis. She just says it's my own fault for havin' more kids than I can handle. But I'm here to tell you I can't do this no more."

"But, honey, we got no choice. We had the young'uns, and now we got to take care of 'em."

"Yeah. *We* got take care of 'em. But *we* don't take care of 'em. *I* take care of 'em. I take care of them and you too!"

"But anytime I try to help, you say I'm doin' it all wrong, makin' things worse."

"That's just an excuse, Eustis Trydell. And you know it."

"No, it ain't—"

"Well, you never do it right, that's for sure. Just give it a lick and a promise, then go back out the door fast as you can. So I've decided what I'm gonna do. Somethin' that'll make you understand what I'm talkin' about."

I don't like the way that sounds, but I say, "What's that?"

"I'm leavin' y'all for a while."

"Leavin'? What are you sayin'? You can't leave."

She stands up and points her finger at me. "No? Just watch me. I'm gonna go stay in Turkey Creek with Susie and Matt for a while, that's what I'm gonna do. Then we'll see what you can figure out."

I feel like somebody hit me in the back of my head with a brick. "What? Stay with your sister? You can't leave us here. Anna Jean's only . . . what? Four? Five?"

"I'm goin' in the mornin'."

I got no idea what to say. "But . . . I don't know nothin' about takin' care of girls. I mean, I . . . I . . . "

She stares at me. "It's just natural, like you're always tellin' me, Eustis. And if it's natural for me, then it is for you too. You'll manage. You're a big tough man."

"But . . . but . . . it's natural for *you*, not me. *You're* the mama."

"Maybe somebody from the church would be willin' to help you out. Or maybe your brother."

I shake my head. "My brother? Ollie don't even have kids. And I ain't gonna ask nobody from the church. I ain't askin' for charity."

"So do it your own damn self," she says. "Like your daddy did." Then she gets up and leaves.

The next mornin', Mazie don't say a word to me, but she fixes breakfast, and after she gets the big girls off to school, she brings Anna Jean out back to me. I notice she's carryin' a satchel along with a bag full of somethin', clothes it looks like. "Bye," she says. "Susie's here to pick me up." Then she turns to go.

"How long you goin' for?" I say, breakin' out in a cold sweat as I watch her walk away. My stomach's in a knot. I feel like I've just got throwed off a cliff or I'm about to walk the plank on a pirate ship.

Anna Jean runs after her mama 'til Mazie stops and gives her a hug, then points her back to me. After Mazie's gone, I take a deep breath and tell Anna Jean to go play with the barn cats while I muck out the chicken coop.

Around noon we go up to the house for lunch, and that's when I notice for the first time that I don't know where nothin' is in the kitchen. I hadn't fixed myself somethin' to eat since I left home when I was nineteen.

Anna Jean helps me make a couple of sandwiches, and after we eat 'em, she tells me she'll wash the dirty dishes—that her mama'd showed her how. I pull a chair up to the kitchen sink for her to stand on and head back outside. Not five minutes later, I hear her screamin', "Daddy! Daddy!" I take a deep breath, turn around, and go back inside. There's broken glass all over the kitchen floor, and Anna Jean's standin' barefoot in the middle of it.

"Help!" she shrieks. Tears are runnin' down her cheeks.

I crunch through the glass, pick her up, and sit her on the kitchen table. "I broke the pitcher! Mama's gonna be mad." Then she holds her legs straight out and points to her feet. "Look! My feet! There's blood!"

I look down, and sure enough, she's cut both her feet, and one of 'em is bleedin' pretty bad. "Oh, Anna Jean," I say, "you're all right. You ain't gonna die or nothin'."

She looks up at me, sobbin' like she's scared to death. "It's blood! Where's Mama? I want Mama."

I grab a dishtowel and start wipin' the glass from her feet, but she keeps jerkin' away. "Ouch! Ow! You're hurtin' me!"

I pull back, irritated, then look her straight in the eye. "This ain't no big thing, Anna Jean. Don't be such a baby. You're gonna be fine."

"But it hurts!" she cries.

"Stop it, now," I say. "It don't hurt that bad. It's just a few little cuts."

She pulls her right foot up and looks at the bottom of it. "The blood! There's blood!"

I cross my arms and take a deep breath. Since bein' nice ain't calmin' her down, I say, real stern, "Anna Jean Trydell! You stop it. Right now!"

She yowls louder. "I can't!"

I raise my voice. "I mean it, Anna Jean! Right this minute." Don't make no difference.

I pick her up, still screamin', and take her to the bathroom, where I sit her on the side of the tub and run water over her feet. When I get the blood and dirt off, I can see there's still a few splinters stickin' out. With all the callouses on my hands, I can't get hold of 'em, and I can't find Mazie's tweezers. When I try to squeeze 'em out, she jumps and twitches around and screeches like a banshee.

"Anna Jean," I say, "sit still, dammit! You don't sit still, I ain't gonna be able to get these out."

"It *hurts*!"

"I know it hurts, but you're gonna have to be brave. I got chores. I can't spend all day in here."

"I want Mama," she sobs. "Mama can fix it."

Well, to make a long story short, I end up sittin' her on the livin' room couch with her feet propped on a pillow, gettin' her some books to read, some oranges to eat, and turnin' on the radio. After I clean up the glass and I'm ready to go back to work, I tell Anna Jean to get her sisters to help her with the splinters when they get home from school and to tell 'em to wash the dishes and think about what to fix for supper. She's still snifflin' when I leave, but I can't wait no longer.

As I come in the back door of the kitchen later that afternoon, I hear Patience and Harmony arguin' over what to cook for dinner. They look my way when I walk in, and both come runnin' over. "Why'd Mama go to Susie's? When is she comin' back?"

Then Faith and Innocence come in too, ready to cry. "Where's Mama? What happened?"

Anna Jean calls in from the livin' room, "Daddeeey! I can't walk! They got the glass out, but I still can't walk."

"Okay, okay now," I say to the girls. "Just take it easy. Let's go in the livin' room where Anna Jean can hear."

When they're finally all sittin' down and quiet, I say, "Your mama's gone to stay with Susie and Matt for a little while. Needs to get away from all the arguin' and fightin'. Says she can't stand it no more."

"When's she comin' back?" Harmony asks. "We need her. She's supposed to have a new dress finished for me to wear to church on Sunday."

"I ain't exactly sure," I say. "She didn't tell me. But she's not far away. She'll be home in a few days, I reckon."

"I want to talk to her," Innocence says. "I want to call her."

"Well, remember Susie and Matt ain't got no phone. I'm sure she'll be back soon."

"Don't she love us no more?" Faith asks in a quivery voice.

"Of course she loves you," I say. "She's your mama."

"What about my feet?" Anna Jean whines. "I can't walk."

I feel like I'm gonna fly into a million pieces. "All right, girls. Everybody just settle down." I'd heard Mazie say that a thousand times. And to my great surprise, they get quiet. Then they all turn and stare at me.

"We can live without your mama for a few days."

"But I don't want to!" Anna Jean wails.

"Me neither," Faith whines. "Let's just go get her and bring her home."

"No," I say. "We ain't gonna do that. We'll give her a few days, and then she'll come back on her own."

Then they all start talkin' at once. "She can't leave us!"

"Don't she care about us no more?"

"Mamas ain't allowed to run off!"

"QUIET!" I yell. "Stop it."

And again to my great surprise, they shut up.

"Patience, you and Harmony go fix supper."

Harmony glares at Patience, then looks at me and says, "How about chicken soup, Daddy? That would be good."

Patience pipes up. "Oh, no. Chicken is all we ever have. And you don't know how to cook it. I'm gonna make meatloaf—"

"*NO!*" Harmony screams back. *"Chicken soup!"*

"SHUT UP!" I say. "The both of you! Just go fix somethin'."

They both glare at me. But then they get quiet.

"NOW!"

They start toward the kitchen. Harmony looks at Patience and says in a bossy voice, "We're gonna have chicken soup."

"Are not. Mama was gonna make meatloaf tonight, and that's what—"

Harmony yells at her, *"CHICKEN SOUP!"*

"STOP IT," I holler in my meanest voice. "Right now!" I wish to God I knew what Mazie does when things get like this. I can't seem to remember to save my soul . . . maybe 'cause that's when I always head out the back door.

When I've finally gotten 'em calmed down for a few minutes, I go take a shower. For the first time, I notice that when I stand directly under the showerhead, I can't hear the fussin'.

After I'm cleaned up and dressed, I go to the livin' room to listen to the radio like I do every night. I'm tryin' to hear the news when Innocence comes runnin' up to me. "Daddy, Miss Carrie June gave us spellin' homework, and I need you to call out the words for me."

Damn! Homework? One more thing Mazie does every night. "All right," I say, thinkin' maybe I can listen to the radio while I help her. "Show me what I need to do."

While I'm callin' out the words, I hear screechin' in the kitchen. "Harmony! You pushed me into the stove. You burned me!"

"I didn't touch you!" Harmony screams back.

"Did so!"

"Don't try and blame me."

I can feel my temper risin'. "Girls!" I holler, louder than I mean to. "Stop it!"

I'm about ready to get up and head for the kitchen when Faith comes runnin' in, whinin'. "Daddy, they won't let me help. I want to help."

"Stop fussin' and just sit down here and help Innocence with her spellin' words."

"I want to cook! I don't want to do homework."

"Faith!" I yell. "Dammit! Sit down on the couch and be quiet."

"But Daddy . . ."

"Stop it," I say. Now!"

She gets quiet, then starts cryin'. When I give her a dirty look, she hushes up.

It's an hour later when we sit down to eat. I grit my teeth when I say the blessin', 'cause I sure ain't thankful to the good Lord for puttin' me in this spot. Nobody talks much, the soup tastes like dishwater, there's no biscuits, and there's too much sugar in the tea, but I know better than to complain. The kitchen looks like two raccoons had a fight in there, and the twins say that since they cooked supper, the other girls have do the dishes. Anna Jean's cryin', sayin' that she can't help 'cause her feet hurt. I know I can't just walk out the door, much as I want to, so I take a deep breath and start wipin' off the counter in the the kitchen while Anna Jean keeps askin' me why my face is so red.

By the time everybody gets to bed, it's almost ten o'clock, and I think to myself that there ain't nothin' I won't do to get Mazie back here as quick as I can. No wonder my daddy was so mean.

The next mornin', I tell Harmony to make a big pot of oatmeal and that's what everybody's havin' for breakfast. Period. And I tell the rest of 'em that we're not gonna sit down to eat until they're all dressed and ready for school.

Right off, Faith starts whinin' that Anna Jean stole her last clean pair of underpants and she can't go to school without 'em. Innocence can't get her hair in braids by herself, and when Patience tries to help her, Innocence yells that she's pullin' all her hair out, and Patience says the tangles are so bad, she ought to just cut it all off, which makes Innocence start cryin'. And Harmony comes in to help Anna Jean, who says she still can't walk good and her feet hurt more than ever and since she's not goin' anywhere, she doesn't need to have her hair combed at all and even tries to bite Harmony, who throws the hairbrush down and stomps away.

After I finally get the girls off to school, I bring one of the barn kittens in for Anna Jean to play with, then go out on the front porch with a cup of coffee to think. This house is like a war zone. I'm so het up that I need to go chop some wood or wrestle a bear before I slap somebody silly. How can everything get in such a mess so fast?

When I'm just walkin' out the door to feed the chickens, Anna Jean yells out, "Daddy, the kitty peed on the couch and it's gonna leave a spot. Mama's gonna be real mad."

Five long days go by, and the only things that get better are Anna Jean's feet. And now that she can get around, she wants to help, but she ends up spillin' the chicken feed in the chickens' water bowls and breakin' six eggs and slowin' me down so much, I'm startin' to feel like choppin' wood again.

Have to say, and it's an awful thing, but these past few days, I been noticin' the way I'm talkin' to the girls. Sometimes I'm yellin' so loud, I wonder if the veins on my neck are stickin' out like my daddy's did. Makes me feel sick to my stomach to think I could be like him.

For the rest of the week, I spend all my time when the girls are home tryin' to break up arguments and get them to cooperate with each other. It's a constant battle. The twins want to run the show and boss the little ones around, but I remind 'em that I'm in charge—even if all I really want to do is leave.

Saturday mornin', after I feed the chickens and livestock and make sure the kids have breakfast, I tell the twins they got to watch their sisters while I go to see Mazie at Susie and Matt's house.

I take a deep breath and send up a prayer before I knock on Susie's front door. "Well, hello there, Eustis," she says. "Thought we might be seein' you. Come in. Mazie's out back. You go on and have a seat, and I'll get her."

I sit down on the couch, surprised she's bein' so nice to me. Lord only knows what Mazie's been tellin' her. When Mazie comes in, she ain't smilin'. I get up and try to hug her, but she pushes me away and sits in a chair across the room.

"How you been?" I ask, sittin' back down. That's when it occurs to me that I should have thought more about what I was gonna say.

"All right," she says in a flat voice.

"Um . . . we all miss you a lot, the girls and me. We really do, hon."

She crosses her arms in front of her, then crosses her legs and looks out the window.

At least it occurs to me to start with the accident. "Anna Jean cut her feet pretty bad on Monday. Was tryin' to help by washin' the breakfast dishes and broke a pitcher."

She opens her eyes wide and puts her hand on her heart. "Is she all right?"

"Yeah. She is now. But she was real scared. I think it was seein' the blood. And she wanted you there."

"Eustis! You shouldn't ever let a five-year-old wash dishes by herself! Use your head!"

"Mazie, I really want you to come home. We all do."

"I'll bet you do, Eustis. Ain't so easy, is it?"

I don't say nothin'. I sure don't want to say the wrong thing.

She rolls her eyes and kind of sneers at me, then says, "It's nice and calm here. Nobody argues. And there ain't six other people here for me to worry about takin' care of day and night and nobody ever sayin' 'Thank you' or 'Need any help?' I don't ever hear it from the girls. And I sure don't hear it from you."

"But Mazie, you got a husband and five young'uns to take care of. We need you. Bad."

She grabs the arms of the chair and leans forward, squintin' her eyes. "You need me for a workhorse. That's the only reason you need me. To cook your meals and clean your house and raise your kids. Not for no other reason."

I know I got to say the right thing here. I think hard before I talk. "Well, it's true we do need you for them things. But we all love you, Mazie. The girls miss you, bad. Before this, they'd never even been away from you for one night in their whole lives. And they were all real upset when they found out you was gone. Especially the least ones. And, 'course, I miss you too."

It's quiet for a little bit, then I say, "What's really wrong at home, Mazie? I know you're outdone with the kids. But kids fight. That's what they do."

"You think I don't know that? I know them kids better than you ever will. I'm wore out, Eustis. I'm the first one up in the mornin' and the last one to bed at night. All I do is take care of everybody else. I keep the house, help you out back when you need it, tend to all of you when you're sick, and fix three meals for seven people every day. Sometimes when I can't stand it no more, I shut myself up in a closet and scream as loud as I can." Her voice gets quivery. "I didn't want nobody to know how bad I feel, but I finally got to the point where I don't care what people think anymore. Some days I don't even care about you and the kids." She looks down and shakes her head. "Maybe I shouldn't ever have married you and had all the young'uns. Maybe it was a big mistake." She wipes her eyes with the hem of her dress and looks up at me.

My heart sinks. This don't sound good at all. "Oh, Mazie. Why didn't you tell me?"

She glares at me. "Goddammit, Eustis, I have told you. Over and over. But you don't want to hear it."

"But you ain't ever told me all this stuff."

"I have so. Just not sittin' down serious like this. I've told you in bits and pieces a thousand times. At least."

"Well, then, I'm sorry, honey. Could be you're right. Maybe I didn't want to hear it. But after bein' alone with the girls all this time, I know you work hard. And I've been tryin' to think about what I've been doin, bein' the man of the house and all. And really, it seems to me I do my part. I provide for you and the girls, we always got enough to eat and a roof over our heads. I don't go over to Schniticker's Tavern more than once in a while, I'm nice to the neighbors, and I go to church regular, at least twice a year. I love you and the kids, and I work hard every single day."

"Yeah. And that's all you do. You don't hardly even know your own young'uns, Eustis. You're glad to be with us, long as everything's goin' along smooth. When somebody kicks up a fuss, you get up and hightail it. Every single time. You leave all the trouble for me to clean up. But I help you anytime you ask me to. I drop whatever I'm doin' and go do what you want. You don't ever do that for me."

"Come on, Mazie. You know how I grew up. With a daddy who was always hollerin' at us and beatin' us. I don't want to be the kind of father he was. That's why I leave. I don't want to be mean. I want 'em to love me."

"Well, to love you, they got to know you. And don't none of us know you, Eustis. You're like a . . . a . . . a shadow."

This ain't goin' too good here, but I gotta say *somethin'*. "So . . . what can we do to make it better? Me and the girls, we're willin' to do whatever it takes to get you back home. They really miss you."

"Instead of what y'all are gonna do, how about what are *you* gonna do?"

Uh, oh. "Um, well, you tell me what I'm supposed to do. And I'll do it. I promise."

"No, Eustis! Damn you! I'm not the one to fix everything. YOU decide how to make things better. I'm sick of bein' the only one to try and solve every little problem."

"Oh . . . um . . . how's about if the girls help more with the cookin' and the housework?"

"We're talkin' about what *you're* gonna do, Eustis. Not the girls."

"Well, I don't know. I thought I was doin' my part, Mazie. Honest to God, I did."

"Well you ain't."

"Okay, then. Let's see. You need some help with the cookin' and cleanin, I reckon."

"That's a good start."

"Why don't the girls help—"

"I'm too tired to fight with 'em over it, that's why. And you don't ever get on to 'em for nothin'. Don't ever say, 'Mind your mother,' or 'Go to your room,' or nothin'. You just march out the door when things head south."

"Oh! I can do that, Mazie. I can tell 'em to mind you."

"And what else?"

"What else? I don't know. Let's see, we could make a plan where one of the twins helps you cook every night."

"But you'd have to back me up on it."

"I will. I will, honey. What else?"

"The twins got to stop fightin' all the time."

"I'm with you on that one, hon. You just tell me how to stop 'em, and I'll do it."

She leans forward and talks to me through clenched teeth. "If I knew how to do it, Eustis, it would be done! *You* figure out what to do. I'm done tryin'."

"Okay, okay, I'll talk to 'em," I say, feelin' like there's hope. "I have to admit, I'd never noticed how much they fight all the time 'til you left. I just didn't know."

"You figured if you wasn't around much, you wouldn't have to mess with 'em. I know you started that truck garden to get away from us, Eustis. I ain't stupid."

I sure ain't gonna say nothin' about that. Instead, I say, "Really, Mazie, I been tryin' hard not to be mean like my daddy was, hollerin' at us kids all the time, switchin' us for no reason, tellin' us we was idiots and fools. That was his favorite sayin', idiots and fools. So I just figured I'd steer away from anything that looked like trouble."

"Like I said, you didn't w*ant* to know."

"Yeah, well, now I do. Boy, do I. From now on, it'll be us against them."

"Okay," she says with a little smile.

I think for a minute. "Well, how about whenever they get in a set-to, they have to go to their room?"

"They'd just keep fightin' in there. And when I yell at 'em, don't nothin' change."

"Okay, um . . . tellin' 'em it's the Christian thing to do?"

"They don't care about that."

"How's about they get a switchin'?"

"Well, I've thought about—"

"No, wait," I say. "That sounds like my daddy. How about maybe an extra chore instead. One they hate. Like cleanin' the oven. Or washin' windows. Or moppin' the kitchen floor. Somethin' like that."

"Okay," she says, lookin' interested now. "That might work for the older ones. And the little ones can go sit in a corner or somethin'." She leans forward. "And everybody has to make their own beds every mornin'. If the little ones need help, their sisters can give them a hand, not just leave it all for me. One of the twins can help me cook supper, and the other one can help me wash dishes and clean up every night. They can take turns. And Faith, Innocence, and Anna Jean can wipe the table off after supper."

"Good idea," I say. "And we'll sit down with 'em all together and tell 'em what the new rules are. I'm gonna do my part, Mazie, I will. We'll both make 'em do it. Both of us. Together."

She stares at me. "That sounds good, Eustis. But there's one more thing. I want you to start goin' to church with us on Sundays."

I groan. "Aw, Mazie . . . "

She scowls. "I mean it. How you think your young'uns feel about a daddy who don't never go to church?"

"Don't seem to bother 'em so far."

"How would you know? You ever ask 'em?"

"Okay, I'll go. But just every other week."

She looks at me and smiles. "Okay. Every other week."

"And if you'll give me a back rub once in a while? I don't complain about it much, but since I fell off Rooster, my back ain't never been the same. Even if he is the best horse ever born. It would really help me. Would you do that if I go to church?"

She smiles at me. "Okay. I reckon so."

I'm already thinkin' I'll start goin' to church every other week, and before long, I'll get it down to once a month at the most. I say, "Okay," then get up and give her a big hug and a kiss.

I reach over and hold her hand while we drive home, and I hadn't done nothin' like that in a long time. Before we got out of the car, I gave her a big kiss. 'Course, the young'uns hear us pull up and all come flyin' out of the house at the same time, so glad to see their mama.

Well, now, I ain't gonna tell you we went home and laid down the law and everything fell right into place, 'cause that wouldn't be true. Like, for one thing, the twins couldn't ever agree whose night it was to help their mama, so I finally hung a calendar up in the kitchen and wrote their names on it and told 'em they had to do it.

We found out that givin' 'em extra chores for punishment worked real good, and the house was a lot calmer. Me and Mazie stuck together on makin' 'em do stuff, and it wasn't near so hard as I thought it would be. And for some reason, the twins settled down a lot, and when they got along better, the rest of the girls did too. That part surprised me.

Lookin' back on those days now, I see that up 'til then, I'd thought Mazie had it pretty easy, stayin' inside the house all the time with the kids and not havin' to do the heavy work out in the heat of the day. But I sure learned my lesson. Her and me get along lots better too, and I told her that there ain't no way I'd ever trade jobs with her. Not for anything in this world, 'cause her job was harder than mine. That's when she started snugglin' up with me at night.

And them backrubs was great. Before too long, things was more like when we first got married, if you get my meanin', and I went to church every other week for a good while. Who knows, maybe that had somethin' to do with the fact that about a year later, I finally got me a son, Eustis Jr.

Lillie and the Bean

by Patience Trydell

Smitty and Midge Mallet's daughter, Lillie, is six feet tall and skinny as a cattail and has a great sense of humor, which is what you always say about somebody who ain't good-lookin'—either they have a great sense of humor or a good personality. Anyway, Lillie really was funny in high school, always crackin' jokes. How else could she have married Bean Benson, who wasn't but five foot three and a quarter? Lillie's daddy runs the hardware store here in town, and I'm her best friend.

Now, the Bean had a different look about him, was a little chunky with dark skin that came from his great-great-granddaddy's Seminole Indian blood, and he had his mama's Irish blue eyes and curly red hair. He had just the right combination of both sides that all together made him look kinda . . . well, let's just say that once you saw him, you'd remember him.

They first met one Saturday night when we were all over at the roller skatin' rink in Plant City. Everybody was goin' round and round when the Bean tripped over his skates that were two sizes too big 'cause they didn't carry men's shoes that were small enough and his feet were too wide to fit into the ladies'. He was hell-bent on goin' skatin', and nothin' stopped the Bean once he made his mind up about somethin'.

Lillie was racin' with me, and she was behind him. When Lillie looked back over her shoulder to see how far she was ahead of me, she didn't see the Bean sprawled out on the floor. She tripped and flew right past him, landin' way over on the other side of the rink. But I landed right on top of him. Then people started pilin' up. Before it was over, there were six skaters lyin' on the floor, one with a broken leg and three with sprains of one kind or another.

It was the biggest pileup in the history of the Slidell Roller Rink, and that record was never broken 'til the place closed when Old Man Slidell went to jail for lyin' on his taxes.

Anyhow, the Bean pushed until he got me off of him, then lay back on the floor hollerin' that he'd pulled his shoulder out.

Once Lillie got up and saw she wasn't hurt, she was mad as a raccoon caught in a garbage can and lit into the Bean right there with all the boys hollerin' and the girls all cryin', tryin' to see which of their bones were broken. The Bean just stayed on the floor where he fell, 'cause once he got me to move, he found out that along with the bad shoulder, he'd hurt his knee and couldn't get up. So he just sat there with his mouth hangin' open, watchin' Lillie skate from one side of him to the other, givin' him a piece of her mind. That Lillie had a temper hidin' down there among all them jokes she liked to tell, and once it saw the light of day, there was no stuffin' it back in.

That was when them two met, but they didn't get together 'til a few months later, and by that time they was both livin' in Tampa. The Bean had just started workin' at Mason's Furniture Store over on Franklin Street, and Lillie was lucky enough to have gotten a job in the steno pool for the state attorney's office.

Lillie and I had been ridin' the Central Avenue streetcar one Saturday afternoon when she glanced over and saw the Bean. She remembered his dark skin and curly red hair and that brought the whole skatin' rink fiasco to mind. She smiled at him but it seemed like he wasn't nearly so anxious to strike up a new acquaintance, 'cause he looked away real quick and stared at the back of the streetcar driver's head.

"Hello," Lillie said. "Do you remember me?"

He slid his eyeballs her way, then, real slow, he turned his head toward her. "Um, no. I don't think so."

"At the skatin' rink in Plant City a while back. I guess I lost my temper that night you fell down."

"Oh," he said. "Oh, yeah. That's okay. I didn't pay it no mind."

Then she allowed as how she was really sorry and wanted to make it up to him in some way. When she asked him to go to dinner with her and she'd pay, he looked surprised.

"Here's a better idea," he said. "Why don't we go over to the A & W Drive-In and get a hamburger. I'll borrow my uncle's car."

"Okay, I'd like that."

"But you ain't payin' for it," he says. "That would never do. I'll pay."

And that's how they started goin' out. At first, she told me that they kept runnin' into small problems, like kissin' for instance. Now, Lillie had only been kissed three times and only once by a boy taller than her. She liked the way it felt, holdin' her face up like that, and she lifted her foot the way they did in the movies. Turned out the tall fella wasn't as good as his kisses though, 'cause he never called her again. But after that she always wanted to look up to a man to kiss, and even though it would only help a little, she tried to get the Bean to buy some cowboy boots so he'd be taller. But he said anything to do with cowboys went against his Indian blood, and his daddy would tear him limb from limb if he found out. Finally, Lillie just got down on her knees so she could look up at the Bean when they kissed. 'Course, she couldn't lift her foot the right way, but it would have to do.

On their third date, they went to see *Horse Feathers,* that funny movie with the Marx brothers that was showin' downtown. The ticket seller, who started school with Lillie but ended up a grade behind because he had the scarlet fever, he thought the Bean was some little kid and that really set the Bean back to where he started talkin' about gettin' some shoes with real thick soles he'd heard the shoe stores could order. But in the end, he just couldn't get up the gumption to do it.

Lillie told me once that at first her mama was worried about how serious they were gettin'. She always thought Lillie should set her cap for Earl Skeets, who was a lot better lookin' than the Bean and taller to boot. But Lillie wasn't about to listen to her mama.

After a while, people started callin' Lillie and the Bean *the String and the Bean,* 'cause besides bein' tall and skinny, Lillie had been savin' bits of special kinds of string since the second grade, and she had a ball that was twenty-seven and a half inches around, and when you think about it, the Bean *was* shaped a little like a butter bean. I'm the one who come up with the names, I'm proud to say.

Anyway, about two months after Lillie and the Bean got married, he had to quit his job at Mason's Furniture Store after he threw his back out tryin' to help lift one of those big old Naugahyde sleepin' couches onto the back of a delivery truck. After that, the only job he could find was makin' black beans and yellow rice and Cuban sandwiches on the day shift over at the Columbia Restaurant in Ybor City, where he heard all kinds of wild stories about the gangsters that hung out there. And *they're* the reason he got into trouble.

Now, settlin' into married life wasn't all Lillie thought it would be, what with the Bean decidin' that now that he was the head of the household, she would have to keep workin' 'til she had a baby and they were gonna save every little penny towards buyin' a house someday. They put all their paychecks in the bank, and he gave her a measly little allowance to buy groceries, and accordin' to him, they couldn't hardly even afford a movie show or goin' to the A & W or Goody Goody's for a hamburger. Lillie told her mama that the Bean must be related to Landis Perkins, who was the cheapest person ever born on this Earth and mean to boot. But if you ask me, the Bean wasn't all that stingy, 'cause when Lillie would joke and tease with him, once in a while he'd give in and she'd buy some extra sugar to make cookies or a cake, or they'd go to a movie—but no root beers on the way home.

Before the whole thing was over, it came out that Lillie had a few irritatin' ways herself that the Bean let slip to his best friend Jasper who was never supposed to breathe a word to anybody, but if you want to keep a secret, the last person on earth you'd tell is Jasper Mullins. I figure the Bean must have had a few beers, and you know how that devil liquor can loosen the tongue.

For one thing, the Bean said it made him mad as a homeless hornet when Lillie decided he should lose a little weight so she put the cookies and sweets up on the top shelf where he couldn't even see what was there much less reach anything. And she'd leave the shower head aimed toward the back wall when she knew good and well that it was so high he couldn't reach it, 'cause Timmy Alford, the fella who built the house, was six foot eight and had it put in special for himself. Anyway, the Bean would have to stand on the side of the tub to aim the shower-head down, and once he slipped and damn near broke his tail-bone, and after hurtin' his back at Mason's Furniture . . . Well, you can see his point. But Lillie said she'd just forget to aim the shower back by accident and he was just bein' silly. She'd told him a million times that if he'd call her, she'd come and fix it, but no, she said, he was too proud to do that.

For their first anniversary, Lillie was bein' real thoughtful and got the Bean a big old secondhand easy chair, for "the man of the house," she said. And really, it wasn't her fault that it was so high his toes didn't even touch the floor.

But the thing that bothered him most was that damn ball of string she'd been addin' pieces to since she was six. Lillie would have a hissy fit if he ever threw out even the tiniest piece, and that made him want to unwrap the whole damn thing and wind it around her long, skinny neck. But there was one good thing, he said. At least she didn't put up a fuss when he started playin' poker on Saturday afternoons with Carlos Ochoa and Jacky Wills and Hack Hilton. She'd just come over to Toad Springs to tell me all the latest and to see her folks.

Well, after that first year or so the Bean decided it was time to start workin' on havin' a family, since no babies were showin' up on their own. He told Lillie that even if she was taller than him, that he was the man of the house, and anyhow, they were both the same height when they were layin' down. You might even say since he was so round that he'd be taller than her . . . if you see what I mean. Now, personally, I think things like that should just be kept private, but since she told me . . .

Well, anyhow, they worked on makin' babies real hard 'til Lillie was so tired of the Bean that she started leavin' all the sweets down where he could reach 'em in hopes he'd leave her alone. And finally, he did.

Now, by this time, Lillie had moved up workin' at the state attorney's office and was typin' up warrants and writs and them habeas corpus things or whatever they are. She knew the names of people the cops were after, and the Bean was workin' down in Ybor City, minglin' among them same criminals, so the two of them had plenty to talk about at the supper table.

In the evenin's, Lillie would fix dinner while she listened to the news on the WDAE radio station, and the Bean would read the Tampa Daily Times, which was the evenin' paper. Sometimes they'd find out the fella they'd talked about at the dinner table the night before was in jail tonight. Lillie loved havin' the scoop before it was general news, and she'd drop little offhand tidbits on her visits over here with us and scare the livin' daylights outta her mama and daddy. Her mama thought Lillie was bein' too nosy for her own good and was sure to get herself killed, talkin' like she did.

So this one day, Lillie was typin' up papers about some fellas who were mixed up with some harlots, if you know what I mean, and she ran across the name of Carlos Ochoa, who played cards with the Bean. She was surprised, but when she saw the Bean's name there too (Caleb was his real name Caleb Benson AKA the Bean Benson) she nearly keeled right over. Accordin' to the papers, the Bean was supposed to be consortin' with prostitutes (and she knew what *that* meant) and sendin' 'em customers too. Well, Lillie was just downright flabbergasted, and her temper was risin' inside her, that temper that always got her in trouble. She went and got her a cup of coffee and tried to sit back down at her desk, but she was so mad she just couldn't stay there. She told the girl at the next typewriter that she was sick and had to go home.

Then she took the streetcar over to the Columbia Restaurant and marched right through the front door, which everybody knows she shouldn't have done 'cause the kitchen help always had to use the back door in a fancy place like that—don't want no riffraff minglin' in with the customers. Anyway, she saw where the kitchen was, 'cause somebody was just walkin' out the door with a big tray of food, and she stormed right in. There stood the Bean, talkin' to a flashy-lookin' lady who was wearin' the tightest red dress Lillie had ever seen on a body, and she had a pretty good idea of that girl's line of work.

When the Bean looked up and saw Lillie, his eyes got real big. Then he said, "Hey, honey. What you doin' here?"

And Lillie told him in no uncertain terms what she was doin' there in a voice you could hear all the way over at the tobacco factory, and he just stood there, pretty much like he did at the skatin' rink the night he first met her, with his mouth hangin' open, just starin' at her.

Well, accordin' to Lillie, he said he didn't know what she was talkin' about and he hadn't ever done nothin'—ain't that what they all say—and when Lillie looked around to see that person the Bean had been doin' nothin' with, she was gone. Lillie had never been this mad in her whole entire life, not even when she got cheated out of first place in a cake-bakin' contest. Said she was just about to slap the Bean upside the head when she looked around and everybody in the kitchen and half the lunch customers were gathered around, starin' at 'em. Right away, she grabbed the Bean's hand like he was a little boy and marched him right out of the front door of that restaurant.

She was too mad to wait to catch the streetcar, so they walked all three miles home, her hangin' on to his hand and goin' so fast the Bean had to run and skip alongside her to keep up, and her hollerin' at him the whole way. By the time they got there, she'd calmed down a little, she said, and just sat on the couch while the Bean went to make her some iced tea. Took him a while, 'cause he had to drag a chair into the kitchen to look through the cabinets for the tea bags, but finally, he came out and handed her a glass.

He scooted up into his easy chair and let his feet dangle down while he looked at her, sittin' there, sippin' her tea. After a long time, she said that she didn't want to hear the details but did want to know if he'd been messin' with some other woman, and if he had, she'd never sleep with him again.

And he came back sayin' that sure, maybe him and Lillie'd been sleepin' in the same bed, but all she'd been doin' was sleepin' since they tried so hard to get them a baby that time, and he was the head of the household and who would ever blame him if he did go somewhere else since she just gave him cookies instead of lovin'.

And she said that he didn't have no consideration for her feelings and that she wasn't no cow just to breed and there must be somethin' wrong with him since they hadn't had any babies anyway.

And he said he was a strong, healthy man, frisky as a spring colt and even had Indian blood runnin' through his veins and God knows *they* had plenty of babies, so it must be her fault she never got in the family way.

And she said he'd probably be goin' to jail for the rest of his life for foolin' around with those undesirables they talked about at supper every night, so there wouldn't be any worryin' about how she was gonna get in a family way with him in jail anyhow. And he'd better just tell her if he'd been messin' around with somebody else, and if he had, he'd pay for it for the rest of his life.

Well, the Bean was in a helluva fix, and like he told Jasper— in secret of course, like always—in a way, he did love Lillie, but at the same time she made him as mad as a sack full of cats. But then, he didn't know if he could ever find anybody else who would marry him. So he told Lillie that gal had been workin' on him for a while, tryin' to get him to go off with her but he never did even once 'cause he loved Lillie and would never be unfaithful to his wife, he was just not that kind of man. Now I don't know how much truth there is in that but I reckon time will tell 'cause like Aunt Birdo always says, men are just like dogs. Once they get to rollin' around on dead frogs, they always go back sniffin' for more.

For a long time, I didn't think Lillie believed him, but in the end, the String and the Bean decided to stay together. The Bean had to get a new job downtown at Knight and Wall's Hardware and tell 'em about his police record, now that he was gonna be on probation for two years for aidin' and abettin' a criminal. Most folks said he was lucky to have got off that easy, but if you ask me, even if Lillie did have a good sense of humor, livin' with her just might make goin' to jail seem like a vacation.

It's Your Lucky Day!
by Chuck Barber

My name is Chuck Barber and I come to Toad Springs after my cousin Andy Barber promised he'd help me find a job. I didn't have two cents to my name and he let me come and stay at his house. I always figured he started up his barber shop just 'cause of his last name, but I wasn't never gonna do nothin' like that. Since Andy knew everybody for miles around, he figured we'd come up with somethin' for me. Turned out the only jobs I could find was workin' out in the orange groves or helpin' with some of the other crops—you know, tomatoes or carrots or collard greens and such. Now, I ain't never done nothin' like that, where you're out there sweatin' in the hot sun and crawlin' around in the dirt.

I always been a city man, myself, more of a thinkin' man. I like comin' up with new ways to make things run better. I'd had this job back in Tampa at the Park Movie Theater and since I pick things up real easy, I learned how to run the place. I was in charge of the ushers and makin' sure the right movie was set up to show. I tell you, I had them fellas hoppin' like fleas on a fat hound dog, and things was runnin' better than they ever had before. Everybody said so. The only reason I got fired was 'cause the owner's daughter took a fancy to me and he didn't like that too good. I couldn't help it if that gal fell for me. That's when I thought to come over here and figure out a way to make this backwater town a better place. And the good Lord knows it needed work.

Anyways, I decided that Toad Springs needed a movie house so more folks would visit. We could put up a place right on Main Street, just a few blocks down from the gator ranch where everybody'd see it when they come to town. I even went to the trouble of drawin' up a plan – laid it out kind of like the Park Theater, but not as big. It wouldn't have to be fancy, just somewhere folks could come to spend their money on movies and popcorn.

I started remindin' everybody how the closest theater to Toad Springs was all the way over in Bartow and that was a far piece to have to travel to see a show. I talked it up to the old fellas at Smitty's Hardware and around town to anybody who'd listen. In the end, the only one besides me who thought it would be a good idea was Angus Hewitt – figured he might sell more at his Blue-Eyed Gator Restaurant with more folks comin' to town but he didn't have no money to put into it. For sure, the only fellas around who had any money, Hank Plenty and Bubba Stroudamore, said there wasn't no way Toad Springs needed a picture show and they wasn't interested.

So I put my thinkin' cap back on, and the next idea I come up with was to open a little zoo. We could just catch critters out in the woods, like snakes and bears and maybe even a panther or two, and stick 'em in cages and get people to pay to come see 'em. I figured we could snag us some birds, you know, cranes and egrets and the like. Maybe even a few flamingos. It would be kind of like the gator ranch but with lots of different animals. Now, I know folks around here wouldn't have no reason get excited about somethin' like that, but them tin can tourists that are always comin' to Florida, they're all dumb as a sack of turnips. The only thing they know we got down here is gators.

More folks liked that idea, but then, somebody would have to buy the land to put it on and then feed all them animals, and that could end up costin' more than you'd think. Nobody had any extra time to take care of the place, and I sure as hell wasn't gonna get stuck doing somethin' like that. And besides, the money men,

Hank and Bubba, they wouldn't give me the time of day. Old
Hank says to me, "You oughta spend less time comin' up with
things for other people to do and more time puttin' some elbow
grease into a real job." I told him I was the imagination man and
I don't do the grunt work, but didn't nobody take too good to that.

The best idea I come up with was to start my own little bolita business like the one over in Ybor City. Now, in case you
don't know about bolita, it's really just a game of chance. It ain't
gamblin' or nothin'. They take a bunch of balls, put some numbers on 'em, and throw 'em in a sack. Then they sell tickets to
folks who want to bet on one of the numbers. After that, once a
week, they get somebody to pull out one of them balls and everybody who bet on the number on that ball gets to split the jackpot.
Simple as pie. Don't have to buy no property or build no buildin'
to do that. I figured that might be somethin' I could do myself.
Didn't sound too hard. I could get Andy to sell tickets at the barber shop, Smitty to sell 'em at the hardware, and Halt to sell 'em
at the grocery, and I'd just go by once a week and collect the money. Then I could keep half of it for my trouble and the winners
would split the other half.

First person I talked to about it was Andy 'cause, after all, I
was livin' with him. I picked a day when he was in a real good
mood and told him my idea. He rubbed his chin while he listened to me and said, "You know, that just might could work
out. Sooner or later, every man in this neck of the woods comes
into the barber shop and I could put up a little sign sayin' I'm sellin' tickets. I might could sell a lot of 'em." He cocks his head to the
side and looks at me. "So what's in it for me?"

"For you? Whatcha mean for you?"

"I mean if I'm gonna be sellin' stuff for you, I need to get paid
somethin' for it. Man's gonna work, man's gonna get paid."

"Well, I wasn't thinkin' it would take a lot of your time. Just
when folks are payin' for the haircut, they could pick up a ticket."

He looks at me over the top of his glasses. "Ain't nobody in
town gonna sell stuff for you without gettin' some of the pay,
Chuck Barber. Use your head, man."

"I am usin' my head. I come up with a great idea, didn't I?"

"So, how you gonna pay for the stuff you need? Balls and tickets and such. You been hidin' money from me, Chuck?"

"No, sir. I told you I ain't got two cents to my name."

"Well, you gonna need a little money to get started, for advertising and such. Where you gonna get that?" Andy rolls his eyes. "When you decide to pay me, I'll sell them tickets for you."

"All right, Andy. I'll see what I can come up with." As I walk out the door I'm thinkin' about how I'm already givin' half the money away and I got to end up with somethin' for myself. The more I think on it, the madder I get. He's got a nerve, tryin' to tell me how to run my business. But on the other hand, I was kind of countin' on him to lend me the money to get the bolita up and rollin'. So . . .

After that, I go over to Smitty's Hardware and play a couple of games of checkers with the old fellas out front. When it looks like Smitty's inside all by himself, I go in and say howdy.

Smitty's standin' behind the register and waves over at me. "Hello there, Chuck. Found any work yet?"

I wave back. "Well, not yet."

"Hank Plenty always needs help at the dairy. He's got him so damn many cows now . . . and you know it ain't everybody who likes gettin' up at five o'clock every mornin'."

"I'm a city man, Smitty. I don't know nothin' about cows."

"You ain't too dumb to learn, though. I mean, there ain't nothin' hard about milkin' a cow."

"Yeah, yeah," I say. "I just want to do somethin' different – I don't much like workin' with my hands. Like workin' with my head better."

"Good luck with that." He laughs. "Got somethin' in mind?"

"Well," I say, lookin' around to make sure nobody's come up behind me. I lean toward him over the counter and talk low. "I'm thinkin' about startin' up a little bolita business right here in town."

"Bolita, huh?" Smitty says. "Bolita? Like they got over in Ybor City?"

"Well, yeah. Somethin' like that."

He looks at me with squinty eyes. "You mixed up with them Mafia guys, are ya?"

"Naw, man. No, no, no. Just figured if people can sell tickets over there, I can sell 'em over here. I ain't gonna do nothin' illegal."

Smitty rubs his chin just like Andy did. "Hmmmm . . . I ain't too sure about that."

"I was thinkin' of askin' if you'd like to sell tickets for me. Right here."

He looks surprised. "Me? Oh . . . I don't think so, Chuck. I mean . . . I reckon . . . that is, I ain't gettin' messed up with any of them Mafia fellas. They don't think nothin' of killin' a man just 'cause they don't like his looks."

I put my hand down on the counter and lean in toward him. "I ain't got nothin' to do with them Mafia guys. I just want to start a business like theirs, that's all. They got their bolita, and I'll have mine. It's all separate. I'm just lookin' for an honest way to earn a little money." I pause to let it sink in. "And I think Andy's gonna sell tickets for me at the barber shop. He thought it was a good idea. Maybe you ought to talk to him about it."

Smitty shakes his head. "So . . . if I was to sell tickets, what would I get out of it?"

This time I'm ready for that question. "You're a smart businessman, Smitty. You'll get customers comin' in here to buy tickets who wouldn't be comin' in otherwise, and they'll likely buy somethin' from you that they hadn't planned to get. So you'll be earnin' money that way."

"That's all? I don't get no cut?"

"Well, not that I was thinkin' of . . . "

He shakes his head. "I don't know, Chuck. Seems like I'd need a little somethin'. After all, the wife would be givin' me holy hell, I can tell you that."

"Okay . . . okay. I'll see what can I figure out."

"All right, then. You say you're gonna pay me, I'll talk to Andy."

Then I think maybe that ain't such a good idea, him talkin' to Andy, 'cause the two of them'll probably want to steal me blind. But it's too late by then.

After church the next Sunday, Andy and Smitty say they want to talk to me, so we go over and sit on a bench under a tree in the churchyard. Andy starts out, "We got a problem, Chuck. Now, you know Rusty Heppner, the fella who cuts hair with me at the barber shop?"

"Yeah."

"Well, when I told him what you was thinkin' of doin', he about threw a hissy fit. Went on and on about how everybody knows the mob's in the bolita business and they'd be over here tryin' to get money out of anybody who's sellin' tickets. Ain't no way in hell it would be safe to do somethin' like that. Any fool who tried would be riskin' their lives and the lives of everybody in Toad Springs."

I'm gettin' riled up. I can feel it. "Come on, man. Rusty Heppner's just a kid. Still wet behind the ears. You're crazy to listen to some fool like him."

Smitty stands up and looks down at me. "Let's just say you're gonna have to come up with some fast talkin' to get me to go along with this. I'm tellin' you, boy, if them Mafia guys hear the words *Toad Springs* and *bolita* in the same sentence, trouble's gonna start."

I just sigh and start walkin' back to Andy's house when I get a whopper of an idea. I just won't call it bolita. I'll call it somethin' else. Somethin' different so them fellas in Ybor won't even know what I'm doing. Then we'd all be safe. Then it would work. Let's see now, maybe I could call it something like . . . maybe . . . say . . . It's Your Lucky Day. Now, I like that. *It's Your Lucky Day.*

I could always say I never heard of bolita, just dreamed up this idea by myself. Instead of puttin' balls in a bag, I could make little square pieces of wood with numbers on 'em and put 'em in a box to shake 'em up. That would work.

It took me a while and lots of fast talkin', but I also managed to get Halt Brisco to sell tickets at the grocery and Angus Hewitt to sell 'em at the restaurant. Problem is, I have to pay 'em two cents for every ticket they sell. It's highway robbery, if you ask me, but then I just ain't got no choice.

I make me up a bunch of little squares of wood chips out of some oak and sand 'em down 'til they're all the same size. I write numbers on 'em from one to fifty in ink, to where they can't get erased, and then make me a special Lucky Day box to put 'em in. It's got a round hole in the top that's just big enough to get your hand into but you can't see what number you're grabbin', so that oughta work out okay. And I ain't gonna be the one to pull 'em out. Instead, I'll ask whoever's around if they want to do it, and that way nobody can think I'm tryin' to cheat 'em.

So I put out the word that we got somethin' new and excitin' in Toad Springs, somethin' like they got in the big cities all over the world, our own little game of chance. Folks in these parts deserve to be able to come into some money by spendin' just a few pennies and havin' a little bit of luck. And I'm just the man to help 'em do that. I got Andy to lend me some money, and I put an advertisement in the *Toad Springs Hopper*. That got everybody talkin' about it right off, just what I wanted.

The first week we sold twenty-three tickets for twenty cents apiece, and that come up to four dollars and sixty cents. Then, I had to pay ten cents to Halt and twenty-three cents to Angus and eight to Andy, so that left four dollars and nineteen cents. I got half of that – which all went to pay for the expenses - and the rest was for the winners. Now, I'd been hopin' to sell lots more tickets, but I told myself it was better to start small. Anyway, the ad in the paper said the winnin' number would get drawn at the Blue-Eyed Gator at seven o'clock every Saturday night. Angus was more than happy to let me do that. Bring in more customers to the restaurant, dontcha know.

At about five minutes before seven, I come into the restaurant carryin' my Lucky Day box under my arm, sit down on one of the stools at the counter, and start countin' the people. There's sixteen of 'em there and I can't stop smilin'. Then Angus comes out of the kitchen to announce that we're gonna draw the numbers. He claps his hands, then hollers out that it's gonna be somebody's Lucky Day! And for everybody who's got a ticket stub to take it out.

There's some big smiles and mumblin' around, and when things settle down a little, I say, "I'm so glad to see y'all here tonight for the very first It's Your Lucky Day drawin'." Some folks look a little confused, but other ones hold up their ticket stubs and grin real big. "Now, I'm gonna tell you just how it works. Like you folks already did, you pick a number between one and fifty, buy a ticket, and write that number and your name on the ticket. Then I get the ticket and you keep the stubs. On Saturday night of that week, I get somebody to pull a number out of a box and read it, and that's the winner. If anybody else gets that same number, they split the pot. And if nobody gets the number, that money is added to next week's pot. Now, since we're just startin' out, there ain't a whole lot of money to split, but the pot'll get bigger when more folks buy tickets."

Darwin Brown waves his hands and yells, "But we already done all that!"

I wave back at him. "I know, I know. Just want to make sure folks understand how it works. Now, tonight the prize is gonna be two dollars and seven cents." I hear a little grumblin', but I can feel folks gettin' excited.

I clear my throat. "Now, I want everybody to know that I'm on the up and up here. And just to prove it, I'm gonna ask for one of you pretty ladies to draw out the number and let's see who's the big winner." So some gal who'd come over from Mango pulls out number forty-two.

Right away, Ginger Perkins yells loud enough to wake the dead, "It's me! I won! I got forty-two!" That gal's as happy as a dog with two tails even if it wasn't a hundred dollars. All the rest just grumble and wad up their tickets and toss 'em on the table.

I tell 'em all, "The more people who buy tickets, the bigger the prize is gonna be, so get your neighbors to pitch in. We're gonna be right here every Saturday night, and you can get your

Lucky Day tickets from Angus or Halt or Andy or me. Maybe you'll be the big winner next time."

For the next little while, things are comin' right along, and one week, we sold seventy-eight tickets, some to folks in Turkey Creek and Mango. I'm feelin' pretty damn good, just beginnin' to think that maybe I've found my callin'. And that's when the trouble started.

One Saturday afternoon, I'm sittin' in the livin' room at home while Andy's at the barber shop. I'm tryin' to think of where else I can sell tickets when this feller comes up on the porch, looks in through the screen door, and says, "Chuck Barber, just what do you think you're doin', tryin' to corrupt this town and drive us all to wrack and ruin?"

I get up and go to the door, and it's Preacher Mayfield from the Fiery Freedom Holiness Baptized Church, mad as a sack of wet cats. The only way I know it's him is 'cause folks had pointed him out to me. I hadn't never been to his church or nothin' like that. He's one of them fire-and-brimstone fellas, and they say sometimes he gets carried away.

I know why he come to see me, but I just play dumb. "Why, Preacher Mayfield, how are ya? What in the world are you talkin' about?"

"You know damn well what I'm talkin' about, you no good . . ." He grabs the handle and snatches the door open, but I don't move, so he can't come in. Then he says, "You come out here on the porch and talk to me, you damn heathen."

"I don't know what you're talkin' about," I say, tryin' to act all innocent. "I ain't broke no laws 'cause this ain't bolita. I ain't done nothin' wrong."

He backs up, and I come out on the porch and point to one of the rockin' chairs. "Have a seat, Preacher." Then I sit down in the other rocker and try to look calm. I say, "Now, why don't you just go on and speak your mind? 'Cause I ain't got no idea why you got a knot in your tail."

"Yes, you do," Preacher says. "You know damn well that game you've started up around here, that Lucky Day idea, that ain't nothin' but gamblin', and gamblin's a sin. It says so in the Bible. Thou shalt not gamble. Jesus said it hisself. Them very words, he did. At the Sermon on the Mount, I believe."

"It ain't gamblin'," I say. "Ain't nothin' more than a game of chance. A way for folks to put a little extra money in their pockets. Heaven knows the people around here need to be able to do that. For sure! Now, times is hard these days—"

"A game of chance ain't nothin' but gamblin'. Any fool knows that."

"Is not. You callin' me a fool?"

He's gettin' loud now, and his face is turnin' red. He leans toward me and shakes his finger in my face. "Is so. Look what happened over in Tampa. Just look at it. The Mafia moved in to Ybor City and took over the whole place. Now it ain't nothin' but a den of iniquity, full of sinners and whores. Ain't nobody safe there." He shakes his head over and over.

"Now, you listen to me," I say. "This ain't no bolita thing. This ain't got nothin' to do with the Mafia. It's just me. Only me. And I ain't gonna hurt nobody. Why, I'm just tryin' to help folks bring in a little cash."

"You're a heathen and a liar," he says. "You got to stop sellin' them damn tickets right now. And if you don't, I'll . . . I'll . . . I'll report you, that's what I'll do."

Now I've got him. "And who you gonna report me to? Constable Grogan's the only law around here and he done bought three tickets himself."

"Why . . . why, I'll report you to the United States government, that's who. I'll report you to the FBI! The Federal Bureau of . . . of . . . Instigation! And they'll come down here and put you in jail. No, wait. Not just in jail. They'll send you way off somewheres. To a prison. A real one. One of them government prisons where you'll never get out."

"Come on, man. I'm tellin' you, it's all on the up and up. I ain't tryin' to cheat nobody, and that's what's different from bolita. Like I keep sayin', I'm just tryin' to help folks." I lean back in my chair and look him straight in the eye. "And I ain't gonna stop."

Mayfield's quiet for a minute, then gives me the sideways turtle eye. "So, just tell me what you're gettin' outta this. I mean, you ain't just doin' it out of the kindness in your heart."

"I get the good feelin' of helpin' folks, that's what I get."

He squints his eyes at me. "You mean you don't take none of that money for yourself? You can't tell me . . . "

"I just take enough for the expenses," I say, tryin' to look innocent. "You know, it cost me somethin' to make up all them chips and put numbers on 'em. And then I got to buy the tickets to sell. Just expenses, stuff like that."

"So that means you're just livin' off Andy? Is that it? Livin' off your cousin? You just takin' advantage of your own flesh and blood?"

"Now, Andy and me, we got our own agreement . . . "

He squints at me. "You just listen to me now. In my line of work I get to know how evil and dishonest and mean folks can be. I'm onto you and your tricks."

"Well, from what I hear around town, you ain't so lily-white yourself, you ain't."

"You don't need to be listenin' to no gossip. The Lord says—"

"Well, how's about this?" I say, leanin' back in the chair and foldin' my hands in my lap. "Andy told me that you was married to two gals at the same—"

"Andy don't know what the hell he's talkin' about."

"Wait a minute now. Let's see . . . who was it . . . " I look up at the porch ceilin' like I'm thinkin'. "It was Smitty Mallet. That's who it was. He told me the same thing."

"Smitty's a fool. He don't hardly go to church. Just spreadin' rumors–"

"Seems like you was married to one gal and had a bunch of young'uns, then married some other gal–"

"That ain't true!" he hollers out. "And anyways, we're talkin' about you, not me."

"Yeah, but you ain't nothin' but a man who's broke God's law–"

"Me and God, we got things straight between us," he says, all red in the face. "Ain't none of your concern."

"Well then, my business ain't none of your concern neither."

"Gamblin's against God's law."

"Yeah, but look who's talkin' about breakin' God's law."

"I just want you to know that if you don't stop this, I aim to put you out of business."

"Oh yeah? Is that so?"

"That's so. This Sunday, when I stand up in front of them good, God-fearin' people who come to church, I'm gonna tell 'em just exactly what you're doin'. You're tryin' to cheat us all, and any fool knows you'll be keepin' most of that money for yourself."

"Talk all you want. That don't mean they're gonna listen to you."

"Oh, they'll listen to me, all right. They always do. 'Cause I speak the truth." Mayfield waves his hand in the air. "And I can shut you down just like that," he says, snappin' his fingers. Then his voice gets quieter. "Now, I'd hate to have to do somethin' like that to a good man like you, I sure would."

I lean forward, elbows on my knees. "Then don't do it." Now he's got me thinkin'. Sales are just startin' to pick up, and I don't want to stop now. All of a sudden, an idea hits me right between the eyes, and I sit up straight. "You know, it come to me just now that It's Your Lucky Day would be good for the church too. The folks in your church give you money when they pass the plate every week, like . . . what's that word . . . they tithe, right?"

He stares at me.

"And it makes sense that the more money they got comin' in, the more you got comin' in."

He looks out in the yard for a minute but don't say nothin'.

"It just makes sense, dontcha see? Folks have more, they'll give more."

He rolls his eyes. "Gamblin's evil and wicked."

"Come on, now. Ain't nothin' wrong with bingo, now, is there?"

"Well . . . "

"I hear tell you folks have bingo games at the church picnics."

He looks up at me from under his eyebrows.

"And one of the old fellers at Smitty's was sayin' you need a lotta work done on that buildin' so folks can worship proper like. Told me the floor was startin' to rot out and there wasn't enough money to get it fixed."

Mayfield nods and squints at me, then says, "I ain't gonna have folks thinkin' they can just gamble whenever they want. 'Cause it's a sin."

I have to think for a minute myself. Then I say, "Well, maybe it would help if I made sure folks know it's just a game of chance. Nothin' wicked or immoral like gamblin'." I glance over, and for sure, he's takin' it all in. "Somethin' like that," I say. "You know, so folks would know they ain't breakin' none of God's laws. Then you could get the church floor fixed."

He's quiet for a few minutes. "Well, could be . . . Maybe the Lord *is* on your side, since you come up with that idea. He knows if we don't fix that floor, we ain't gonna have nowhere to meet. Maybe that's God's way of helpin' out. Maybe He's sent you here to help us fix the place up."

"Makes sense to me," I say, tryin' not to sound too happy.

"Heaven knows we wouldn't need to be talkin' like this if folks all gave their fair share, like Jesus tells us to do. But they don't. Some of 'em don't give more than a nickel a week, and that ain't hardly enough to keep a church goin'."

I just listen.

Then he points his finger at me. "And you need to join the church too," he says. "Don't sound to me like you spend much time cleansin' your spirit . . . and we'd welcome you with open arms." He reaches over and pats my shoulder. "And we got us some pretty young gals comin' every week. Mighty pretty young ladies. Yes, sir."

I don't say nothin'. Goin' to church ain't on my list of things to do, especially not his. And I can find my own girls.

He turns to watch a dog amblin' down the road. Then he looks over at me, squintin' his eyes again. "Saints above, Chuck. I reckon that if I could count on extra tithin' money comin' in every week, I might could afford to look the other way. The money would only be used to do God's work, of course. Wouldn't be for me."

That's when I start to smell somethin's rotten in Denmark. "What are you sayin'?"

"The tithin' money. What you'll be givin' me."

"You want *me* to give you tithin' money?"

"Well, sure, just be a nice easy way . . . "

"Oh, no," I say. "I'm tellin' you that the folks in your church'll have more money comin' in when *they* win, and *they'll* be givin' you more money. Not me. I don't go to church and ain't gonna be startin' now. No way in hell."

Mayfield looks surprised, then shakes his head. "Well now, that ain't quite what I had in mind here. What if nobody in my flock ever wins? Then I get nothin'. But you, you always win. Every week, since you're collectin' the money."

"I already told you. I ain't goin' to church."

"Look here, sonny. You don't go to church, the deal's off. And if God ain't gonna be gettin' nothin' out of it, then it looks like it's gamblin' to me. I mean, if it ain't attached to nothin' holy, then it's a sin. That's all there is to it. And sinnin' is somethin' we all got to go against." He stands up. "You don't join the church, then I reckon we ain't got nothin' more to say to each other."

Dammit, I don't know what to do. I don't want to give in and start payin' this fella for nothin'. But I don't want to give up my idea neither. "Let me think it over," I say. "I'll let you know."

For three solid days and nights, I try and think of some way to get him on my side without sayin' I'll go to church. And let me tell you, it ain't easy tryin' to figure out how to fool somebody with such a sneaky mind as a preacher.

I still ain't come up with nothin' when a week later, I hear that old Mayfield's preachin' hard about how there's somebody in town who's tryin' to get folks to forsake all their good sense and church lessons and start gamblin' right and left. He tells 'em that God's watchin' their every move, and if they forget it for even one minute, they can end up burnin' in the fiery furnace for eternity. He tells 'em that the good Lord give us all rules about what's right, and he expects people to do the right thing all the time. And he points out that since it ain't always clear what that right thing is, that it might take a man of the cloth—like him, of course—to let people know what's what.

Well, I'm hopin' maybe all this'll just blow over one way or another, 'cause I sure ain't gonna be givin' away none of my money. Even if I have to give up my dream and quit sellin' tickets. 'Course, if it come to that, he'd win and I'd be the loser, which don't sound good to me.

For a while there, things slacked off a little, but then I got a great idea. I start tellin' folks that they ain't sinnin' if they don't make any money on the tickets they buy. So what they can do is just buy tickets for each other, and that way they don't get no profit from it. If somebody was to buy a ticket and give it to you, I told 'em, it would just be a gift—you wouldn't be sinnin', 'cause you didn't buy nothin'. They're just sharin' what they have with you, which is a Christian thing to do. And if you buy somebody else a ticket, you ain't gonna benefit from it, so you ain't gamblin' neither. Lucky for me, folks buy into that idea and Preacher can't talk 'em out of it.

It works out fine at first, but after a while folks start gettin' mad when the tickets they buy and give away as gifts earn more money than the tickets they get as gifts. They start thinkin' I'm cheatin' and makin' sure folks I like get more. I do my best to convince 'em that there ain't no way I could do that, but in the end, there's so much bad feelin' everywhere I decide to move on to greener pastures.

Will She or Won't She?

by Violet Mooney

My mama's aunt Birdo was a royal pain in the ass who never once in her whole life thought about anybody but her own self. She was skinny and had pale skin and thin dishwater blonde hair. When she was young, she went out with Nate Hawkins for a while, and he even wanted to marry her, but she left that nice man standin' at the altar while she went to see *The Battle of the Sexes* over at a movie theater in Bartow. It was a real scandal at the time, kept folks whisperin' to each other behind their hands for weeks. But like everybody said later on, Nate turned out to be damned lucky, cause the older Aunt Birdo got, the bigger the lies she told 'til it was riskin' your good name to be in the same room with her.

Back when she turned twenty-one, she decided to change her first name to *Bordeaux*. A neighbor told her that name come from France, and since it sounded like *Birdo,* probably some fool had just spelled her name wrong. Reckon it didn't matter that her mama's middle name was Birdo.

Anyhow, she really liked the idea of bein' French. She started puttin' on airs and tellin' folks to call her *Bore-Dough* and sayin' she was related to Napoleon. Her Sears catalog and her other mail-order stuff started comin' to Bordeaux O'Brien, but around Toad Springs, everybody still called her Birdo.

I don't know how, but she got 'em to call her *Bore-Dough* at the train depot over in Mango where she sold tickets for forty years. And couldn't nobody figure out how she managed to keep her job that long, ornery as she was. She told everybody that she was real important, that they couldn't run the depot without her, and anytime she talked about leavin', they begged her to stay. "Oh, Bore-Dough," they'd say, "we need you here," and "We couldn't run this place without you," and "Who would keep everybody in line if you wasn't here?" She always batted her eyes and tried to look modest when she told that little tale.

There was this one big old burly engineer she took a dislikin' to—probably 'cause he looked like her uncle Arnie who had beady eyes and a bad reputation—and she always gave that man a hard time. She'd start when he walked in the door, fussin' at him that his train was late or that he was trackin' mud inside and tellin' him, "The railroad's got enough troubles with everybody drivin' cars instead of ridin' the train these days. And people like you ain't helpin'."

At first, he tried to explain his side of things, and when that didn't make any difference, he ignored her. And that made her madder than she already was. Thing was, he got along just fine with everybody else.

Anyway, one day, she finally went too far. She started in on that fella as usual, and when he laughed in her face, man oh man, she lit out after him like a duck on a June bug, chased him down the platform, hittin' him with the stick they used to herd cows off the tracks, hollerin', "You no-good son of a bitch! You don't do nothin' right. You're a goddamned fool." And that was her last day at work. She told us that she quit, but we all knew without askin' that she'd finally got herself fired.

Now, she'd always lived with her mama, and Aunt Birdo was almost fifty when her mama died. Since there wasn't no will, she figured she'd get the house 'cause she'd lived there since she was born. But her sister, Ruthel, didn't agree. She said she'd been born there too, and since their brothers had all moved away and didn't want nothin' to do with 'em, her and Aunt Birdo should split it fifty-fifty. And if Aunt Birdo wanted to keep on livin' there, she'd have to pay Ruthel for her half. Well, Aunt Birdo near about lost her mind over that. Couldn't stop talkin' about how mean and selfish her sister was 'cause she was married and had a house already and besides that, she wasn't near as good to their mama as Aunt Birdo had been. Them two argued about that for a couple of years 'til finally, Ruthel's husband told her if she didn't just let Aunt Birdo have that damned place that he was movin' out 'cause he was sick to death of the arguin'. After Ruthel agreed, Aunt Birdo said she'd been generous about it and offered to give her their mama's old overstuffed chair that needed to be recovered in the worst way. Said her feelings was hurt when Ruthel wouldn't take it. Them two hardly ever talked to each other after that. But truth be told, they hadn't talked much before then either.

Every so often, Aunt Birdo would ask one of the men cousins to come over and unclog a drain or kill a rat or somethin', and as soon as they left she'd call some other relative and swear that feller had run off with two of her best towels and her last jar of homemade strawberry jam or scratched her antique dinin' room table (which wasn't no antique, just a ratty old table) or stole money out of the cookie jar when she wasn't lookin'. If she caught a cold and one of the ladies brought her some chicken soup, she'd say they tried to poison her or left dirty dishes in the sink for her to wash, sick as she was. Me, I got no idea why anybody ever bothered to help her out with anything, but they did.

My own mama, Maggie Mooney, took that woman to the Fiery Freedom Holiness Baptized Church in Toad Springs every single Sunday, where Aunt Birdo sat in the front with the old ladies and Mama sat in the back. One day after church, when the old ladies were standin' over on the side starin' at Mama and whisperin' to each other like they did every so often, Mama went over, pointed her finger at 'em, and said, "If you won't believe what she says about me, I won't believe what she says about you," and then she walked off. Myself, I think Mama took her to church 'cause she felt like she needed to put a few extra stars in her crown for when she went to the great beyond, but ask me, she sure enough earned them the hard way.

Somehow or other, don't nobody really know quite how, Aunt Birdo ended up ownin' this little old house out on Grasshopper Lake. She acted real sneaky and wouldn't tell anybody how she got hold of the deed, so Hank Plenty got Constable Grogan to look into it. He said the place used to belong to a John Smith, who Aunt Birdo said she didn't know, but somehow, she knew he'd moved to Canada—or maybe it was Mexico, she wasn't sure. It was one of the two. When Constable Grogan was done with his checkin', he said it sounded suspicious, but unless John Smith wanted to do somethin' about it, he couldn't do nothin'. So then, Aunt Birdo had two houses. After she got the second one, she thought she was so rich, she signed up to be a Republican.

Once in a while, she'd invite folks to come out to the lake house for the day, but we had to bring along our own food, even butter and salt, since Aunt Birdo said she was just a poor old maid with nobody to take care of her and she had to squeeze the copper out of her pennies (even though she owned two houses and was a Republican). She said if anybody went out there without her permission, she'd call the constable on 'em in a flash, especially the young folks, 'cause God only knows what they'd do without her there to keep 'em in line. Too bad. With all the young'uns in the family, that old place could have been put to better use. But it's too late now. They're all grown up and gone to the dogs.

Aunt Birdo didn't put a lot of work into keepin' up with either one of them properties. She never even thought about fixin' up the lake house—said it was supposed to look *woodsy* out there. And she got so tired of pullin' weeds in the yard of the house in town that she got a fella to come and pull everything up—grass, weeds, flowers, down to just the dirt and two sad-lookin' crocus bushes in the front. Then, when the weeds started growin' back in, she'd let 'em go 'til they was knee-high, then get somebody to pull everything up and go back to dirt again. And she had this rule that she wouldn't get the leaky roof fixed until she had at least three buckets collectin' water inside. Then, when they come to fix it and told her that she'd waited so long to call 'em that they was gonna have to replace the rotten wood, she'd cuss 'em out and say they was just cheatin' her, but in the end, she had to let 'em do it.

When she was about sixty, Aunt Birdo rented out a room in her house in town to a Mr. Matthews, a fella who looked to be in his late forties, from Jacksonville. Nobody even knew his Christian name. We'd see the two of 'em of an evenin', sittin' on the front porch, talkin' and laughin' to pass the time, and he came to a few potluck church suppers with her. Once in a while, they'd even have somethin' to eat at the Blue-Eyed Gator Restaurant.

He was quiet, a nice enough fella, but in spite of that, everybody knew somethin' had to be wrong 'cause it seemed like for a while there, Aunt Birdo just wasn't herself. Why, folks said she'd smile at you in the grocery store, and you could almost have a whole conversation with her before she started accusin' somebody of cheatin' her. Some people thought she was just glad to have a man around to fix a broken window or clean the gutters and her not have to pay for it. Others wondered if she was fallin' in love or somethin', even though the feller was a good fifteen years younger than her. That should'a been a real scandal, but folks just looked the other way 'cause she was so much easier to be around.

Then, all of a sudden, he was gone. Poof! One Sunday, when Mama and I took Aunt Birdo to church, Mama asked, "Where's Mr. Matthews? Ain't seen him around lately."

"I don't want to talk about it," Aunt Birdo said in a snippy voice.

"Seemed like a nice enough man. Seemed to lift your spirits."

"You can't never tell about people," Aunt Birdo said.

Mama let it drop, but the next week, when they were sittin' on Aunt Birdo's front porch drinkin' sweet tea after church, Aunt Birdo turned to her out of the blue and said, "That bastard just turned on me. After I been so good to him, givin' him a home, cookin' his food, puttin' up with them damn cigars and all like that."

"What are you talkin' about?"

"That Mr. Matthews."

"Oh . . . what you mean, turned on you?"

Aunt Birdo took a deep breath and started rockin' back and forth in her chair like she was mad enough to strangle him. "We was sittin' right here one night, like you and me are now, when he looked at me real innocent and had the nerve to say, 'You know, Bore-Dough, I'd like to drive out with you one day and see the little place you got on the lake.'" Then she stops rockin', looks at Mama, and narrows her eyes.

"Yeah? And . . . " Mama says. "What did you say?"

"I ain't no fool. I knew just exactly what he was up to, that no-good son of a bitch. Right then and there, I told him to go collect his stuff and get out of my house and don't never come back. Made him leave the next mornin'."

"Just 'cause he asked about the lake house?"

"Oh, he was actin' all sweet and nice, all right, pretendin' he was surprised I was onto him, like he didn't know I could see right through him. Tryin' to make me believe he didn't mean nothin' by it." She stops rockin' and slaps her hand on the arm of the chair. "Well, I'm way too smart for him."

"What was wrong with that?" Mama said. "He just wanted to see the lake house."

Then Aunt Birdo's face got red, and she started yellin' in her screechy voice, "That lousy bastard was just layin' the groundwork so I'd put him in my will! He was plannin' to cheat me out of every penny I own. I wasn't born yesterday. He wasn't puttin' nothin' over on me."

Later on Mama told me she knew there wasn't never any use in arguin' with Aunt Birdo, so she just said, "Okay. If that's what you think." Then we got up and Mama said, "Reckon it's time for us to be gettin' home and all."

After Aunt Birdo's mama died without leavin' a will, she always told everybody that she wasn't gonna write one either, 'cause you have to get a lawyer to sign it or somethin' and they'd charge you for it, and anyways, lawyers were all crooks. She'd smile and say, "Y'all will just have to figure it out when I'm dead and gone. That's what me and Ruthel done when Mama died, and it worked out just fine." Like usual, what she was sayin' didn't really make much sense to anybody but her. But then, we was all used to that.

Finally, when Aunt Birdo was ninety-nine and a half, she passed on over to whoever had to take her next, bless their hearts. In a way, I'm surprised she ever died at all. Mean as she was, not even the devil would have wanted her. And she may have been gone, but her story wasn't over. I'm tellin' you, the Lord works in mysterious ways.

As soon as word got out that she died, the family started squabblin' about who'd get what. Folks all over town start comin' up with things of Aunt Birdo's they wanted. Landis Perkins said he'd loaned her seventy-five dollars over the years and he figured he should get it back—even though that fella's got money to burn. Hester Brisco said that three years before, she gave Aunt Birdo her old washin' machine for the lake house when Hester could have sold it for five dollars and that's what she was owed 'cause she'd gotten the house key and gone out there and done a load of laundry and that machine was still workin' just fine. The Stroudamore boys put a new roof on the lake house years before, and Bubba Stroudamore said Aunt Birdo'd promised to leave the place to them. And on and on and on.

Eleven relatives from all over the state, not countin' the ones who lived here, said they was comin' in for the service. It was surprisin' how many people there were when you think about how none of 'em ever wanted anything to do with her when she was alive. Mama said it was the two houses that done it.

Since everybody knew Aunt Birdo didn't leave no instructions about who'd get what, the cousins in Toad Springs all met at Mama's one afternoon to try and figure out how to be fair about sellin' her property and dividin' up the money. Some thought it should be split equally among everybody, others thought the old folks should get more than the young ones, and the young folks said it should be the other way around. The poorest ones thought the folks with the least money should get the most—that was only Christian—and then somebody pointed out that there was a nephew who'd run off a couple of years before and should they keep his share out and save it for him in case he come back some day or just split it up with all the rest.

The day before the funeral, Aunt Birdo's third cousin Louise and her husband, Frank, come blowin' into town from Raiford. Now, just between you and me and the barn cats, we always thought that Raiford was the right town for them folks to be livin' in, 'cause the state prison's up there and Louise already had an uncle on her daddy's side who'd got hisself put away for a few years, and you know what one bad apple can do to a family. Besides that, Frank had some odd relatives—one gal with a wanderin' eye that rolled around on its own all the time so you couldn't think when you was tryin' to talk to her, a brother who stuttered and did lots of cussin', and the gal who'd had three sets of twins in five and a half years and was crazy as a betsy bug . . . but that ain't no wonder.

Besides that, Aunt Birdo had already told us that both Frank and Louise had took to the drink, and Aunt Never, the Toad Springs telephone operator—who was also the town gossip—had just heard that their youngest gal, Sissy, had run off with a girlfriend. We already knew that Louise and Frank's other two girls both had love children. Little bastards, Aunt Birdo called 'em.

Anyways, when Frank and Louise got to town the day before the funeral, they was invited to the last meetin' about how to split things up. Everybody was crowdin' into Mama's livin' room again—some sittin' on the furniture, some on the floor, and some on the dinin' room table—when Mama said, "Let's call this meetin' to order and get everything decided once and for all." When it was quiet, she said, "I'm gonna read y'all what we come up with about how to divide everything," and she started openin' up a piece of paper she had in her hand.

"Now, just hold on a minute," Frank said. "Birdo left a will."

Folks said, "What? What are you sayin'?"

Somebody called in from the dinin' room table, "She said she wasn't leavin' no will."

"Yep," he said, smilin' and rubbin' his hands together. "But she did. And she give the papers to me."

"To you?" Mama said. "Why would she give 'em to you? You ain't even a blood relation."

He smiled and looked down at his hands. "'Cause she left everything to Louise."

At that, everybody started yellin' at him. "You're a lyin' scoundrel!" and "You ain't gettin' away with this."

"Now, now," Mama said. "Just settle down for a minute." She turned to look at Frank. "Aunt Birdo always said she wasn't gonna leave no will. And she made sure we all knew it."

He puffed his chest out. "Well, that may have been what she said. But it ain't what she done."

"I'm gettin' a lawyer!" somebody hollered out.

"If you got a will, let's see it," Mama said.

Frank rolled his eyes. "Oh, we got it, all right," he said, lookin' at Louise. "We just ain't got our hands on it at the moment."

"Either you got it or you don't!" Never Riley hollered out. "Sounds to me like you're lyin'."

Louise spoke up. "We got it, all right. Had it for years."

Mama held out her hand. "So . . . let's see it."

Louise turned to look at Frank, then back to Mama. "We just ain't got our hands on it right now," Louise said. "Can't find it."

"And why is that?" Mama said.

"Well, I hid it in a suitcase so it wouldn't get lost," said Louise. "And right now, Sissy's got it, and we don't know just where she is."

"What's that supposed to mean?"

"I'd have took it out if I knew Sissy was leavin', but she sneaked away in the middle of the night and just left a note sayin' that her and Gloreena was runnin' away to start a new life in a better place."

"Gloreena?" Aunt Never asks. "Who in hell is that?"

"Her best friend. Gloreena Pashonsky. A few years back, I folded up the will and hid it down underneath this little flap in the bottom of the suitcase. I didn't tell nobody I was doin' it, thinkin' that would make it real safe—nobody'd look for it there."

"I don't believe you for one minute," said Aunt Never. "Birdo made sure we all knew she wasn't gonna leave nothin' to nobody— that way, she thought she could look down from heaven and watch us all fight over it."

"She'll have to be lookin' up, not down, you ask me," Mama said. "And Louise, if you ain't got no proof, I say we should just go on and split it up even-steven between all the nieces and nephews."

"No way," said Frank. "She said we always treated her better than anybody else in the family, so she left it all to us and that's that. Just wait 'til Sissy comes home and we'll show you."

One of the cousins from out of town hollered out, "I'm gettin' a lawyer for sure!" then stomped out. Pretty soon everybody followed him.

There was a big turnout at the graveside funeral the next day, with folks waitin' to see if the preacher could find somethin' good to say about Aunt Birdo. And he did, said that she kept a job for forty years and came to church every Sunday. But mostly, he just talked about Jesus.

On her way to the car, Louise hollered out to Mama that she'd call as soon as Sissy got home. And Mama yelled back to Louise that if she didn't get the will in two weeks, she was gonna go on ahead and split everything up.

After that, there was as much gossip flyin' around Toad Springs as there was when we found out Preacher Mayfield over at the Fiery Freedom Holiness Baptized Church was married to two gals at the same time and one of 'em had gone to visit the other one.

Louise called a week later, sayin' Sissy finally showed up complainin' that her and Gloreena had too many fights and she'd decided maybe she'd give men another try. Said they'd gotten the will back and Frank took it to a lawyer in town, who said it looked good to him.

Now, Mama, who never once in her whole life thought of what she might get when Aunt Birdo died (other than a couple of stars in her crown), decided that if somebody was gonna be inheritin' that stuff, it sure as hell shouldn't be the Raiford folks who never had to take that grouchy old woman to church or to the doctor or put up with all them lies she told. The next mornin', Mama called Schick and Schick Attorneys at Law over in Bartow and talked to 'em about what was goin' on. When word got out that Frank and her was talkin' to lawyers, the phone lines for the whole fam damily were buzzin', and opinions were flappin' like fresh-caught trout.

When Mama's lawyer, Cooper Schick, finally got ahold of the will, he called Mama, and I went over to Bartow with her. While we waited to see him, I watched his secretary type out four copies of the same thing on her typewriter all at the same time, usin' somethin' they call carbon paper. I'd never seen that before. What'll they think of next?

Anyway, when we went in to see him, he was sittin' in a big fancy chair behind a great big desk like he was a judge or somethin'. He opened up a file, unfolded a piece of paper, and pushed it our way. It looked old and dirty and was all wrinkled. Mama took it, and I leaned over to read it with her. It said *I, Bordeaux O'Brien, give both of my houses and all the stuff in them houses to my dear cousin Louise and her husband Frank. Don't nobody else need to get any of it.* And it was signed with an X.

Mama looked up at the lawyer. "Aunt Birdo didn't write this. It's not her handwritin'."

"She could read and write?" Cooper Schick asked.

"Yeah, of course she could read and write. She worked at the railroad depot for forty years, sellin' tickets and such."

"Well, anyhow, the lawyer in Raiford says your Aunt Birdo told Frank what she wanted to say and he's the one who wrote it all down. Then she signed the X."

"Why would she do that? Why wouldn't she write it and sign it herself?"

"He said she'd hurt her right hand and had to sign it with her left hand. That's why she just put an X."

Mama leans back in her seat and looks him straight in the eye. "I bet I know what happened here. She did it just to start trouble. That's all that woman ever knew how to do. And she was smart enough to know this would get everybody in an uproar, even told us she wasn't gonna leave a will on purpose so she could watch us fight over everything."

"Hmmmm," he says. "Looks like she's gettin' what she wanted."

"She usually did."

"But to tell you the truth," he says, "this whole thing looks suspicious to me. I've checked around, and it looks like this will wasn't ever filed. It doesn't have any witness signatures on it, and since it isn't in her handwritin', I think we have somethin' here we can work with."

"So can I just go on ahead and split everything up, then?"

"Well, not yet. Louise's lawyer is sayin' that it's legal and bindin' and that Louise and Frank should get everything."

"So what do we need to do?"

"We'll have to file a lawsuit to contest what they're sayin'. I'll be glad to do the paperwork, but I'll need fifteen dollars to get it started."

Mama's face falls. "Fifteen dollars? That's an awful lot of money."

"Well, I'd suggest that since you're handlin' this for the family that any money you put into it should be returned to you before the funds are dispersed. That way, you won't be losin' anything."

Mama gave him the money, and as we left his office she said, "Goddamn lawyers."

Well, Cooper Schick told us that him and the other lawyer was arguin' back and forth and back and forth, Cooper Schick sayin' the will didn't look to be legal and the other guy sayin' it was and Cooper Schick sayin' we need to get an expert to look at it and that'll cost more money and the other lawyer sayin' if you was willin' to make a deal just say what it would be, and Cooper Schick sayin' if you want to make a deal you come up with an offer and like that 'til the we could tell lawyer's bills was addin' up way too fast.

Finally, Mama called Louise long distance and asked if they couldn't sit down together and try to figure somethin' out, 'cause all this fightin' was costin' too much. And Mama was kind of surprised when Louise said she'd come down and visit for a few days.

Now, her and Mama didn't really know each other very well since they lived in different parts of the state, but Aunt Birdo always told us that Louise was dumb as a mullet and had a nasty temper on her and had took to the drink. And that she'd lie at the drop of a hat. And she'd cheat her own grandma. So ten minutes after Louise said she'd come down, Mama was thinkin' twice about invitin' her.

I went with her to meet Louise at the station over in Mango. The train was late, and we had to sit there in the broilin' August heat for an hour, so neither one of us was in too great a mood by the time Louise got there. And Louise didn't look none too happy neither.

I could tell Mama was drawin' up all her patience and good manners before she gave Louise a little hug and said, "Hello there, hon. Good to see ya."

Louise frowned, leaned her head to the side, and fanned her neck, then said, "Long day on that damn train. Hotter than the hinges of hell."

"Ain't it?" Mama said, tryin' to smile. "Come on, now. We'll get home and have some nice cold sweet tea."

When we got to the house, I went to make the drinks while Mama showed Louise where she was gonna be sleepin'. When the tea was done, we all took our glasses and went and sat in the rockin' chairs on the front porch.

"Well," Mama says, "before we get into talkin' about Birdo, why don't we catch up on the family? It's been a long time since we've sat down and talked. How's things been goin' up your way?"

"Not all that good," Louise says, shakin' her head. "First of all, Frank ain't worked in a while 'cause he fell off a ladder and hurt his back. And he says he's in so much pain that he's started drinkin' again. He drives me crazy, lyin' around all day, tryin' to make me wait on him hand and foot. Tell you the truth, I was glad to have an excuse to get outta there."

"Oh, my," Mama says. "That don't sound like fun."

"And we got these new folks moved in next door that are always hollerin' and screamin' at each other loud enough to take the top of your head off. And if you go over there and ask 'em real nice to try and keep it down, they'll start tellin' you what they're yellin' about and try to get you to take their side. Idiots, all of 'em. And we can't close the windows in this heat, ya know, so we're stuck with it."

She takes a sip of tea. "And then there's Sissy. She's always into somethin' or other. Now she's found herself a boyfriend from Mississippi who come to town lookin' for work. At least that's what he says, but ask me, he's just lookin' for a free ride."

"Oh, my," Mama says. "How's your other two girls?"

"They're fine. Both married now, and they each have two young'uns. How about you?"

Mama leans back in her chair, "Well, life ain't been easy, a woman by herself with a couple of kids, but I'm lucky I got a job down at the Blue-Eyed Gator Restaurant. They let me bring leftovers home, and it keeps food on the table for Violet and Sweetie and me, but we don't have a lot extra. But I'm real proud of both my girls. Violet's gonna graduate this year."

Louise nods at me. "Good for you!" Then she lights up a cigarette and turns to Mama. "Why didn't you ever get married again, Maggie?"

"Ain't nobody around these parts I'd want to even go out with, much less marry. I don't need some man bossin' me around, tellin' me what I'm doin' wrong. Me and the girls' daddy got along real good for the first month after we got married, but after that we couldn't agree that water was wet and I don't need no more of that aggravation."

"Well, I know whatcha mean," Louise says. "Some days I wonder why I ever married Frank. But don't tell him I said that."

Mama laughs. "No, I won't. Where'd you meet him anyways?"

Louise takes a puff and blows out the smoke. "At school. He was just a little bit ahead of me, and I thought he was the bee's knees. I was sixteen when we got married, seventeen when we had the first young'un. And he's been okay, I guess. Except for the drink. But the truth is, you don't have no idea who you're marryin' 'til it's too late."

"I thought you got married later on," Mama says, "in your twenties. I remember Birdo tellin' us you were goin' out with a different boy every night."

She looks surprised and shakes her head. "That ain't true. Frank's the only fella I ever went out with."

"Hmmm," Mama says. "I should have known . . . Birdo."

Louise looks at Mama, real curious. "What else did she say?"

"Oh my, let's see now. I don't know if I should . . . I mean, we know how Birdo was."

"Come on now, Maggie. Tell me. Please?"

"Well, let's see . . . She said you had a nasty temper and was always sassin' your mama right to her face. And . . . that you wouldn't go to church."

She looks at Mama sideways. "Hmmm. Well, I did talk back once in a while, but I always went to church. Every Sunday. Did she say anything else?"

"Well . . . " Mama glances over at me and gets quiet, like she don't know whether or not to say somethin'.

"Well, what?"

"I just don't know if I should . . . I mean, it might make you mad or somethin'."

"What? Come on now. Tell me."

Mama looks at her, then down to her lap. "Well, all right. She said that you went to visit some relative up in Ohio for six months, some relation Birdo'd never heard of, then come back home tryin' to act like you hadn't had a baby."

Louise's eyes get wide and her mouth falls open. "No! Really! She said that?" Then she turns red. "My first baby may have got started a little early, but I never . . . Oh, my dear Lord, did she tell that to everybody?"

"Afraid so. 'Course, she always said not to pass it on. You know how good that works."

"I know, I know. Anything else? There must be more."

"Let me think now . . . She said that you stole money from your mama all the time and she didn't know what you did with it, but she'd smelled the drink on your breath when she went up to visit y'all, so she figured you was buyin' liquor. Said you was just an old drunk. Couldn't even take care of your young'uns."

By now, Louise's face is bright red and she's lookin' mad. "Why, that old witch! I ain't never touched liquor, even if Frank does. Now, you just tell me, if she thought all that, why would she want to leave everything to me?"

"I got no idea. Maybe she liked y'all better than us. She was a funny old bird, that's for sure." It's quiet for a minute, then Mama says, "I hate to think what she told you about us."

Louise smiles. "Oh, I can remember a few things, all right. But they're probably not true."

"Oh, Lord. What? Do I even want to know?"

"Sure you do. I got to hear mine." She pauses. "Let's see now, she said you wouldn't let the girls go to school, made 'em stay home and work takin' in washin' when they were little, maybe eight or ten years old. And then you kept all the money for yourself, wouldn't ever buy 'em anything new, but you had real nice clothes. All the kids ever had was hand-me-downs from charity."

Mama puts her hand up to her mouth. "No! She didn't! Why, that old cow! I just told you Violet's about to graduate. Neither one of 'em hardly ever missed a day at school."

"And she said you been havin' affairs right and left since your husband died. Just go off and leave the girls on their own almost every weekend."

Mama looks at me with her mouth hangin' open, then back to Louise. "That ain't true! You can ask anybody!"

"I believe you. You know that old woman was crazy. And mean, besides."

"It's funny when you think about it," Mama says. "Everybody around here always knew you couldn't believe nothin' she said, but if the gossip was juicy enough, they believed it anyways. Guess it gave 'em somethin' to do."

All of a sudden both Mama and Louise start laughin'. When Louise spews out a mouthful of tea, they laugh even harder 'til they're both holdin' their bellies and have tears runnin' down their faces.

The next mornin' at the breakfast table, Mama says, "Now, tell me about when Frank wrote Birdo's will."

Louise takes her last bite of scrambled eggs and leans back in her chair. "Well, she come up to visit years back, and that's when they done it. I wasn't there, but Frank told me about it after she'd gone back home."

"So you didn't see her sign it?"

"Nope. Frank just told me about it."

"Hmmm. The lawyer told us she'd hurt her hand. Was that before she got to your place or while she was there?"

"You know, that's the odd thing. I don't remember her hand bein' hurt. But since Frank didn't even tell me about it 'til months later, I wasn't sure. My memory ain't the best sometimes."

I can see the wheels turnin' in Mama's head. "Well, Louise . . . do you think it could be that Frank just wrote it all up and put the X there hisself? I mean, our lawyer said nobody else signed it, and it's supposed to have two witnesses."

Louise looks at Mama and narrows her eyes like she's thinkin'. "When Frank takes the pledge and don't drink, he can be a pretty good fella. But when he's drinkin' . . . I guess I wouldn't put it past him."

Well, after that conversation, Louise agreed with Mama that Birdo's stuff should be divided up equal, and they dropped the lawyer. After everything was sold, Mama got the money back that she'd spent on Cooper Schick, and she was just waitin' for

Frank to ask for the money they paid their lawyer. But it turned out that their "lawyer" was just some friend of Frank's whose brother-in-law was a real lawyer and that friend was pretendin' to be one. Frank hadn't paid him anything.

So in the end, even though Aunt Birdo spent most of her life goin' out of her way to stir up trouble and didn't even leave a will, probably just to aggravate us, everybody went away from the funeral feelin' good about how things worked out.

And I sure hope she's been watchin', whether she's lookin' up or down, 'cause that would make her madder than a boar with a sore tail.

Fishin' for a Livin'
by Deloyd Stroudamore

The thing I always loved best in the world was goin' fishin'. I never would have thought it could get me into such a helluva mess.

I was born in Fort Pierce and lived there with my mama and daddy and big sister, Jolinda. We were right near the Indian River, and I can remember my daddy takin' me fishin' when I was almost four years old. Wasn't too long after that he run off and Mama moved us over here to Toad Springs. Later on, Jolinda told me that Daddy was real bad to drink and that's why he left. Him and Mama was always fightin' over it, she said.

When I was four or five, my daddy's brother, Uncle Bubba, started takin' me fishin'. He said I was the best little fisherman he'd ever seen, and man, I'm tellin' you, I took that right to heart. We'd dig up these big fat worms or catch grasshoppers for bait, or sometimes we'd get us some lures at Smitty's Hardware and Feed. Uncle Bubba taught me where the best fishin' holes were, which sort of grass the different kinds of fish like, and how they mostly hang out in the shade of the big old mossy trees. That man was a second daddy to me. In more ways than one.

One summer when I was around twelve, this feller they called Old Man Redfish come visitin' from Fort Myers. He had a bushy grey beard that he said used to be red and he hung out at Smitty's, smokin' a dirty old corncob pipe, drinkin' coffee, and pla-yin' checkers with the other old guys.

I'd pull up a stool and listen to him talk about when he'd had his own commercial fishin' boat out of Fort Myers. He was always sayin' that fresh water fishin' is for sissies and can't nobody make a decent livin' that way. Commercial fishin's what brings in the cash, but it's hard work, haulin' up them big old heavy lines with a bunch of fish hooked on, gettin' the catch all stowed away in the cooler just right, and keepin' it so the ice don't all melt before you can get everything back to the docks and sold.

He told these great stories about seein' big schools of dolphin and how sometimes the sharks would come after the fish they were tryin' to reel in and that late at night once in a while, you could hear a ghost moanin' out on the water. But the best story was about the time they got caught in a big old storm. "We got hit by a ninth wave," he said.

I asked, "What's that?"

Old Man Redfish takes a puff off his pipe and leans back from the checkerboard. "It's somethin' you don't see very often, son, and somethin' you don't never wanna run into. It's the big-gest wave of all."

"Why do they call it that?"

"Well, sir," he says, "It can turn up when the weather's turnin' bad. What happens is that the waves start out small, then one by one they get bigger and bigger. The ninth wave to come along is the biggest one of all and can flip the boat over in a flash. Lotsa sailors went to meet their maker after runnin' into a ninth wave."

I'm so wrapped up in his every word I'd have listened to him forever. "Where'd you see it?"

"Well, sir, we was caught in a bad one about thirty or forty miles out in the Gulf—must be twelve, fifteen years ago now, I reckon. It'd got pretty rough, but I sure wasn't expectin' nothin' that big. Drowned the engines, bilge pumps wouldn't work, and I didn't think we was gonna make it. Closest I ever come to dyin'."

I can hardly breathe. "What did you do?"

"Held on best we could. Wasn't nothin' else we could do. Just rode her out. Took 'em five days to find us, and we were damn lucky they didn't give up. By that time, we'd run out of fresh water and were drinkin' melted ice from the fish boxes that was mixed up with fish slime." He sucks on his pipe and looks out into the street.

"Yuck," I say. "Were you scared?"

"Me?" He looks around at the others, pulls his pipe out of his mouth, then leans over my way and whispers, "Well . . . I don't tell this to everybody, but I'll tell you. I wasn't scared, but I was right nervous."

Just hearin' him talk, I'm afraid, myself. I feel like I'd been right there with him. He goes on and on about how the work ain't easy but he come away with good money. After hearin' all his stories, by the time I'm sixteen, my plan is to get my own fishin' boat.

But then, Helen Jamison moves to town. She's tall with these bright green eyes and long wavy brown hair, the most beautiful gal I ever seen. I don't know why she ever give me a second look, but the minute she smiles at me, I'm a goner. She's always doin' nice things, like bakin' my favorite peanut butter cookies, tellin' me how smart I am, or sometimes takin' my hand while we walk along the street. I'm tellin' you, them cookies was so good, I gave her the nickname Peanut. I was happy as a barnacle at high tide.

Not long before graduation, we're sittin' on her front porch swing of a Sunday afternoon, and she says, "I hear Landis Perkins has been needin' some more hands out in the groves. Think you might want to go to work for him when school's out?"

"Naw," I say. "I'd never work for that guy."

"How about your granddaddy's gator ranch? If you went to work there, I bet when he dies, he'd just pass it down to you . . . "

"Not a chance," I say. "I ain't about to have that cranky old man bossin' me around all the time. He thinks the only way to do everything is his way, and if you don't go along with him, then you're sassin' him and you'll shut the hell up if you know what's good for you. Ain't one man in Toad Springs I'd want to work for. You know . . . fishin' is what I got my mind set on."

"Come on, Deloyd. I mean, you'll be gettin' married one of these days . . . " She glances up at the porch ceilin' real flirty, then smiles and looks back to me. "Won't you?"

"Well, yeah. But I already told you I want to get me a boat and do commercial fishin'. Out in the Gulf. Ain't nothin' better than catchin' a big old fish." Then I notice she ain't lookin' too happy, so I give her a quick hug. "Except you, of course, honey," I say. "I love you more than anything."

She pulls away and looks at me with a pouty face. "Come on, Deloyd. How you gonna buy a boat when you got no money?"

"Figure to hire on with a fishin' crew first, so I'll be earnin' a livin' while I learn the ropes. Then when I've saved up enough, I'll get my own boat."

"Well, Deloyd," she says, kinda snippy. "Last time I looked, there wasn't no Gulf close around here."

"Yeah, but John's Pass ain't all that far."

She crosses her arms in front of her and stares at me.

"C'mon, hon. You go out for four or five days, or maybe even a week or two, so it's not that far."

She looks me in the eye real serious. "A week or two at a time? What are you—"

"Now, Helen. Don't get all . . . "

"You've never even been out on one of them big boats, have you?"

"Well . . . I told ya—"

"Never even been fishin' in the Gulf at all. Have you?"

"Have so. Uncle Bubba took me over there three or four times . . . " She gives me a real dirty look and I know I'm in for it now. "Just simmer down, girl. I ain't decided nothin' for sure. Least not yet."

"You ain't decided? You? What about me?"

"Aw, come on, Helen . . . "

"Well, I'll just tell you right this minute. You for sure ain't never asked, but if you was thinkin' to marry me, I ain't movin' off to John's Pass. Or any other godforsaken place you might—"

"Honey, this can't be no big surprise. You know how much I love to fish."

She stands up, puts her hands on her hips, and looks down at me. "Deloyd Stroudamore! You always said you loved me! We'll just see who you love more! Me or some old dead fish." And with that, she stomps in the house and slams the screen door behind her. I get up and go home.

Over the next few days, I do a good bit of thinkin', and I decide I'd better say I'm sorry. Then, after I marry her, when things settle down some, I'll bring it up again. Things'll look different to her by then.

She won't hardly speak to me all that week. The next Sunday evenin', we're on the front porch swing again. She's way over to one side with her arms crossed in front of her and a frown on her face, but this time, I'm ready.

I say, "Helen, honey, you remember what we was talkin' about before?"

She looks at me, then straight ahead.

"Well, I just want to make sure you know I love you more than fishin'."

She smiles just a little and folds her hands in her lap. "I love you too," she says, lookin' down at her hands.

I slide off the swing and kneel in front of her. "And I want you to marry me," I say. "I don't have no ring or nothin' right now, but will you be my wife?"

She holds her hands to her mouth, then lets 'em drop and hugs me. Tears come into her eyes and she says, "Oh, Deloyd, honey. 'Course I will." She takes my hands, and when we both stand up, she gives me the best kiss I've ever had. Then she says, "But we got it straight about the fishin', right?"

"Sure, honey. You're more important to me than fishin'. Like I said, I love you more than anything on this earth."

She gives me another big kiss. Then we go inside so I can ask her daddy for his permission, to be proper and all. He says he'd be proud to have me for a son-in-law, and her mom gives me a great big hug.

A few days later my mind starts sneakin' up on me while I'm not watchin', and I'm gettin' mad. All the way along, I'd told her I wanted to be a fisherman. She always knew that, and never one time did she say I shouldn't do it. Not until that afternoon on the porch.

Now all she talks about is how nice it'll be to get our own little house that she can fix up like she wants with brand-new furniture and fancy pictures and nice flowerpots of ferns along the front porch. And how she's livin' here in Toad Springs for the rest of her life, right near her mama and daddy.

All that talkin' starts stickin' in my craw, but I tell her that I'll keep workin' here in town—to make her happy.

But then, the more I think about givin' up my dream, the madder I get. One day I think I can't live without her, the next day I can't live without fishin'. Now, this don't make no sense even to me, but while I'm so mad at her, at the same time, I love her so much, I can't imagine losin' her.

I talk to Uncle Bubba, but he ain't got no advice. Says he's never once in his whole life come out on the winnin' end of an argument with a woman. I think about talkin' to Pastor Blander, but Mama always says he just tells everybody to pray to the good Lord and the answer'll come. He don't give out any advice worth listenin' to. So I don't bother.

After I spend too much money on a ring and we're officially engaged, the only job I can find is workin' in the groves for Landis Perkins, and he turns out to be a stingy old so-and-so, just like I thought he would be. He treats his hired hands like we're all a bunch of morons, but I do it for her. We get married in the Church of Everlasting Liability in June, on her mama's birthday like she wants, and she even talks me into buyin' a new suit that I'll never wear again except for funerals.

We rent a little house for next to nothin' after I agree to replace some rotten wood in the floor and paint the whole place, inside and out. I'm real handy when it comes to fixin' things. I do everything I can to make Helen happy. When she says she don't really like me callin' her Peanut, I stop callin' her that. Why, I even promise we can name our first boy after her great-grand-daddy, Orsimus, which is a crazy name if I ever heard one.

The only thing she don't like is that I come home from work in a snit every day 'cause Landis Perkins is so sure he's always right and everybody else is always wrong. Don't know how his boy, Worthy, ever put up with him. After a few months I think I'm gonna have to kill that man, so one day I just up and quit. I knew that job wasn't gonna last long, but at least it got Helen to feelin' sorry for me.

It takes some tall talkin', but I convince her to let me try out the fishin' stuff, at least 'til we have enough for a down payment for our own house and get it all fixed up. Then I'll come back and work in town.

She says that maybe I need to get it out of my system before our young'uns come along. My plan is to go work on a boat and come home with a wallet full of money. That way, we can both have what we want. She'll be able to see the cash pilin' up so we can get our own place, and she can buy new stuff for the house. And I can see what fishin's really like.

I go over to John's Pass and get hired to work on this boat called *My Betty*—Captain Shay named it after his wife. Takes me a while to get used to the boat rockin' all the time and get my sea legs, but little by little, things get better. By the end of the first full day of fishin', I barely got the steam left to crawl in the bunk and go to sleep. But by the end of the trip a week later, I'm keep-in' up with the captain and the other fella and got new muscles to boot. Then, when we get back on the dock, I have to get used to walkin' on dry land again. Didn't know that was gonna happen. It's real odd, the way your legs feel kind of rubbery, like the land is supposed to be movin' but it ain't.

But the fishin's even better than I thought it would be. It's in my bones. Bein' so far out and away from everything is real qui-et and peaceful. When we stop at night, you can hear the boards creakin' as the boat rocks back and forth in the water. Why, the way the stars sparkle up in that black sky at night—a million, at least—and the sunrises and sunsets on the water are so purty, I can't even tell you. Then there's that clean, salty sea smell when you're way out in the middle of the Gulf. It ain't like nothin' else in this world.

Captain shows me all the ropes, and in the evenings we sit around playin' poker while him and the other fellas tell fishin' stories like Old Man Redfish used to tell. That trip, we make a great big haul of grouper and I bring home some good money. For sure, I'm hooked. But then, like I promised Helen I would, I hire on with Hank Plenty. He's a lot better than workin' for Landis, but after fishin', workin' on a ranch in Toad Springs is real hard. I stick it out there for three long months, but I'm so unhappy all the time that Helen's sick of lookin' at my grumpy face.

I reckon she really does love me a lot—either that or she likes havin' more money than Hank pays, 'cause after a while she agrees for me to go back and work with Captain Shay, just 'til we have all the money we need for the down payment on a house. So then I'm out fishin' two weeks and home two weeks workin' on the house we're rentin'. After six or eight months, we get a real good deal on buyin' one of the old Riley houses, but it needs some repairs before we can move in.

It's about the same time that Captain Shay tells me about this feller, Sweet William, who's lookin' to sell his boat and asks do I want to go over to see it. Now, I know I'm damned lucky Helen's goin' along with things like they are, and I shouldn't do anything that'll stir up a hornet's nest, but when I hear about this boat, I can't stop myself. Ain't no harm in just checkin' it out, I figure. Just take a look-see . . . I know I'll never be able to buy it. But I tell myself that I'd be a fool not to talk to the man.

By this time I know a lot about boats, and she's a beauty, even if she needs some work. She's forty-five feet long with bent oak ribs and cypress plankin'. The cabin's big—twenty feet long—and the roof goes pretty much from the front of the cabin back to the stern, with four bandit reels screwed onto the gunnels. It's got four boxes to keep the fish iced down in, but the engine needs a little work. The paint's peelin', and the hull's pretty beat up, but I figure since I can build just about anything, it couldn't be that hard to fix.

I start lookin' for somebody with some money who'd be interested in goin' into business with me, knowin' all along I shouldn't be doin' it. No need to bother Helen with it, I tell myself. Don't need to have her all upset and raisin' sand when probably nothin's ever gonna come of it. Any reasonable man would have done the same thing.

I keep tellin' myself it's just a dream that can't ever come true. But then I think if I had my own boat, maybe I could go out two weeks at a time and have somebody else go the other two. 'Course, I'd have to pay 'em.

Well, ends up old Sweet William gives me the answer. He knows just the right feller to go in with me, some skinny little city slicker from New York called Charles Vanderhoff. The three of us sit down and talk over a beer, and even though Charles has only been on a boat a couple of times—and then the *boat* was an ocean liner—he says he can learn on the job like I did. And the best part is that Charles's folks say they'll make the down payment and pay for all the boat repairs, so I don't have to fix nothin'.

Now, in the back of my mind, I'm thinkin' somethin' must be wrong here—this is too good to be true. But I convince myself there ain't no harm in tryin' it. Turns out Charles's daddy has money—one of the few fellas who come through the Great Depression all right—and him and his wife'll do just about anything to get rid of their boy for a while. Seems like everything Charles touches goes straight to hell. 'Course, nobody told me that part 'til later.

I know I'm doin' wrong, gettin' into all this behind Helen's back, but I tell myself this ain't costin' me nothin', and she'll be so happy with the money that she won't care. I'll buy her a brand-new Maytag washin' machine and a new Hotpoint electric stove, and she'll be the talk of Toad Springs. And I tell her to pick out the newest style furniture for the whole house while I'm still fishin'.

Once I get the captain's license, there's no turnin' back. I want to name the boat after Helen, like Captain Shay named his after his wife, but Charles says that ain't fair and we can both name it. Helen can be one of the names, and he'll pick the other one. He comes up with Blazes for his name—*Helen Blazes*—and I like it, but I don't much think Helen would.

Since I'm only plannin' to go out two weeks a month, we got to have somebody else in charge who can fish with Charles the other two weeks, and Sweet William says he knows this feller by the name of Uncle Chunk from Mississippi, who used to be a boat captain there. He don't smell too good, what with eatin' beans three times a day, but he's a great big guy, and strong, and I'm glad to get him.

On our first trip, Charles gets seasick before we're even out of the harbor, and he wants to go back in. "No," we say, "you'll get used to it." And he does, but it's three days before he can walk on the deck without holdin' on to somethin' and eat without hangin' over the side. Soon as he's better, we start teachin' him about pullin' in the lines and navigation and readin' the weather, and it gets clear real fast this fella knows as much about an honest day's work as a hog knows about Sunday. He complains that the navigation don't make sense and pullin' in the fish is leavin' blisters on his hands. What the devil did he think was gonna happen?

And I'd said no liquor on board, but that don't stop Charles and Uncle Chunk from bringin' all they want. Let me tell you, it ain't good when the owner of the boat don't have a world of experience and the deckhands are always higher than a Georgia pine.

We get back in from that first trip with a fairly good catch even though when Charles isn't seasick, he's drunk. When we're back at the dock, we find a couple of rotten spots in the hull. We have to put the boat in dry dock to get it fixed, but we're lucky that we only miss a week goin' out. And at least Charles's daddy pays for the repairs.

I call Helen and tell her that the boat I was workin' on had to be put on a cradle and hauled out but the captain asked me to stay and make sure it's fixed right so I'll be gettin' home a week late. She don't like that at all, but I remind her I'll be paid for the time I'm here. Don't know what excuse I'll come up with when I don't have the money, but I'll worry about that later.

When I finally get home, she's a little testy at first, but I bring her a bracelet and some pretty silk cloth I bought in Tampa and she calms down—never does ask about the money, which ain't nothin' short of a miracle. By now, my conscience is really botherin' me. Bad. I can't believe I've done all this behind her back. That ain't the kind of man I thought I was. But then I think about the fishin'. God, I love fishin'.

If I told Mama what I've done, she'd say I'm bein' selfish, that I need to put my wife ahead of everything else. I figure she says that 'cause when they were still married, Daddy never put her ahead of anything, especially his drinkin'. Every time I come home, I plan to tell Helen about gettin' the boat, but I don't do it. A few months go by, and I'm finally feelin' so guilty that I decide I have to fess up. I write down what I want to say, even memorize it so I'll say everything just right. Then it crosses my mind that I could maybe just mail her a letter that she'd get while I'm still out on the boat. But I know better. At least I didn't go spendin' our money without tellin' her.

When I walk in the door the next Sunday night, probably still smellin' like fish, she runs up and gives me a big hug.

"Hi darlin'," she says. "I'm so glad you're home."

"Me too," I say, huggin' her back. "Somethin' smells good."

"That's apple pie. And I'm fixin' your favorite supper too."

"Aw, that's real nice, honey. You didn't need to go to all that trouble." She sure ain't makin' this easy.

She pulls away from me. "I love you so much. Just want you to know how much I miss you when you're gone."

"Aw . . . honey, aw . . . honey," I say, feelin' lower than a ga-tor's belly. "I love you too."

"You go on now and take a bath while I put supper on."

The whole time I'm gettin' cleaned up, my stomach's in a knot. She's too good. I don't deserve her. When I come to the table, she brings out a whole platter of fried chicken along with mashed potatoes, gravy, green beans, and coleslaw.

"Sit down, honey," she says. "Hope you're hungry."

"Starved for some home cookin'," I lie, pullin' up my chair. I feel sick to my stomach and a little dizzy, but I pick up a knife and fork, take a deep breath, then say, "I've got somethin' to tell you."

She looks at me and smiles. "What is it?"

I put the knife and fork back down. I have to get it over with. "Well . . . " I take another deep breath. "Well . . . somebody of-fered me a way to get my own boat."

She looks surprised. "What? You want to buy a boat?"

"Well, not exactly."

She frowns. "Either you do or you don't."

"Well, there was this boat for sale, and Captain Shay thought I oughta see it."

She's squintin' at me, and her face is red. "*Was* for sale? *Was?*" She slams her napkin down on the table. "You bought it? You bought a boat?"

"I didn't buy nothin'. Did not spend one penny on it."

Her smile is gone. All that happiness. Gone. "I knew some-thin' was wrong. What the hell have you done?" She stares at me.

I tell her the whole story, and she's so mad, she's spittin' nails. Didn't help at all when I told her I'd named it *Helen*. Might have even made it worse.

"You lied to me, Deloyd Stroudamore!" she hollers, standin' up. "You *lied*!"

"I did it for you, honey. For us. So you could have all this new stuff for the house. You know the money's been real—"

"You did NOT do it for me. You did it for your ownself."

"But, Helen . . . "

She leans over and pounds her fist on the table. "You can't do this. You swore—"

I stand up too. And now I'm gettin' mad. "Helen, I didn't swear to nothin'. I was real careful not to promise somethin' I couldn't stick to. And you're the one who was so excited about gettin' all the new stuff. Fancy, brand-new washin' machine, an electric stove, even got you the latest refrigerator. Look at what all that money's bought you."

"Well, I got somethin' to tell you too. You ain't the only one with news. While you were gone, I started up my own business. So you wouldn't have to work so hard and be away from home all the time."

I feel like somebody just slapped me in the face. "What?"

"Yes, sir! That's right." She gives an ugly laugh. "I'm bakin' stuff to sell at the grocery, cakes and pies and stuff, and I've already made twenty dollars, lots more than I ever dreamed I could do. I've got lots of orders in the next two months for Thanksgivin' and Christmas. And stupid me, I was thinkin' you could help me. But of course, that won't be happenin'. You'll be out on that damn boat!"

I can hardly get words to come out of my mouth. "I didn't . . . I mean . . . I don't know what to say!"

"I think you've said plenty."

I manage a fake smile. "I'm just surprised, that's all. But I'm real happy about your job." I get up to hug her, but she turns away.

After I sit back down, she picks up her plateful of food and slams it into the sink. I hear the dish break. Then she turns around and glares at me. "You're sellin' that goddamn boat. Or you're gettin' out of whatever deal you made with them people."

I shake my head real slow. "Don't know if I *can* get out of it, Peanut." Soon as I say Peanut, I know I just made everything worse.

"First of all, don't call me Peanut. Second of all, you're gettin' out of it. I ain't gonna live here all alone for weeks at a time. You're gonna have to choose. One way or the other."

"Okay, okay," I say, holdin' my palms up to her. "Just listen for a minute. Charles's daddy made me sign this piece of paper sayin' we're both owners of the boat, me and him, but that I'm the one who'd be takin' it out."

"Who the hell is Charles? And why can't he take it out?"

"Well, 'cause the only thing he can do a good job of is drinkin'. Don't know squat about fishin'."

"Then you'll just have to sell it, that's all."

"Aw, Helen . . . it ain't that easy, I'm tellin' you."

She puts her hands on her hips. "Don't 'Aw, Helen' me."

"I told you I'm sorry. Really, truly sorry."

"Well, ain't that nice? I just want to know what you're gonna do about it." She stomps out to the front porch.

When the screen door slams shut, it hits me that we sound just like my mama hollerin' at my daddy all them years ago.

That night, I get to stay on the new couch, but I can't sleep a wink, thinkin' I'm gonna have to give up my dream. I go back and forth between bein' mad at her and mad at me. The next mornin', I wake up feelin' sick, but Helen looks worse.

Can't hardly stand to think of it, but I reckon I'll have to get rid of the boat one way or another. Don't matter no more that there ain't nothin' else in this world I want to do to earn a livin'. But in a way, I feel like my life is over.

When I call Charles's daddy and tell him I'm gonna have to give up fishin', he blows his top, says I signed a contract that I'd be workin' with Charles for at least a year and I got four months to go. Says I'm supposed to be helpin' his boy and he'll take me to court if I try to get out of it. And he's got the money to do it too. Now, I don't remember nothin' in that paper I signed about helpin' Charles, but when I go back and look, the part about workin' for at least a year is right there. Must have been so excited about ownin' half a boat, I just didn't notice.

Helen hears me talkin' on the phone to Charles's daddy, and she comes in and sits right beside me while I'm readin' the papers, so she knows I got no choice. But it's just 'til the year's up. She ain't happy and neither am I, but for different reasons, if you see what I mean. Figure I'll be able to get eight more trips in before I have to give up the only work I was ever meant to do.

When I head back over toward John's Pass the next time, I'm thinkin' I better enjoy it while I can. We get everything all loaded up, and we're off. Standin' in the bow of the boat, feelin' that nice cool breeze blowin' in my face and the smell of the salt water makes me glad I'm alive.

We have some real good catches the next couple of months, but the last trip out is when we get the most. The fish boxes is full of red snapper and grouper, and we're headed home when the water gets choppy. Next thing I know, Charles is hollerin', "Look! Over there!" He's pointin' off to the west where rain's headin' our way and the sky's dark as pitch. You can't even see the skyline. Don't know how all three of us missed seein' it, but in no time flat, it's all we can do just to hang on.

I'm scared to death and tryin' to think what Captain Shay would be tellin' me to do when the rain starts comin' in sideways, hittin' us so hard it stings. The wind is howlin' so loud that we can't understand each other even though we're yellin' as loud as we can. I got no idea how I done it now, but I get the bilge pump runnin, and I'm prayin' that the engine don't get swamped. We tie everything down, drop the anchor line all the way out, turn off the engines, and head for the cabin. We crawl into the bunks, but the boat's rockin' so bad we have to brace ourselves against the hull to keep from gettin' tossed out.

Charles is cryin', "Oh, my God! Please, dear Lord, if you get us out of this I promise I'll change my ways. I'll work hard. I'll do whatever my daddy says. I promise."

"Oh, shut the hell up!" Uncle Chunk says. "Don't be a God-damned sissy!"

I look out the front window and a wall of water is headed at us. "Hang on!" I yell in a panic. "It's a ninth wave!"

When it hits, it knocks out the front windows. Water's sloshin' around in the cabin, and I'm sure we're gonna flip. Or go under. The boat's still rockin' so bad that it's all we can do just to hang on.

By mornin', the rain stops, but for a day and a half, the high winds and rough water keeps battin' us around. Everybody's seasick, and the cabin smells worse than death itself. Finally, finally, the winds let up, and the seas go calm.

Holdin' my breath, I try to start the engine. This is it. If it don't crank up, they'll never find us this far out in the Gulf. I try it once. Nothin'. I try it again. It spits and sputters but don't catch. It starts on the third try and we're all yellin' and huggin' each other—even Uncle Chunk. Then we head for home. It's a goddamn miracle, for sure.

When we pull in, I tell myself I don't care what Charles's daddy does. He can sue me up one side and down the other but I'm done with fishin' in the Gulf. I ain't never goin' through anything like that again. Now I know why folks kiss the ground when they get back to dry land.

Soon as we pull up to the docks, before we even unload the fish that's still on ice, Charles calls his daddy and tells him he's a new man. Had an epiphany, whatever that is. He's turned over a new leaf, and he'll do whatever his daddy wants. Except for one thing. He ain't never goin' out on a fishin' boat again.

Turns out Charles's mama is the one who *finally* talks his daddy into givin' up on the boat, so I didn't have to worry about gettin' sued after all. When it finally got sold, he even wrote me out a check for half the profit, sayin' this is the first time they'd ever seen a real change in Charles.

Me and Helen's got ourselves a little girl now, with another one on the way. If it's a boy, I reckon I'm gonna have to give in and name him Orsimus. But I'm gonna make real sure that's his middle name.

And, like Helen is always remindin' me, now I've got my own ninth wave fishin' story to tell when I'm old and grey and sittin' around playin' checkers at Smitty's Hardware and Feed.

I never did tell Helen that the boat's whole name was *Helen Blazes.* And if she ever found out, she didn't let on to me.

Be Careful What You Ask For
by Ginger Perkins

When I was a kid, I wanted to move to Tampa and live the city life where you could go see a movie every night if you wanted, swim at the Sulphur Springs pool any Saturday you felt like it, and shop at big fancy stores. I wasn't gonna be like everybody else in Toad Springs, gettin' married and livin' the rest of my life on some dairy farm or orange grove, spendin' my days cookin' and cleanin' up after a husband and a passel of babies. But that's where I ended up.

There's been days I wondered why I ever thought bein' a mama was a good idea, like when I'm choppin' collards for supper with one young'un on my hip, another one with a runny nose cryin' and hangin' onto my apron, and the oldest ones fightin' out on the porch. I love my kids, 'course I do, but nobody ever told me how much work all this was gonna be.

My folks just had the two of us. My little brother, Worthy, was the smartest person ever born in Toad Springs, but he hated a fight worse than anybody I ever seen. That's why he was Mama's favorite. He'd just bite his tongue and do whatever she wanted. Me, I'd fight back—I've even been known to do stuff on purpose to make her mad 'cause I didn't like her always tellin' me what to do.

Why, she was the strictest, most orderly person God ever put on this Earth. Every little thing had to be just so all the time, even the salt and pepper shakers set in just the right spot on the kitchen table, to the left of the sugar bowl. And I couldn't ever do anything right. If I missed as much as one little drop of water when I was dryin' the cast-iron skillet, she'd pitch a hissy fit, hollerin' how it would go all rusty. If I didn't make my bed every single day with the bedspread smoothed out just perfect, she'd have a conniption. I was even supposed to dry off my toothbrush!

Mama was always the first one up every mornin', took the coffee pot off the back right-hand burner of the stove where it always sat, and put the coffee on to perk. Next, she went into the livin' room, did twenty jumpin' jacks, then lay down on her special little rug and did ten sit ups, stuck her legs in the air one at a time, and rolled from one side to the other. Did the exact same thing every day.

After Mama got up from her exercises, she turned down the heat under the coffee and then took a hot shower. Just before she got out to dry off, she always turned the faucet way down to cold—said it closed up her skin pores and kept all the dirty germs out. The picture I got in my head of all them little holes in her skin squeezin' shut always gave me the willies. Still does.

I remember this one time when I was fourteen and I'd gotten into trouble with her. It started when she wouldn't let me go to the church picnic one Saturday 'cause I sassed her. Then Monday, she said I couldn't go anywhere after school on account of me gettin' a bad mark in comportment on my report card—Old Lady Heppner wrote this ugly note sayin', "Ginger talks in class when she should be payin' attention to her studies," but that wasn't true. I never talked any more than anybody else. Anyway, the next day, Mama said I couldn't leave the house after school 'til I'd cleaned my room. I was mad as a hornet, but I swept and mopped and wiped and folded and polished everything in there. Of course, she found a little tiny speck of dust under the bed and a blouse that wasn't folded just right and said I had to do it all over. By that time, I was so mad I wasn't gonna do one thing she said, and 'cause of that, she wouldn't let me leave the house for a week. Still makes me mad to think about it.

Know how it is when you got that angel on one shoulder sayin', "Honor thy mother," and the devil on the other side sayin, "Your mama's so mean, it's okay for you to get back at her," and you start leanin' toward the devil? Well, I figured I'd had enough. I ain't proud of it now, but here's what I done.

I moved some things out of their rightful place, which don't sound exactly cruel . . . unless you know my mama. I put the coffee pot away down with the pots and pans instead of leavin' it sittin' on the back burner of the stove, I put the bath soap up on the window sill next to the tub where it would leave a mess instead of in its special little soap dish, and I hid Mama's little exercise rug underneath the couch.

At first, when she started slammin' around lookin' for things, I was glad. Felt like I'd gotten her back for treatin' me so bad. But then, when I heard her cryin', I was ashamed of myself. I never did anything like that again, even though there were a few times when I thought about it.

When I was seventeen, I started goin' out with boys. Me and my best friend Elsie Lou Only spent hours and hours talkin' about 'em—who was cutest and who'd make the most money. I had big plans. I wanted a boyfriend, but at the same time, I was bound and determined to leave Toad Springs. I was gonna live in the city and make somethin' of myself.

Elsie Lou, on the other hand, had a sad love affair with an encyclopedia salesman, and after that, she said she was just gonna wait and see what happened. The right man would come along. Back then, we all knew there was only one man who's perfect for every girl, and she was sure he'd find her.

'Course, soon as I fell in love, I forgot my big city plans, married Grady, and stayed right here. And Elsie Lou ended up marryin' Darnell Swigfellow, who was down here visitin' his aunt and uncle in Turkey Creek, then moved back to Nashville with him. So much for plannin' out your life.

After Daddy'd gone on to his great reward—which Mama said he probably wouldn't get since he liked the drink and he never went to church—anyway, after that, Mama took over runnin' the orange groves on her own. Things went along fine for a good while, but then a freeze hit. It wasn't a real bad one, but everybody knows you got to be ready for cold weather—it can show up without a bit of warnin'. Turned out Mama didn't have what she needed to stave off the cold in the groves. Grady'd told her a hundred times to get them smudge pots in workin' order and lay out some old railroad ties behind the barn that they could drag over to the groves and burn durin' a freeze. And she said she was doin' it, but she wasn't. That seemed odd, 'cause she was always so careful about havin' everything just perfect. Turned out it was the first sign that she was headed downhill. So Daddy's old grove that had won blue ribbons at the Florida State Fair for so many years and was known all over the state brought in nothin' at all that year.

Well, when Mama seen what a mess she'd made, she got mad at everybody else, blamed us for not helpin' her enough, even though she wouldn't let us. Said the whole town was talkin' about what a fool she was and how we'd all turned against her when she needed us most. After a few weeks of actin' like that, she just melted into a nasty, sticky puddle, like meringue that hadn't been beat long enough and was droolin' off a lemon pie. For four or five weeks, she sat in her livin' room in a dirty old bathrobe and drank coffee and stared at the wall. She stopped doin' her exercises every mornin', left dirty dishes in the sink, and wouldn't sweep the floors or wash her clothes, much less do anything about the groves.

One day while I was over there tryin' to get her to eat somethin', Sorrey May Only—that's Mama's best friend *and* Elsie

Lou's mama—come by to visit. She was braggin' like she always does about how excitin' Elsie Lou's life was in Nashville, how her and her singin' group, the Swinging Sisters, was makin' a record.

"Ree," she'd say to Mama, "just look at these fancy dresses." And she'd hand over pictures Elsie Lou had sent her. "Did you and Landis ever think my baby girl would get so famous?"

Mama would just smile and nod at her. Made me wish I had Elsie Lou's life, I have to say.

Out of Sorrey May's four girls, Elsie Lou was always the good daughter, never sassed back, was always helpin' her mama around the house. Not like me. I used to tell her she wouldn't get anywhere in life bein' so nice all the time, but it looks like I was wrong. After her and Darnell had them twins, she got herself a Nashville singin' career. 'Course, after that, all the girls we went to school with was sayin' she was their best friend, but she really *was* my best friend. You can ask her sometime.

I always thought it must be heaven to be able to get all gussied up and sing a few songs and be earnin' all that money while you're doin' it. Just imagine havin' all them folks clappin' for you. What a life! I've never even owned a fancy dress, myself. And if I did, there wouldn't be anywhere to wear it around here.

Anyway, when Sorrey May was through braggin' on Elsie Lou and started in on the latest gossip, I noticed that Mama wasn't payin' much attention or askin' any questions. And that wasn't like her. That very night, me and Grady started talkin' about her movin' in with us and Grady takin' over the groves. We knew my brother, Worthy, wasn't gonna be no help. He'd moved away and was a big shot in a phosphate company. After Daddy died, he didn't hardly ever come back, and I heard he'd taken to the drink. Just like Daddy.

It wasn't my first choice to take Mama on, but I was hopin' it maybe could work out since she didn't care about keepin' things clean no more. I was even hopin' that she'd maybe help me with the kids, especially Zekie.

I was close to forty when that baby was born, and he screamed his head off night and day—had the worst colic anybody'd seen in seven counties. While I was pacin' the floor with him, I had lots of time to think about Elsie Lou and all the fun she had every day of her life and how her twins never give her a minute's trouble, accordin' to Sorrey May.

Now, I'd had four babies before Zekie come along, and not one of them ever had the colic. I tried it all—quit eatin' anything spicy so my milk would be good, even drank a nasty old beer every evenin' for a whole week. I tried puttin' a warm washrag on Zekie's belly, floatin' him in tepid water, and walkin' him for hours on end with him screechin' in my ear like a banshee—think I lost some of my hearin' on my left side. I tried movin' his legs like he was ridin' a bicycle, layin' him over my lap on his stomach, drinkin' chamomile tea, givin' him chamomile tea in a bottle, givin' him a sugar tit, bouncin' him up and down, singin' to him, not singin' to him, keepin' him inside, takin' him outside. Even give him a drop of whiskey one time, but mostly, I thought about wringin' his little neck. Didn't one of them things make a lick of difference.

So I was just barely keepin' my wits about me when Mama moved in. And for some reason, bein' with us pulled her right out from all her sorrow and misery. She went straight from feelin' sad to bein' hateful.

She started right off sayin' Zekie had the colic 'cause my milk was weak—and sour besides—and that was 'cause I had a bad attitude. She hollered about how our young'uns was disrespectful to their elders and how my greasy cookin' in my dirty kitchen give her the worst heartburn she'd ever had. Grady tried to get me to believe that she was just embarrassed about the mess she'd made with the groves, but I knew better.

By the time a month had gone by, the idea of murderin' somebody was soundin' pretty damn good. And it was hard to say who'd come first, her or the baby. Then, just when I thought I couldn't stand it one more day, the miracle happened. Almost overnight, Zekie stopped cryin'.

By that time, Mama'd agreed to let Grady rent out her old house to pay the taxes, so, of course, as soon as folks had signed the lease and moved in, she wanted to move back home. Since she couldn't do that, she got it into her head that Grady was the cause of all her troubles. She called him a sneaky weasel who was tryin' to butt into her business and rob her blind, when really, Grady was just tryin' to help.

Mama'd go on and on about how awful we all were 'til I started feelin' like I was gonna end up as crazy as her. Finally, I called Pastor Blander, and for a couple of months, that patient man come over at ten o'clock every Tuesday mornin' and sat with Mama for an hour. I know she was tellin' him that we'd forced her to move out of her own house and were plannin' to steal her property right out from under her, but by that time, I didn't care. At least I didn't have to put up with her while he was there. After she told him off one day and said she wouldn't be goin' back to church 'cause of what all God had put her through, he quit comin'.

Sorrey May'd drop in to visit Mama every whipstitch or so—so she could brag on Elsie Lou, I'm sure. But this one afternoon, she come in all excited. She'd just been at a circle meetin' at the Church of Everlasting Liability and told Mama they really needed her to help out with the big July Fourth celebration, only six weeks away. Seems like Carrie June and Gladys just had a big blow-up at the meetin' over whether they'd have horses in the parade this year. Gladys said the dung droppin's they left behind was just too nasty to even abide, and Carrie June said her great-grand-daddy was the one who founded Toad Springs and havin' horses was a tradition they needed to stick by. And when Carrie June said that Gladys should be in the parade herself and walk behind the horses with a shovel, that did it. Ended up Gladys was so mad that she said she wasn't even gonna go to the parade.

I'll never know why, but the big July Fourth shindig was enough to get Mama back in the swing of things. Her and Sorrey May got together one day and decided just how they was gonna set up the whole thing—have some high school girls twirlin' batons, marchin' in front of fellers playin' the drums and flutes, all dressed up like they'd been wounded in the Civil War, and the 4-H Club carryin' big posters showin' what they'd been doin'. Also, the Stroudamores were makin' a great big green papier-mâché three-legged gator with a red, white, and blue halo around his head to ride on a float and advertise their prize gator, Precious, at the gator ranch.

Mama and Sorrey May were hell-bent on keepin' the horses in the parade, even added a few extra ones just to irritate Gladys. They'd have the big shots ridin' horses, and behind them, a horse-drawn wagon full of little kids dressed up like toads—they'd all have to wear brown clothes and put on funny little toad hats with big old buggy eyes that Aunt Never said she could knit when she wasn't puttin' through phone calls at the switchboard. And they could sing "There's a Hole in the Bottom of the Sea," but when they got to the part about the frog, they'd call it a toad. And between songs, they could holler out "Ribbit! Ribbit!" while they rode along.

Then I come up with the best idea of all. "Mama," I said, "why don't we ask Elsie Lou to be in the parade? We could get her to come down from Nashville! She could wear one of them sparkledy dresses Sorrey May's always braggin' about, the ones she wears when she's singin' up on the stage."

Mama's lookin' interested.

"It would be a huge surprise for the whole town. She could ride on that big fancy wagon of Hank Plenty's."

Mama smiled. "That might could work, Ginger. But I don't know if she'd come. Sorrey May talks about her all the time, but truth is, that gal don't ever come to see her own mama."

"Well, we could ask her anyways. I'm gonna call her long distance. Even if Grady gets mad."

Elsie Lou sounded tired when she answered the phone, but I could still tell it was her. "Ginger!" she said. "Oh, God. What's wrong? Did Mama die?"

"No, no. Sorrey May's just fine. How are you? How's the twins? And Darnell?"

"We're all just fine too, honey. I hear you got five young'uns now yourself."

"Sure do. Keep me right busy."

"So . . . how come you're callin' me long distance?"

"Well, our mamas are plannin' the July Fourth celebration, and I thought you could be in it, singin' up on a float in the parade."

She didn't say nothin'.

"Elsie Lou? You there?"

"Oh, yeah," she said after a second. "I'm here."

"Think you could come? You been gone so long. It would be like old times."

"Well . . . " she said. "I don't know."

"It would be so good for Toad Springs. We'd have our own famous person in our parade. Folks are already comin' from Turkey Creek and Mango to see it. Even some from Bartow. If you were here, they'd come all the way over from Tampa."

"I ain't all that famous," she said. "Nice that you think I am, but I ain't."

"Around here, you are. You just don't know how much everybody loves hearin' about you. Sorrey May keeps us all up to date. You know your mama."

"I sure do." She's quiet, like she's thinkin, then says, "Well . . . my wardrobe's in pretty bad shape these days. I just ordered some new dresses, but they ain't finished yet. I reckon it would depend on—"

"We don't care about your clothes, Elsie Lou. Hell's bells, Sorrey May could make you a new dress right here."

"Well, like I said, I'll see what I can do. But don't say anything 'til I know for sure."

"No, no. I won't. I promise."

Elsie Lou finally called me two weeks before the parade and said she and Darnell and the kids would be comin'. She was hopin' they might could hang around a few extra days, but they'd be stayin' with her mama. And since Sorrey May never took kindly to Darnell, they probably wouldn't be here long.

When I told Mama, she gasped, then put her hands to her heart and grinned. "I knew it! I knew it!" She was so happy, I thought she was gonna cry.

I got the house cleaned up all spick and span and was sittin' out on the front porch shellin' peas and watchin' the young'uns when Elsie Lou and Darnell pulled up out front in an old Ford that could have used a paint job. I ran down the steps and hugged her around the neck. I reckon I was expectin' to see a movie star or somethin', but when I leaned back and saw her face up close, I was surprised at how thin and pale she was, had these dark circles under her eyes.

I know she seen it on my face, 'cause she said, "Oh, hon, it's been a long drive with the kids and all, and I'm just gettin' over a touch of the flu. That's why I look like this."

"You look just fine," I lied, then turned to the rest of them. The twins were five years old, and you could tell they was sick of bein' cooped up in the car.

Daisy scrambled out first, a chunky little thing, her blonde hair all a mess. She must have just woken up. Davey was skinny as a rail, and his hair was almost black, like his daddy's. You'd never have known them two was twins, I swear.

I gave Darnell a hug, and he was nice and all but felt stiff, like he didn't want to be there. "Grady'll be here directly," I said. "Come on inside. I got somethin' for you young'uns."

We sat the kids around the dinin' room table, and I passed out cookies and lemonade. They got on just fine right off the bat. The grownups sat in the livin' room with the rotatin' fan goin', drinkin' sweet tea. I could hardly believe Elsie Lou was really here. Seemed like fifty years since I seen her.

"We ain't been out to Mama's yet," she said. "Tell you the truth, I ain't lookin' forward to it."

I held the plate of cookies out to her, but she just shook her head. "Can't say as I blame you," I say. "Sorrey May ain't never been the easiest person in the world to get along with."

Just then, Mama come in from workin' on the parade, carryin' a bunch of decorations. "Why, Elsie Lou," she said, droppin' the box on the couch and givin' her a big hug. "We're so excited you're here! Sorrey May's been on pins and needles waitin' for you. You seen her yet?"

"Well, no," she said. "Not yet. Since y'all live on the way to her place, just thought we'd stop by here first."

"Want to call her? We got us a party line."

"We'll just rest a few minutes if that's all right," Elsie Lou said. "Then we'll be on our way."

Mama sat down next to her and said, "Guess Ginger done told you about all the big plans. You'll be on the best wagon in town, Hank's big fancy one. And one of his cowhands is gonna play the guitar for you. You'll have a nice throne to sit down on when you want to—one where you won't mess up your fancy dress—and a post to hold on to when you're standin' up and singin' to everybody. We even got a megaphone that'll carry your voice if you want it. When the parade gets to Smitty's Hardware and Feed, we'll stop, and you can sing three or four songs there. We're hopin' one of 'em will be about the travelin' man."

"That sounds fine," Elsie Lou said, "but I have to tell you them new dresses I ordered didn't come in, so I'll have to wear one of my old ones. They ain't near as fancy as the pictures I sent Mama. Just want you to know that ahead of time."

Mama looks like her heart just broke. "Oh no! I been tellin' everybody we'll be able to see all them pretty—"

I give her a dirty look, then turn to Elsie Lou. "Oh, it don't matter. It's your pretty voice we want to hear."

We talked a while about the town folks, who'd died, who'd got born, who was mad at who, and like that, but she'd already heard most of it from Sorrey May on those phone calls every month. After a while, she says they'd better get goin'.

Elsie Lou's the last one out the door, and she stops me for a minute and says in a low voice, "Ginger, I hope there's gonna be time for us to visit. I ain't got nobody up at home I can talk to."

"Why, sure, hon," I said. "I'd love it. Come over in the mornin' and we'll have some coffee. Mama's gonna be down at the town hall all day, gettin' everything ready. About ten o'clock?"

"I'll try," she said, givin' me a hug. "For sure, I'll try."

The next mornin', I make a fresh pot of coffee, but ten o'clock comes and goes and no Elsie Lou. Can't say I'm surprised, knowin' how once her mama starts talkin', you can't pry yourself outta there with a shoehorn. If you even try to leave, she acts like you're bein' mean and hateful and pretends she's all crushed. And to be fair, it's true she ain't seen Elsie Lou in a good while.

It's about two, and the kids are takin' naps when Elsie Lou finally turns up all by herself. Seems like Darnell and Sorrey May had a big set-to before they'd been at the house an hour—them two never could get along for nothin'—and after breakfast that mornin', he took the young'uns and went out to Grasshopper Lake. Elsie Lou can't get away 'til Sorrey May goes to work on the parade. I fix us some sweet tea, and we go out and sit in the rockers on the front porch.

"I want to hear all about everything," I say. "It must be so excitin', you bein' in show business, gettin' all fixed up and singin' in front of all them folks. Me, I spend half my time cookin' and the other half washin' clothes and wipin' noses and bottoms. And I love my mama, but havin' her livin' here don't make life no easier."

Elsie Lou reaches up and twirls some hair around her pointy finger. "It's okay. I love music—always loved it. But show business ain't all it looks to be."

"Oh, honey, you sing like an angel, and it has to feel so great, all them folks clappin' for you. I can hardly wait to hear you in the parade."

"Well, I like the music and the applause. But the rest of it, it ain't what you think."

"What are you talkin' about? Is it them gals you sing with? Don't you like them?"

"Oh, they're all right. They're both single, and the men are always sniffin' around 'em after the shows—most of 'em ain't what you'd call nice guys either. When I tell 'em I'm married, it don't make any difference. After they've been drinkin', which they mostly have, they can get downright ugly."

"Oh, my," I said. "I never thought of somethin' like that."

"And Darnell. He don't like show business. He wants me to quit."

"Well, I can see how he—"

"And our manager is a jerk. Some of the places that hire us make us wear these short skirts and strapless tops and sing songs that ain't all that nice. The other gals think it's fun, but I don't like it."

"Why don't you just say you ain't gonna do it?"

She shakes her head. "If I do that, we lose all our good payin' jobs 'cause them two can't sing without me. They tried it, and it don't work. It's the harmony we got with the three of us. And I can't just leave 'em in the lurch. Besides, if we can get a hit, we'll be makin' real good money. Then we can dress any way we want."

I don't know what to say. I never had no idea.

She looks down at her lap, then back up to me. Her eyes are full of tears.

"Honey," I say. "What's wrong?"

She looks around and leans over close, even though we're the only ones here. "Promise not to ever say anything if I tell you?"

My stomach churns up in a knot. "Sure, I promise. 'Course I do."

She leans back in her chair but keeps talkin' low. "I . . . I met somebody."

"What? What are you talkin' about?"

"One night a few months ago, we was playin' at a place called the Purple Moon. After we changed clothes and were headed out the back door, there was some guys waitin' for us. 'Course, they claimed all's they wanted was autographs, but that wasn't true. They only want one thing." She looks at me out of the corner of her eye.

"There was this one feller who kind of hung back from the others, leanin' against a brick wall. He was real handsome. Made me think of your little brother—with wavy brown hair just like Worthy. Anyway, I was tryin' to squeeze around the edge of the crowd and get out of there when this drunk grabbed my arm and pulled me over like he wanted to kiss me. I started screamin' and hittin' him, and it was David who pulled him away and rescued me. I was so bumfoozled that he took me to a little place across the street and bought me some coffee. He's such a gentleman. So sweet."

"David. The one who looks like Worthy?"

"Yeah."

"Good thing he was there," I say. "And then what happened?"

"Well . . . "

I turn and look right at her. "Well, what?"

Elsie Lou swirls the tea around in her glass, then takes a sip. Her cheeks are pink, and she's smilin', the first real smile I've seen since she got here.

"Elsie Lou . . . "

She looks over at me. "Well . . . that's when it started."

"Started? What started?"

"Well, me and Darnell, we hadn't been gettin' on for a while. He don't like me comin' home so late and leavin' him stuck there with the twins, says all he does is work and babysit. He claims I don't have to work because he makes enough money for us to get by, and we could, I guess, but just barely. Says if I want to work, I need to find somethin' where I'm home nights." She looks up at the ceilin'.

"And?"

"And I started seein' David." She bites her lower lip.

I lean back in the rocker. "Oh, Elsie Lou . . . Oh, my." I sigh. I just can't think of anything else to say.

She's tryin' not to smile, but her mouth's twitchin' at the corners. Finally, she turns to me with a big grin on her face, and she looks beautiful, not so pale and tired anymore. "Oh, Ginger, he's so wonderful, anybody'd fall for him. Don't know why he ever even looked at me. But he loves me, and it ain't 'cause I can sing. He loves me for just bein' me. He buys me candy and flowers, and one time bought me a real cashmere sweater. 'Course, I can't ever wear it."

"Oh, my. Oh, my. Are you gonna leave Darnell?"

"Well, David wants me to. He says he wants to marry me, but I don't know. I just ain't sure."

"Does Darnell know anything?"

She looks down in her lap again. "No. At least I don't think so. I don't know."

"My dear Lord in heaven! What you gonna do?"

"I don't know," she says, her smile fadin'. "On the one hand, seems like this is the best thing ever happened to me. On the other hand, it's the worst. The only time I'm really happy is when I'm with David, but I don't know what to do."

"Have you been, uh, you know . . . "

She looks down at her hands in her lap. "Um . . . just a few times. But he's so wonderful, Ginger. You just can't imag—"

"Elsie Lou!! Are you crazy? I mean, what if you get a baby?"

She stands up and starts pacin' up and down on the porch. "You think I ain't thought about that? I'm miserable. I just don't know what to do. And here's the biggest thing." She stops and takes a deep breath. "David says he ain't all that good with young 'uns. Never wants any of his own. And I don't want to give up my kids. I love 'em too much. And what would people say?"

I rock back in my chair. "Honey, I can't even think of any gal I ever knew givin' up her own flesh and blood. I'd never give mine up. Not even for Clark Gable."

"I know, I know," she says, shakin' her head. "I know."

"Around here, it ain't ever all right for a mama to leave her young'uns. The daddy can go, but not the mama."

"I know." She wipes tears from her eyes. "I love my babies. And Darnell is a good man. I just feel so guilty."

About that time, Mama come up in the front yard and Elsie Lou wipes her eyes and says, "I gotta go."

I walk down the steps with her. "What you gonna do?"

She turns and gives me a big hug. "I don't know, honey. I just don't know. See you at the parade tomorrow."

That was the last time I talked to Elsie Lou. She sang in the parade the next day. I especially loved her most famous song, "Don't Never Trust a Travelin' Man." It's about that first fella she fell in love with. She was wearin' just a regular dress, nothin' sparkledy, but her voice was as pretty as any you'll ever hear. She had a big smile on her face, and Darnell and the kids were lookin' up at her real proud. You'd never have known anything was wrong. But they left right afterwards. I figure it's 'cause Darnell wouldn't stay with her mama one minute longer than he had to.

A couple of months later, I heard that that Elsie Lou had run off with some feller. When she didn't call her mama like she did every month, Sorrey May tried to call her. That's when Darnell told her he'd woke up one mornin', and she was gone. Left a note on her pillow sayin' she was sorry but she didn't have no choice, couldn't pass up her one chance for real happiness, she said. She left a little note for each of the twins, tellin' 'em how much she loved 'em and sayin' goodbye.

When I heard about her leavin' her babies, I just felt sick for my old friend. All that time I'd spent wishin' I was her, livin' that glamorous life . . . It's odd, you know. When we were girls, I was the one always arguin' with my mama and could hardly wait to get out of town, and Elsie Lou was such a good girl at home, follⁱowin' all the rules. Now she's the one who's moved off to the big city in Nashville and sings on the stage, and I'm still in Toad Springs with five kids. She's run off with some handsome, romantic fella, and I'm stuck with my crazy old mama livin' with me.

Then it comes to me that I'm damned lucky to have good old, dependable Grady who can fix anything that breaks and loves me and the kids like a mama bear. And I don't know how I'd survive without my young'uns, even if they make me crazy sometimes. I'd never want to live anywhere but right here in Toad Springs, where you can hear the frogs and toads and crickets at night and watch the rain every summer afternoon and don't need to wind no alarm clock in the evenings 'cause neighbors' roosters crow at sunup.

Still, every night, I try to pray for Elsie Lou, that she'll find whatever it is she's lookin' for. But to be honest, I'm really hopin' that someday she'll get her kids back and bring 'em back here to live. Miracles do happen.

Acknowledgements

I want to acknowledge those who have helped me during the writing of this book and without whom there would probably be no book.

I've been meeting with a group of talented authors for many years who have given me invaluable insights and creative support. My thanks to Barbara Schrefer, Abe Spevack, Jack and Geni Vanek, and Richard Erlanger.

And last but certainly not least, I want to thank Sarah Townsend for her amazing organizational skills, and my wonderful publisher, Jason Aydelotte, and the rest of the Grey Gecko staff.

About the Author

Susan's family came to Florida in the late 1800s and has been there for five generations. She borrowed from, as she says, "memories of our old cracker family stories" while working on both books in the Toad Springs series. She also cowrote the memoir *A Quiet Voice* about Vietnam veteran Eugene Hairston and his struggle to overcome addiction, post-traumatic stress disorder, and homelessness.

In a few of her personal adventures, Susan has found fossils in the Peace River in Florida and on Rainbow Mountain in Alaska, tramped for two days through a Philippine jungle to get medical supplies to the natives, and gone zip-lining through the jungle canopy in Costa Rica. She's sipped high tea at the Peninsula Hotel in Hong Kong, trekked to the remains of an ancient castle in the Czech Republic, and gone skydiving.

Susan currently resides in Dunedin, Florida, near her family.

Connect with Susan

Email: susan@susanadger.com

Web: www.susanadger.com

Facebook: facebook.com/AuthorSusanAdger

Grey Gecko Press

Thank you for purchasing this book from Grey Gecko Press, an independent publishing company that focuses on new and emerging authors, bringing readers the best in fiction and nonfiction at reasonable prices in all formats.

With books in nearly every genre of fiction and non-fiction, there's something for everyone, and you can be sure that buying books from us leads directly to the support of independent authors like Susan Adger.

Visit our website to purchase our titles, including special and autographed editions, and pre-order upcoming books at a discount.

And don't forget: all our print editions come with the ebook absolutely free! Email support@greygeckopress.com for your copy today.

Web: www.greygeckopress.com

Facebook: facebook.com/GreyGeckoPress

More from Susan Adger

Seashells, Gator Bones, and the Church of Everlasting Liability

In the 1930s, the fictional town of Toad Springs, Florida, is filled with the adventures and daily what-nots of worthy, down-to-earth folk such as Flavey Stroudamore, owner of a three-legged gator named Precious who also just happens to have a birthmark of Jesus on his side.

Joining Flavey are Buck Blander, pastor of the Church of Everlasting Liability, who honed his preaching skills in prison but doesn't tell his parishioners, and Sweetie Mooney, whose attempt to run a beauty shop in her aunt's home fails after tragedies with head lice and henna hair dye.

This lively, heartwarming collection of tales from the Sunshine State will inspire you to smile!

amazon 📗iBooks

BARNES&NOBLE kobo
BOOKSELLERS

grey gecko press

http://books2read.com/toadsprings1

Recommended Reading

When young Marnie unexpectedly loses her father, her grandmother moves into her home to help her mother and all three women must create a new life together—all while Marnie goes through the trials of adolescence in 1960s small-town America.

Chickens & Hens
by Nancy-Gail Burns

Marnie witnesses unexpected lessons—from the heartwarming to the hilarious—learned by family and townsfolk. She also sees the older women in her life fall in love again. But will Marnie ever find true love herself . . . or has she missed the most important lesson of all?

Find out in this delightful story of three women who will make you laugh, make you cry, and above all, make you proud to be a woman.

grey gecko press
http://books2read.com/chickens

amazon ☐iBooks
BARNES&NOBLE kobo

Returning to her hometown of Lily Hollow, AJ Rhys sets out to fulfill her childhood dream of restoring the old hotel on Aspen Court. With nothing but the legacy of her great-grandfather and the help of two dedicated strangers, she begins transforming the once-grand hotel into her ideal refuge.

The Bookshop Hotel
by A. K. Klemm

Only after the renovations are in full swing does it become clear that the hotel is having an effect on the town and everyone in it. Memories still haunt both AJ and Lily Hollow, but they begin to release their grip as the hotel binds its patrons together.

The first book in a series, *The Bookshop Hotel* is a story of family, tragedy, forgiveness and the power of books. Join AJ and the residents of a small town where the past is never far away and secrets remain just below the surface.

grey gecko press
http://books2read.com/bookshop1

amazon ☐iBooks
BARNES&NOBLE kobo